PRAISE FOR FREYA BARKER

Freya Barker writes a mean romance, I tell you! A REAL romance, with real characters and real conflict.

~Author M. Lynne Cunning

I've said it before and I'll say it again and again, Freya Barker is one of the BEST storytellers out there.

~Turning Pages At MidnightBook Blog

God, Freya Barker gets me every time I read one of her books. She's a master at creating a beautiful story that you lose yourself in the moment you start reading.

~Britt Red Hatter Book Blog

Freya Barker has woven a delicate balance of honest emotions and well-formed characters into a tale that is as unique as it is gripping.

~Ginger Scott, bestselling young and new adult author and Goodreads Choice Awards finalist

Such a truly beautiful story! The writing is gorgeous, the scenery is beautiful...

~Author Tia Louise

From Dust by Freya Barker is one of those special books. One of those whose plotline and characters remain with you for days after you finished it.

~Jeri's Book Attic

No amount of words could describe how this story made me feel, I think this is one I will remember forever, absolutely freaking awesome is not even close to how I felt about it.

Still Air was insightful, eye-opening, and I paused numerous times to think about my relationships with my own children. Anytime a book can evoke a myriad of emotions while teaching life lessons you'll continue to carry with you, it's a 5-star read.

In my opinion, there is nothing better than a Freya Barker book. With her final installment in her Portland, ME series, Still Air, she does not disappoint. From start to finish I was completely captivated by Pam, Dino, and the entire Portland family.

The one thing you can always be sure of with Freya's writing is that it will pull on ALL of your emotions; it's expressive, meaningful, sarcastic, so very true to life, real, hard-hitting and heartbreaking at times and, as is the case with this series especially, the story is at points raw, painful and occasionally fugly BUT it is also sweet, hopeful, uplifting, humorous and heart-warming.

FREYA BARKER

LOST&FOUND
PASS Series

ALSO BY FREYA BARKER

ISBN: 9781988733654
Cover Design: Freya Barker
Editing: Karen Hrdlicka
Proofreading: Joanne Thompson
Formatting: Christina Smith

Cover Image: Jean Woodfin—JW Photography
Cover Models: Hayley Stavenger and Charles Smith

LOST&FOUND

PASS Series

CHAPTER 1

BREE

"*No.*"

I'm fuming.

"It's not a question."

Yanis Mazur, long-time boss and perpetual pain in my ass, pulls up that arrogant right eyebrow of his.

"That's not in my job description."

I fist my hands on my hips. Not that I really believe it would in any way intimidate Yanis, not much does.

"It's an assignment within an existing contract that requires an operative. That's you."

He dismisses me as he goes back to scribbling notes on a legal pad.

That really pisses me off and I lean down on his desk.

"Get someone else to do it."

He emits what sounds like a growl and I watch with some measure of satisfaction as his nostrils flare. Reluctantly his gaze meets my glare.

"Who would you suggest to be an appropriate

candidate to double for a thirty-eight-year-old, five-foot-nothing brunette then? Dimi? At six four and with full-on facial hair? Or maybe Shep, black and bald?"

Dammit.

I don't want to attend a Denver movie premiere, I don't want to pretend to be Bobby Lee Rose, and I really don't want to wear a goddamn dress.

Our client, Boulder Records, hired us last year to provide additional security for some of their A-list artists at certain public events. Now one of those A-listers—country singer Bobby Lee Rose—has landed herself in a private rehab facility for alcohol and substance abuse. Boulder Records desperately wants to keep that information under wraps, so they've requested a double to attend a highly publicized movie premiere in her place. Bobby Lee's latest hit is also the movie's theme song and she is expected to make an appearance.

I have the unfortunate honor to be five foot two, brunette, and somewhat similar in shape and looks to the singer. It saves the record label from having to hire an actress to play the role, thus reducing the risk Bobby Lee's true whereabouts will be found out.

I see the reasoning behind it, but I'm not an actress. I'm a security specialist, and this assignment forces me well out of my comfort zone.

"No one's gonna buy it," I try as a last-ditch effort.

"They will. The right clothes, hair, makeup; you'll be a dead ringer," he reassures me. "Besides, Roddy

Cantrell is going to be by your side."

Ugh. Bobby Lee's on-again, off-again boyfriend is not exactly an incentive. The guy is a sleezeball. Also a country singer for the same label, but more known for his collection of famous conquests than he ever was for his music. If I were Bobby Lee I might've started self-medicating too.

"Nobody better ask me to sing," I grumble, knowing I'm beat.

His mouth stretches in one of his rare grins, unsettling my equilibrium.

"If anyone asks questions, you have laryngitis. Bobby Lee just finished her tour; it wouldn't be a stretch."

With that, Yanis turns back to his laptop and this time I heed the cue and take my leave.

"Oh, one more thing," he calls after me as I walk out of his office. "Lena has your ticket. Sue is expecting you tonight and picking you up at the airport in Denver. You'll be staying at the house in Deer Creek."

I grind my molars so hard my jaw hurts as I make my way back to my desk.

Great.

Sue Paxton is Bobby Lee's personal assistant, and what Yanis so modestly calls the house in Deer Creek is in fact an ostentatious gated mansion about forty-five minutes out of Denver, in the middle of nowhere. I'd rather stay at a hotel in town so I can be on my way home on the first flight out after I make my appearance.

I spend the next few hours at my desk, working on stuff I'd hoped to be able to do this weekend. Not like I have much of a personal life anyway. Not even here at the office where only Yanis and Radar, our computer specialist, have a space of their own. Most days I share the large office space with my colleagues, Hutch and Dimi. Even Kai and Shep, who take care of most of our international assignments, have desks in the bullpen. I've learned to wear noise-cancelling earbuds, play a rainfall soundtrack, and keep my head down when I need to concentrate.

A hand appears in front of my face and I swing around in my seat to find Lena waving a ticket at me. I pull out my earbuds.

"If you still need to pack, you need to leave now," she says, a stern look on her face.

"What time is?"

"Plane leaves in an hour. You need to hustle."

"*Shit.*"

It'll take me ten minutes to get home, five to pack, and fifteen to get to the airport. I'm going to have to run.

I make it onto the plane with just seconds to spare and the annoyed flight attendant waves me to my seat. I shove my pack under my seat and quickly buckle up. It's only an hour flight and I spend almost more time navigating Denver Airport—even with just a carry-on—to locate Sue.

She only has me beat by a few inches but just

like me, Bobby Lee's PA works hard at being inconspicuous, which makes her hard to spot in a crowd. Dirty blonde hair pulled back in a ponytail matching my own, nondescript clothing, and a pair of sensible shoes make her blend in. Anything to defer attention away from her and toward her high-maintenance employer.

"We have to make a stop at Roz Taylor to fit your dress."

She starts talking when we're still ten feet apart.

"Hello to you too."

She almost looks surprised.

"Oh, right, hi. Sorry, force of habit."

"So…a dress? Do I have to?"

"Sorry," she starts, not looking in the least apologetic. "It was commissioned from the designer six months ago for this purpose."

I let out a sigh.

"Fine. But I hate heels, can I at least wear flats?"

That earns me a look of abject horror.

"Roz would have a heart attack. The dress was intended to wear with cowboy boots. Standard two-inch heel, can you handle that?"

I nod. What a relief, I'd envisioned myself teetering across the red carpet on a pair of stilettos.

Roz turns out to be a matronly, graying woman, who looks more like someone's grandmother than the hottest, up-and-coming designer, as Sue claimed her to be on the way here.

The dress she fits me into is an old-style barmaid's

dress. My B-cup tits almost hit my chin when she cinches up the corset that creates an impressive waist on my less than hourglass figure. Tough to breathe, but all I have to do is walk from the car to the theater, sit down in a chair for the two hours or so the movie will take, and then someone can cut the contraption off me.

Forty-five minutes later, we walk out of the studio to Sue's car. Roz is going to drop by the house a few hours before the event to help me 'finish the look.' I don't know what that means. I'm not sure I want to. They whispered something about big hair and a smoky eye while I was in the dressing room putting my own clothes back on. I have my fingers crossed they were talking about somebody else.

I also have instructions to eat light, since the dress is tight on me and I can't be bloated. In my line of work, you eat when you can and you do it hearty. Never know when the next meal will be. My request to stop at My Brother's Bar to pick up a Johnny Burger is nixed in favor of a salad from Parsley I don't think could sustain a gerbil.

I'm in for a long weekend.

YANIS

DAMN.

By the time I get back from my meeting with a new contact at a vineyard out near Palisade, Bree's Jeep is gone. I'd hoped to catch her before she left, maybe give her a ride to the airport and smooth things over with her.

As usual, when it comes to Bree my judgment is clouded. I knew this assignment would push her well out of her comfort zone. I also knew she'd balk, and if I'm honest with myself, that was part of the reason I was blunt with her. I wanted to see that fire. Wanted to know if it was still there, hidden underneath years of being the calm and levelheaded member of this company, keeping the rest of us in check.

Bree has made herself invisible, in more ways than one, since I first laid eyes on that fiery ball of energy about fifteen or so years ago. My God, she was something else. All opinion, all passion, and so damn happy just to be alive, you couldn't help but be drawn to her.

And I had been, like a moth to her flame.

Until I snuffed it out.

"Hey, Boss."

Lena is still behind her desk.

"Shouldn't you be heading out?"

"I will be, right after I finish this report for Bree."

"Talking about Bree, did she get off on time?"

Lena does one of those slow head turns, and when her eyes hit me, they're sparkling. Damn woman always has her antennae up. Little escapes her, which can be a pain in my ass, but it's also what makes her invaluable to this office. She keeps us all in check and on schedule.

"Why, yes. Last minute, of course, but I had Radar check to see if she made her flight and she checked in."

"Good."

I start walking away when I hear her behind me.

"She didn't seem happy about going, though."

"Tough," I say without turning around, and I hear her soft giggle as I make my way to my office.

The bullpen is empty, both my brother and Hutch already home with their women. Even Radar's office is empty. Until recently, he'd almost always be the last to leave, but since he hooked up with Hillary that's changed.

Fucking guys.

Guess I'm happy they're happy, but this domestic bliss shit seems to be infectious, and I'll be damned if I get caught up in the epidemic. Someone's got to keep their wits about them.

I distract myself with work and barely even acknowledge Lena when she sticks her head in the door to announce she's leaving. My discussion with the owner of the new vineyard still fresh in my mind, I start putting a proposal together to protect against the recent wave of vandalism their business has seen since opening. It works for a while, but then my thoughts start drifting.

To Bree.

Jesus, we were both young. Young and cocky as all get out. I'd just started up PASS the year before and Bree had been my first hire. She'd freelanced for GFI Investigations, a company run by Gus Flemming I signed on with after leaving the force. Not only did she come highly recommended by Gus, but I had opportunity to see her in action a few times and had been impressed.

She hadn't disappointed—in any way—and it hadn't been until…

No.

Not doing that now. No trips down memory lane. Not with an entire weekend open before me without one or another crisis to occupy my time and my mind.

Instead, I pick up my phone and dial while I shut down my computer and turn off my desk lamp.

"Been a while," she answers.

"Megan. Busy?"

She chuckles warmly.

"No, actually. Perfect timing. Just got an offer accepted that'll net me six figures, so I have cause for celebration. What did you have in mind?"

I walk through the office and turn off lights before stepping outside, my keys in hand.

"I haven't eaten. Fancy a late bite somewhere?"

"Sure. Where?"

"Ale House? I'll pick you up in ten?"

"Can't wait."

I hang up and get behind the wheel of my Yukon.

Fuck, what am I doing?

Megan Denny is the real estate agent, who helped me find a property less than ten minutes from the office a couple of years ago, where I've since built my house. I bumped into her again at a function a little over a year ago and spent an enjoyable night. That turned into an occasional hookup. I really can't call it much more than that. We scratched each other's itch.

No ties, that was understood. At least I thought it was until I recommended her to Radar when he was looking for a place. That was a mistake on my part because she took that to mean I wanted to take whatever it was we had to a different level. I didn't.

She's a nice woman. Good company over an occasional meal, a good time in bed—hers and never mine—but nothing more than that. She started calling more frequently and I started answering less. I haven't actually seen her in a couple of months.

Calling her was a knee-jerk reaction, because of the direction my thoughts were taking.

They call that jumping out of the frying pan into the fire.

As I pull up to Megan's place, I already know this night is not going to end the way she thinks it will.

And that's on me.

CHAPTER 2

BREE

I'M STARVING.

Over the past twenty-four hours I've had the same amount of food I normally eat in one sitting. All to fit in this blasted dress.

"The plan is for me to keep breathing, right?" I complain as Roz laces the corset tighter yet.

"Only enough to keep you alive," she fires back, already tiring of my grievances, and there have been a few.

For one, my hair—which is voluminous all on its own without my signature ponytail—is teased into the next zip code by Trish. She's the near-emaciated-looking hair and makeup artist, who showed up an hour before Roz to work on my *transformation*.

Dear God, I feel like my face is caked in plaster and I'm terrified if I smile, cracks will form. Looking at my reflection in the mirror, I don't look anything like myself. My gray eyes are hidden by the deep brown contacts I was told to wear. Trish even tightened my jawline with some kind of skin tape hidden behind my ears and under my hair, and what she called *contouring* made my nose look thinner and my cheeks hollow.

Now my tits are straining out of the top of my dress. One wrong move and we could have a repeat of Janet Jackson's Super Bowl performance right on the red carpet in front of the cameras.

I'd asked Sue earlier if there'd be food at this shindig, hoping that once I was strapped into this dress I might sneak in an appetizer or two, but at this point, I'm not so sure I could fit in a peanut. I promise myself as soon as this is over, I'm going to gorge myself on the biggest, greasiest cheeseburger I can find.

The one saving grace is the boots. They're gorgeous and surprisingly comfortable. Although that could be because the rest of me is suffering more.

"I love the boots," I share, mainly to say something positive after being a bear for the past two hours.

"If you can manage not to touch your face or hair all night, you can have them," Sue bargains. The hand I was lifting to scratch an itch on my nose stays suspended in midair.

"Deal."

"What about her hands?"

Trish looks at mine; kid's hands, with wide palms and short fingers. The blunt nails and mangled cuticles evidence I don't indulge in manicures. Who would in my line of work?

"I brought gloves."

Roz, who thankfully is done strapping me in, pulls what looks like a pair of lace stockings from a bag.

"Do not take these off," she warns, pulling the first one up my arm. It goes up all the way past my elbow.

"What if I have to pee?" the practical side of me wants to know.

"There'll be no peeing," Sue says firmly.

Of course, I immediately feel like my bladder is about to explode. Nothing will bring on the urge like knowing you won't be able to make a sanitary stop.

"Limo just pulled up," Trish announces.

Thankfully Sue is heading down to tell Roddy I'll be another few minutes; while I quickly dart into the bathroom and take care of business.

I leave Roz and Trish to clean up in Bobby Lee's opulent master suite and head down the sweeping staircase. Roddy is waiting at the bottom. His white capped teeth sparkling in stark contrast with the artificial tan of his skin.

"A vision…"

He's so full of himself he doesn't even notice the eye roll I can't hold back. Sue catches it and stifles a snicker. Guess she's not a fan of the man either.

"No need for flattery," I announce. "I assure you it's wasted on me."

I have to give it to him, the bright smile only slightly dims, but apparently the dog isn't down yet, because the next moment as he leads me outside to the limo, his hand slides down to my ass.

Without breaking my stride, I turn my head slightly

in his direction.

"Hands off," I snarl, and his unwelcome touch immediately disappears. "Try that again and I'll break every single guitar-picking finger on that hand."

I'm not sure if the bodyguard—whose name is Sam and is part of Bobby Lee's usual security detail—heard me, but his mouth quirks as he holds the door open for me.

If I were planning an elaborate ruse like this, intended to keep sensitive information hidden, I would've drastically reduced the number of people in the know. As it stands, in addition to record label management who set it up, and my PASS team, there are by last count five people in on the gig. That's too many potential loose lips to control in my opinion.

Roddy makes the smart move to slide into the seat across from me rather than beside me. Guess the prospect of a mangled hand was the right incentive. Still, the look in his eyes is predatory.

"So…what is your real name?"

"None of your business."

As the limo starts to drive, I stare Roddy down until his smile slowly disappears and he raises his hands defensively.

"Just trying to make small talk."

"Stick to the weather," I suggest before turning my gaze out the window.

Once in the city I start getting nervous.

"Champagne?"

Roddy, who's been blessedly quiet for most of the

drive, must've noticed, as he holds up a bottle he got from God knows where. I might've accepted had it been scotch, but I don't do bubbles, and there's that bathroom issue to consider.

"Not for me. Besides, we're almost there."

He pours himself a hefty glass.

"We are, but we'll be stuck in a line of limos for at least half an hour. It takes time to unload them all."

That's great. I really look forward to another half hour with Roddy in the confined space. Especially if he starts drinking.

Luckily the wait is not quite that long, but when the limo pulls up to the theater and I see the throng of people assembled, I want to puke.

Smile without teeth and wave without moving your arm.

Sue's words loop on repeat in my head as the bodyguard opens the door and I hear cheering.

Roddy is the first one out and holds out his hand to help me. I would rather be in the Amazon burning leeches from between my toes, or be held at knifepoint in a dark alley in the slums of Mexico City. I'm equipped for situations like those—I have my blade strapped to the inside of my thigh—but a knife won't help with bright lights in the middle of downtown Denver that scare the shit out of me.

Nevertheless, I grab hold of Roddy's hot and undoubtedly sweaty hand—suddenly grateful for the gloves—and let myself be pulled out of the shelter of the limo.

Smile without teeth and wave without moving your arm.

I'm sure I look constipated as I try to follow instructions while letting Roddy guide me along. Good thing too, because I can't see a damn thing with flashes going off and hot lights aimed at me.

"Bobby Lee! Bobby Lee!"

My head automatically turns in the direction of the voice. I can barely make out a woman shoving a microphone in my direction, the camera behind her pins me with a bright beam blinding me.

"Are the reports you haven't been well true?" she asks.

I'm unexpectedly grateful for Roddy's presence when he wraps his arm around my waist and leans forward to answer.

"My girl has had a long tour and was advised by her doctor to spare her vocal cords. But as you can see, she is just fine."

The innuendo is dripping from his last words and his fingers flex on my hip, but like a good sport, I smile without teeth in the reporter's general direction.

Five feet farther down the carpet we're stopped again, this time in front of a group of cameras snapping away. Posing for pictures is apparently something Roddy is quite at ease with. Me, not so much. After several calls to turn this way and that, I pinch Roddy's hand resting possessively on my hip.

"Get me outta here," I grind out between my teeth.

A few beats later we're inside where it's blissfully

cooler, but no less busy. Roddy and Sam hustle me to a row of sectioned-off seats where I gratefully sit down. A few people stop by, some of whom I recognize, but Roddy plays his role well and explains the laryngitis, leaving me with nothing to do but smile and nod.

He tries to get me to join him for the after-party, but I'm done by the time the credits roll over the screen.

Sam is waiting for us when we get to the back of the theater.

"Home?" he asks.

If only. I have one more night in that hideous monstrosity of a house before I can hop on the first plane out in the morning.

"Please," I whisper, ignoring Roddy who seems to be pouting.

I'm whisked out of a service door into an alley where the limo is already waiting. I slip in the back seat, followed by my unhappy companion.

"If you want to go to the party, go," I urge him.

"I don't have a ride."

Great. Now he sounds like a put-out child.

"I'm sure there's plenty of limos around to give you a ride."

"You don't mind?" He can't keep the eagerness out of his voice.

"Not even a little bit."

In the front seat, I hear Sam's deep chuckle as Roddy scrambles out of the vehicle.

"Do you have a knife?" I ask Sam through the open partition.

"Excuse me?"

"A knife, a pair of scissors, or anything to get me out of this damn contraption," I grumble, trying to reach behind me to undo the laces.

"Hang on." He's out of his seat and opening the back door in a flash. "Turn your back."

I realize my mistake the moment I feel the corset release. In a quick move I clamp the front to my chest.

"*Shit*."

"Gimme a sec."

I hear rustling behind me and then a white dress shirt is draped over my shoulders. Slipping my arms through the still warm sleeves, I fasten a few buttons before turning to face him. He's pulling his jacket back on over his undershirt.

"Thank you so much. I was getting light-headed with the lack of oxygen."

Sam grins wide.

"No problem. Anything else before we head to Deer Creek?"

Now it's my turn to grin wide.

"The biggest, greasiest cheeseburger you can find me."

YANIS

I DRAG THE bin I filled with garden waste to the composting pile at the edge of my property behind the house.

Good way to kill off a weekend, gardening. When I first built the house, I contracted a landscaping company to put in the garden and maintain it for one year. Since then, I've done the work myself, even putting in a vegetable garden this spring.

I've discovered it's relaxing, a good way to unwind and still be productive. It's my well-kept secret, if my guys ever found out I spend my time off weeding and pruning, they'd never let me live it down.

Not to mention it gets me out of the house. I'd gone from living in a condo downtown to this remote and rambling, three-bedroom house where it can get lonely. My own fault, since I don't exactly socialize. Last night's fiasco is a prime example why.

I should've let sleeping dogs lie, that much became clear over dinner. Hell, I could read the hope in her eyes when she sat down in the booth across from me, and I felt guilty as hell for putting it there. So I manned up, had an uncomfortable conversation that hurt a good woman, and dropped her back at her apartment an hour later, reminded why I do better on my own.

My sister-in-law is of a different opinion, as she made clear when she called this morning. She invited me over for steaks and beers tonight and wouldn't take no for an answer. Willa is a tricky one. First of all, my brother tells her everything, and furthermore she's a social worker and is trained to assess people. She clearly isn't above using her knowledge and insight to guilt me into accepting.

I dump my load on the pile and stop to take in the raw beauty of the high desert lands I border onto.

Then I head inside for a quick shower or else I'll be late. Dimas and Willa live on the opposite end of town, south of the river.

The door is left open a crack when I walk up to their house. I push it open and step inside.

"We're in the back!" Willa calls out from the kitchen.

She's at the sink with the faucet running, washing vegetables, when I walk up behind her.

"Hey." I bend down and kiss her cheek. "What's the occasion?"

She twists her head and shoots me a big grin.

"All in good time. Grab a beer and take one out for your brother. I'll be a few minutes."

Outside Dimas is scraping the grill clean. He grins at me when I hand him his beer.

"What did she threaten you with?" he asks right off the bat.

"Like I'm gonna tell you. You'll just use it for leverage. All I'll say is you better stay on the good side of that woman in there. She's scary."

Not a chance in hell I'll share how she somehow saw me parked across from Bree's apartment a few months ago.

It was a low moment. Bree had just come back from an assignment in Kenya I sent her on—she hadn't been happy about that one either—and word around the office was she had a hot date with a guy she met on her flight home. I just wanted a glimpse of her, to assure myself she was okay, but ended up parked outside her apartment until I saw her getting dropped off. The guy was driving some fucking European piece of trash car he probably spent way too much money on, but at least he walked her to the door. I noticed, with some gratification, Bree quickly turned her cheek when the guy went in for a goodnight kiss.

I was out there until I saw the lights go off in her apartment before I drove home.

Not one of my finer moments, and I have no idea how the hell Willa found out about it.

"So what's the occasion?" I ask again when we finish dinner.

My brother and his wife share a goofy look and I'm hoping it means what I think it does. Dimas let it drop he and Willa had been trying to get pregnant, without success. Last I heard they were looking at a fertility clinic, but it's not really the kind of topic he and I talk about. I only know because Lena shares some of that stuff with me.

"We're gonna be parents," Dimas shares, grinning like a fool.

"That's great news. Congratulations, guys."

I get up and walk around the table to give him a brotherly slap on the back, before turning to Willa and giving her a proper hug.

"When are you due?"

The moment the words are out of my mouth, I want to take them back when I see the pain flash over Willa's face.

"We're adopting," my brother says, walking up

behind his wife and slipping his arms around her. "It's a little boy."

"I…I had no idea."

"It's still all fairly new to us too," she says smiling. "And we weren't sure if it was going to happen, so we didn't want to get everyone else's hopes up as well."

"Doesn't adoption take a long time?"

"Under normal circumstance, yes," Dimas shares. "But Julie—the baby's mother—is a friend of Willa's sister, Connie. She's single, found herself pregnant, and was intending to have the baby on her own. Five months into the pregnancy she was diagnosed with pancreatic cancer."

"Jesus…" I hiss, feeling for the woman.

"She opted for no treatments until after the baby was born, knowing full well what the risk would be," Willa takes over. "Connie went to see her a few times in the hospital and mentioned at some point Dimi and I were having trouble getting pregnant, so Julie asked to see us. That was six weeks ago."

"I guess she already knew she wouldn't make it," my brother continues. "But she wanted to have a say in what happened to her baby after she was gone." He looks down at his wife, who sheds a few tears. "We didn't have to think about it, we immediately agreed. Connie got Hank involved to draw up the necessary paperwork."

Good. Hank Fredericks is a jack of all trades when it comes to the law and has been on PASS retainer for the past ten years or so. He would make sure any arrangement is airtight.

"Julie is deteriorating quickly, so they're planning to deliver the baby by C-section on Tuesday. You're going to be an uncle."

Those words play over and over in my mind as I drive home. Our parents will be over the moon one of us finally gives them a grandchild to fawn over. I think they've long given up on looking at me for offspring. The thought leaves me grim.

Once home, I flip the TV on for a bit of distraction and catch the entertainment section of the news. The flash of a red carpet catches my eye and I turn up the volume to listen to the anchor talk about the movie premiere I sent Bree to attend. They show a couple of actors arriving and then another limo pulling up. I recognize Roddy Cantrell getting out and reaching his hand out for someone.

I don't even realize I'm leaning forward in my seat, when on the screen a woman gets out of the back of the limo. She's almost unrecognizable. Gone is the tight ponytail, the men's clothes, the combat boots she prefers.

When did her hair get so long?

The dress she's wearing is probably illegal in some states, and when she fully turns toward the camera, a tense smile on her face, I know I'm fucked.

CHAPTER 3

BREE

ONE THING I'LL say for Bobby Lee, she didn't spare a penny on her guests' comfort either.

This bed is the bomb, and despite the gaudy decor of the room, I slept like a baby. It makes it hard to get up when my alarm goes off at five forty-five.

My plane leaves at seven thirty, it was the earliest I could change my original afternoon flight to. Aside from the comfy bed, I'm ready to get out of here.

I don't expect to find Sue up already, waiting in the elaborate kitchen with a fresh pot of coffee and the smell of something hot and sweet in the air. My stomach immediately grumbles, despite the massive burger I ate last night.

"Morning," she chirps.

"Hey, I didn't think you'd be up."

"Can't let you go without something in your stomach."

She slides a mug across the island at me and points at the creamer and sugar on their little tray.

"You can fix it up yourself. I'll grab the cinnamon buns from the oven."

"You didn't have to go to the trouble. I could've grabbed something at the airport."

She pulls out a baking sheet with four massive pastries and immediately spreads cream cheese icing over the tops.

"Nonsense. I owe you at least one calorie-loaded meal."

She winks as she slides one on a plate and hands it to me. I take a large bite and groan at the sweet, warm, buttery pastry melting on my tongue.

I did much the same last night when Sam joined me in the back of the limo, and I had my first bite of the burger he insisted on buying after I discovered I had no money on me. A nice guy, buying me food and literally giving me the shirt off his back.

"Oh, before I forget, I left a man's dress shirt with the gown in the bathroom upstairs. The shirt is Sam's." Sue's eyebrows shoot up. "No, nothing like that," I hurry to explain. "I was so eager to get out of that corset when we got into the limo, I didn't stop to think I had nothing on underneath. He was being a gentleman and lent me his shirt."

"That would've been embarrassing," she says, grinning.

"It was. Although I think more for Sam than for me."

"I wouldn't bet on it; he doesn't look like the kind of guy who embarrasses easily. You may have made his day."

I snort. I seriously doubt it. Without that corset it's not like I have much on offer. Once I pulled a brush through my hair and washed that gunk off my face, I was back to my old plain self.

Shit. I should get going.

"You know, I should probably call a cab," I point out, already pulling my phone from my pocket.

"I've got an airport limo picking you up in ten minutes. I would've taken you myself, but I have a conference call in…" She checks a sleek watch on her wrist. "Five minutes. I better hustle. Feel free to grab one for the road and don't worry about the gate, it's already open and I'll close it again later. It was good to see you again, Bree."

"You too," I manage before she disappears from the kitchen.

I finish my breakfast and wrap a second cinnamon bun in a paper towel for the drive. Then I don my ball cap and sunglasses, sling my pack over my shoulder, and head out the door to find the limo already waiting.

"Morning."

The driver tips his hat and reaches for the back door when I walk toward the vehicle. This is a regular airport limo; I recognize the subtle logo on the trunk. The same company works from a fair number of airports I've flown into.

"Thank you," I tell him, noting he seems more interested in the house than in me.

It feels like I'm sitting on something when I climb

in. I shift and twist around to find a book in my seat.

Suddenly I feel a pinch and a burning sensation at the back of my neck, and a heavy body shoves me down on the seat, trapping my arms underneath me.

"I'm sorry," a voice whispers by my ear.

I draw on my training and jerk my head back, hoping to catch him on the chin but it feels like my head weighs a ton. I don't make contact and when I try to struggle, my entire body feels like it's filled with lead.

I'm trying to think but my brain is sluggish and I'm vaguely aware of the smell of cinnamon.

I fight hard to hang on but it's no use.

Yanis

"Move it to the left."

I adjust the tiny camera as Radar instructs.

The Sunday morning call from the owner of Flynn's Fields was unexpected. I planned to finalize the security layout for the vineyard today or tomorrow, but when Joe Flynn found one of his fermentation vats vandalized this morning, those plans moved up.

I rustled up Radar, loaded whatever equipment we had at the office in the back of my vehicle, and drove out to Palisade.

They did a number on his fermentation tank, using some kind of saw to cut through the steel layers and two thousand or so gallons of wine flooded the facility. The night security guard they hired to patrol the property found the mess but the perps had already taken off. Likely he interrupted them since it looks like they had started on the second of the five tanks. Each of those babies cost upward of thirteen grand. That, plus the wine lost, is a lot of fucking money down the drain.

"You've got it."

I give Radar the thumbs-up and climb down the ladder so I can move on to the next one.

We're installing the handful of stationary mini-cameras we had in stock in and around the production side of Flynn's Fields. We'll replace them with proper ones this coming week as soon as we have a security framework set up and equipment ordered, but for now this'll have to do.

With eyes now on the facility, as well as the access point, we head to the office space where we find Joe talking on the phone. He doesn't keep us waiting long.

"Get it done?"

"For now, yes," I answer him, taking a seat. "We only had enough for the winery, but it's on a live feed. You already had the gate and access to the buildings secured, but it looks like they gained entrance from the vineyard and through the service entrance beside the big loading door. The alarm on that was basic and easily dismantled, so Radar upgraded it."

"Jesus," Joe mumbles, rubbing a hand over his face. "My vines…if there is anything more valuable than the tanks or the wine itself, it's the grapes."

"Already included in the plan I was working on, but the key element here is good security personnel.

You can have top-of-the-line equipment all over this place but unless you have eyes on it at all times, it's useless."

"I thought I had everything covered."

I feel for the guy. He finally had the guts and the means to follow a lifelong dream—which he told me Flynn's Fields was—only to be targeted when he's barely out of the starting gate.

"For normal circumstances, maybe." It's not my style to beat around the bush. "But someone's got it in for you, and until police find out who that is and stop them, we've gotta close this place down tight. That means the right equipment and trained manpower."

"I'm at my wit's end. Whatever needs to be done," he dejectedly concedes. "Can you provide both?"

We set up custom security systems, provide specialized personal security, and a variety of other services, but we don't generally guard properties. To be blunt, it's below our pay scale.

I'm about to tell him so when Joe follows up.

"The cops didn't seem too interested. Even with it being the fourth time I've had to call them in the past month. I could really use some help."

Fuck.

I glance at Radar, who gives me an oh-what-the-hell shrug. It's not like we're swamped with work. Especially now that Bobby Lee is out of commission for the foreseeable future and her tour is done. The contract we have with Boulder Records is for her security only, so it'll be on the back burner until she's back on the road.

It'll probably be good for the team to have something to put their teeth into.

I should get in touch with Bree, get her to start working on establishing contact with the Palisade Police Department. Not sure what time she's coming back today, but if I can't touch base with her, I'll catch her first thing tomorrow.

Thinking about Bree brings back the picture of her in that dress last night. It was the culprit for my lack of sleep. If I didn't know her so well, I'd have sworn she enjoyed flirting with the cameras, but I recognized the discomfort on her face and felt a pang of guilt.

I'm hard on her and I know it. Every time I worry her pull gets too strong, I purposely send her off on some remote assignment or piss her off with one like the red carpet gig. Having Bree angry at me is safer than when she lets that impervious mask slip and I catch a glimpse of the warm woman underneath.

"Okay. We'll see what we can do."

Joe looks instantly relieved.

He directs us to an empty tasting room, where Radar can work on his laptop, and I start making some calls.

My first priority is to get some kind of rotation together so the place is covered at night. The existing night guard will keep patrolling the place, but I want one of my guys on site once the place shuts down. It's less likely they will try something during work hours when the property is not only bustling with staff, but also with visitors.

Bree doesn't answer so I leave her a brief message to call me. She's probably on her way back now. Next is Jake, who doesn't mind doing a couple of shifts. Radar is willing as well, so between those two, Bree, and myself, we can rotate through coverage.

I purposely leave Dimas out of the equation; he's going to have his hands full with the new baby. Still have a hard time wrapping my head around the fact my younger brother is going be a dad.

Shit.

I guess it's inevitable Ma and Dad will show up in Grand Junction sometime soon. Their first grandchild.

Maybe I should schedule myself for the bulk of the vineyard shifts. I love my parents, but they can be a bit…much.

Radar volunteers for the first shift tonight, and with a plan in place, I head back toward Grand Junction. Since I haven't heard back from Bree, I try her again while driving. She should be back by now, but her phone keeps ringing before bumping me to her mailbox. It's not like her to be out of reach for this long.

Once I hit town, I steer toward her building instead of home, but her Jeep is not parked in its regular spot and all lights are off in her apartment. I park and dial Lena.

"Sunday night, Boss? It couldn't wait 'til tomorrow morning?" she grumbles when she answers.

"Bree's flight. What time was it supposed to come

in?"

"Her flight was for three fifteen, she should be home."

I end the call with no more than a grunt.

She's not home.

An uneasy feeling crawls up my spine. Call me obsessive, but I don't like not knowing where she is. As far as I know, she hasn't been with anyone recently but however much that has always eaten at me, I almost wish she was currently seeing someone. It at least would explain why she's not answering her fucking phone.

I pull the Yukon back on the road and head toward the airport.

If she never made it back from Denver, her Jeep would still be parked in the long-term lot.

CHAPTER 4

YANIS

"*D*OESN'T LOOK LIKE her name was on the flight manifest."

That uneasy feeling in my gut expands.

I'm standing beside Bree's Jeep in the airport parking lot and according to the parking attendant, the vehicle hasn't moved since Friday.

"Can you see if maybe she changed her flight?"

"I'll have a look, let me call you right back."

Luckily things are quiet at the vineyard for now and Radar has his laptop on hand.

Not much I can do standing here in the parking lot so I get back in my vehicle and head toward the office. Maybe by the time I get there he'll have answers for me, but at least I'll be able to pull the number for Sue Paxton, the singer's assistant. She'll know when Bree left. If she left at all.

The gnawing feeling in my gut doesn't get any better when my phone rings as I walk into the building.

"Nope. Nothing," Radar says and follows it up

with, "Want me to come in?"

My instinct is to say yes, but I can't leave the client in the lurch.

"No. I'm at the office. Am gonna make a few calls. Stand by, I'll be in touch."

Where the hell could she be? It's already almost ten on a Sunday night and nothing about this feels right.

I try her phone again. No luck. Then I pull up the number for Sue.

"Yanis Mazur, PASS Security. Is Bree still there?" I ask, interrupting the woman's greeting.

For a moment it's quiet on the other side.

"Bree? No. She left this morning."

She sounds confused.

"What time?"

"She changed her flight to seven thirty this morning. The limo picked her up at six twenty."

"Limo?"

"I hired an airport limo. I didn't want her to Uber it."

"And you saw her get in."

"I didn't actually see her leave, I was on a conference call, but I heard the limo drive up and moments later heard the front door close. Is everything okay?"

"No. It looks like she never made it here." My phone beeps with an incoming call. "I've gotta go."

It's Radar.

"She wasn't on any flight out of Denver today."

Ten minutes later I've put calls in to Hutch and

Dimi, who are both on their way in and am on hold with the Denver PD when Lena walks into my office.

"What are you doing here?"

She puts a box of donuts on my desk.

"I talked to Radar. I'm putting coffee on."

With that she walks out and I'm reminded why I hired her in the first place. She is one of the most unflappable and organized people I know. You need someone like that in an office like this.

"Detective Evans."

"Bill, it's Yanis. I have an issue."

I worked with Bill when we were both with the Grand Junction PD, before he left for Denver and I left the force altogether. It takes me a few minutes to explain the situation.

"Airport limo, you say? Hold on a sec."

I hear some muffled voices but I can't make out what they're saying, when he's suddenly back on the phone.

"Brianne Graves, forty-two, thirty-five oh five North 12th Street, apartment twenty-three?"

That gnawing feeling just became a deep burning in my gut.

"Yes," I rasp, clearing my throat before I follow up a little stronger. "Yes, that's Bree. Where is she? Is she okay?"

"Don't know where she is. Discovered her wallet and phone in a bag on the floor behind the driver's seat in an airport limo found on a shoulder near Switzer's Gulch, not far from Deer Creek. There was a pair of sunglasses in the back seat, along with what looks like a crushed cinnamon bun in a napkin."

"*Christ,*" I hiss.

If she left at six twenty and the limo was found not that far from Bobby Lee's house, it means she's already been missing for sixteen fucking hours.

"She there on an assignment?" Bill asks and I confirm, barely able to hold on to my composure. Bill appears to pick up on it. "She someone to you? I mean other than an employee?"

"Fuck yes," I grind out. "She's someone to me."

"Damn, my friend. Looks like she might be in trouble. They found the dead driver slumped over the wheel. Knife wound to the back of the neck, at the base of the skull. Body is at the medical examiner's office, but the detectives on the case are still there with the crime scene unit."

It takes a minute for that information to sink in, during which time Dimi walks in and takes a seat on the other side of my desk.

"If you're suggesting what I think you are, you're barking up the wrong tree. Not her," I tell Bill firmly. My eyes are glued to my brother's worried ones. I'm sure mine reflect the same.

"She wear a blade?" Bill asks gently.

"Doesn't matter. If she had anything to do with this, you wouldn't have found the limo or the body." Across from me Dimi's eyes widen. "And she definitely wouldn't have left her bag with all her information behind. She's smarter than that."

"She could've panicked," he suggests.

"Bree doesn't panic," I fire back. "Someone took her. They would've had to disable her, though. She wouldn't have gone willingly. She's highly skilled in hand-to-hand combat."

"Driver's license says she's only five two."

"And every fucking inch of her able to fight off guys twice her size. Make no mistake."

He harrumphs, making it clear he's not necessarily taking my word for it, but he should. Bree is a force to be reckoned with on all levels. I should know, I haven't been able to shake her power over me for fifteen fucking years.

"I'm flying out there," I announce.

"No flights until morning."

"I'll charter one."

Dimi nods affirmatively and leaves my office. I know he'll be on the phone making it happen before I say my goodbyes.

"Good luck with that," he scoffs.

"Then I'll drive. It's four hours."

"Fine. Call me when you get here. I'll take you to the scene. Smooth the way for you."

"Appreciated," I bite off.

"Yeah, she's somebody special," he confirms to himself.

I don't bother responding and hang up.

Both Lena and Dimi are on the phone in the bullpen.

"Anything?"

Dimi shakes his head.

"Not before six in the morning," Lena shares, hanging up.

Dimas gets off the phone as well just as Jake walks in.

"What now?"

"Load up my Yukon. Arms, tactical gear, surveillance equipment. Bring everything," I announce. "We're driving."

Bree

I SMELL PINE-Sol and laundry detergent.

I struggle to grab hold of that information as it tries to slip from me again.

Soft.

I'm lying on my side with my cheek on a pillow. There's no pain. I can't hear anything and my eyes won't open. It's like floating just below the surface of awareness. I know it's there, I'm reaching for it, but I keep sliding down.

Now I hear something. Voices.

I make an effort to blink my eyes open but something is covering them. A blindfold?

Where am I?

The smell of clean sheets registers and locks in. I'm in a bed, on my side.

I try to move my arm, but my hands are behind my back. It feels like handcuffs.

The voices get louder. Two men approaching.

"...your incompetence. Tell me you disposed of the

driver?"

"Staged it just like you instructed."

I force the clouds from my head and remember the red-carpet event last night. Eating a burger in the back of the limo. Sue in the kitchen this morning. Walking outside, the waiting limo, the waiting driver. Maybe six feet, stocky, Ray-Ban sunglasses, graying goatee. Could've been bald under the chauffeur's cap, I'm not sure.

I'm trying to recall if I heard his voice but I don't think he ever said anything.

Then that burning in my neck. A needle? I was drugged.

I hear the sound of a door opening and force my breathing and heart rate to slow down. Better to let them think I'm still out of it.

"This is not her. Doesn't even look like her."

"She's not wearing makeup. You saw her last night, all dolled up and busting out of that dress."

"Exactly. You're trying to tell me this is the same woman?"

"I watched her go in and watched her come out the house again. I had my eyes on her the whole time, I swear it's her."

"Turn her over."

I let myself go completely slack and resist any reaction as a pair of hands roll me to my stomach. Nothing I want more than to take out the asshole pulling my yoga pants down in the back, but I know I don't stand a chance with my responses sluggish, my hands bound, and two of them hovering over me.

The shiver is almost impossible to suppress when I feel a finger trace down my lower back and come to rest at the base of my spin.

"See that?"

"Don't see nothing, Boss."

Suddenly the finger is gone and I hear the familiar sound of a hammer being pulled back on a gun.

"Bobby Lee has a tattoo there, moron. It's not her, you stupid fuck!"

There is a sound of footsteps running from the room and another set following slower.

Still, the reverberation of a gunshot is so sudden and loud, I can't hold back the involuntary startle.

"You awake?"

The voice is much closer than I anticipated.

If one of them got shot, it means I only have one left to deal with. I just need to bide my time.

Rough hands roll me over again and I feel his hot breath on my face.

"It's close, I'll have to give him that…" he mumbles under his breath.

Then I hear a rustle and a soft metal zing. The hair on my neck stands up; it's the sound of a knife being pulled from its sheath.

"Easy way to tell if someone is faking it, you know," he says in a conversational tone, like we're having a casual chat over coffee.

I feel the edge of the blade scraping the fabric covering my thigh and fight not to react. I need my hands free before I try battling an armed man.

"Real easy..." he drawls as he pulls the knife away.

I know what's coming and force my head clear of all but the need to stay completely motionless.

Even as he stabs the tip of the knife in my leg and drags it through fabric and skin.

I let the hot burn wash over me, focusing on the sound of his heavy breathing above me. I must've managed to keep my face slack and motionless because I can hear him retreating until his footsteps finally leave the room.

I'm not sure how long I lie here. Afraid to move as I hear him travel around the house. The rustling of plastic and then a dragging noise. I'm positive I'm listening to the other man's body being removed. I wait until I hear a door close and the muted sound of a car door slamming before I dare move. I rub my face on the pillow to work the blindfold off and then I open my eyes.

Taking in my surroundings—a large bedroom with a brick fireplace and hewn log walls—I notice two doors, one open and leading to a hallway and a second one closed. A bathroom I presume.

The burning in my leg has subsided some and when I gingerly lift my head, I see the cut is down the front of my thigh but superficial and with minimal bleeding.

If I want to have any chance of escaping, I'll have to get moving.

I manage to get up in a sitting position and wait

until the room stops spinning. I test the cuffs around my wrists. I have small hands but wide palms and am just shy of pulling my left one free. Not allowing myself to think about it, I fold my left thumb as tightly as I can under my fingers, and overextend my wrist in the opposite direction until I feel it pop.

Jesus fucking Christ, that hurts.

Tears burn my eyes as I wrestle my left hand from the cuff, but the next instant I'm off the bed, testing my legs for stability. My first stop is the fireplace where I grab hold of a fire poker with my right hand. The pain in my left is a good cure for any lingering aftereffects of the drug, my head and senses now sharp as I make my way to the door and peek out.

There are two more doors to my right but then the dark hallway ends. To my left it seems to open up into a larger space. Soft light streams into the hallway and I gingerly make my way down.

Suddenly my foot slides out from under me and I land hard on my ass and my left hand, causing me to cry out in pain. I freeze and listen, but there's no sound, no indication there is anyone here.

I try to stand up, careful not to have my feet slide in the puddle of blood I landed in.

The hallway opens up into a large open concept space with another massive stone fireplace and a kitchen at the far end. I steer toward a small lobby in the front and try the door. Too late I realize a fancy log home like this is likely outfitted with an alarm, and the sound is ear-splitting.

The second I have the door open I run out blindly, worried first and foremost to get away as fast and far as possible, and next to find help. The house looks to be in the woods and I dart into the trees on the side of the driveway, to hopefully follow it to a road where I can flag someone down.

The hope to find a friendly neighbor out here diminishes the farther away from the house I get. The night seems to have swallowed up all the light and I can barely see a hand in front of my eyes. It's slowing me down dramatically since I really don't want to fall again, and I can't see where I'm putting my feet.

I have a firm hold on the poker, since I don't have anything else to defend myself with, but I almost drop it when I see headlights filtering through the trees to my left. It looks like a road.

Turning in that direction, I pick up the pace, hoping to be able to cut off the car before it passes. Unfortunately, I trip in the ditch on the side of the road and scramble up the embankment.

The car is already past when I feel the asphalt underneath my feet. I wave my arms and yell as loud as I can. The driver must've seen me because suddenly the brake lights come on, and with a screech of tires the vehicle is thrown in reverse.

Then it picks up speed.

CHAPTER 5

BREE

*I*T TAKES ME a fraction of a second to react.

I stumble back down the deep bank on the side of the road, trying to stay on my feet as I aim for the cover of the trees. Behind me I hear a car door slam and I curse myself for the rookie mistake. Blame it on the lingering brain fog.

Forcing my feet to move, I run into the trees. I have run 5K in under twenty minutes, but that's on a level surface, not through woods with brush and roots providing invisible obstacles in the dark.

Still, I should do better than the average person, even under these circumstances, and judging from the plundering through the undergrowth I hear behind me, the guy isn't an experienced runner. The urge is to pull ahead as far as I can, without losing my footing.

As I try to find a balance between speed and caution, I feel my shoe catch on something and before I can stop myself, I'm flying.

I land hard, slamming my ribs on a protruding root.

With a whoosh the air is knocked out of me and a sharp pain radiates from my ankle. Grinding my teeth against the physical agony, I try to scramble to my feet as I hear him closing in, only to have my ankle collapse underneath me.

Then his body lands on top of me, the pain from my injured ribs forcing a scream from my throat.

"You can scream all you want, my little songbird, but no one will hear you out here."

"I'm not your songbird," I grind out, trying to twist to throw him off me, but my injuries hamper me.

"You'll do until I find her," he grunts behind me as he rocks his hips against my ass.

Bile surges up when I feel his obvious excitement. *Oh, hell no.*

With a surge of adrenaline, I snap my head back, the impact painful for me but worse for him as he yelps and shifts his weight. Enough for me to get my good leg under me and heave him off my back. I use the momentum to drag myself away, making sure not to lose my grip around the only weapon I have.

My eye is on the trunk of a tree so I can pull myself up, but before I can get to it a hand closes around my bad ankle, hauling me back. Ignoring the pain, I flip my body over, swinging my right hand holding the fire poker as hard as I can.

There's a solid thunk when it connects with his head, and without making a sound he collapses, keeping my legs pinned. I immediately scramble to get free, mentally noting a cap of some sort on his head, a black or blue windbreaker, and a silver-colored watch on the wrist of his outstretched arm.

The moment I'm free I brace against the tree, propping myself up. Using my back against the trunk as leverage, I manage to push up on my good leg.

For a second I contemplate going back to the road, to the car, but I don't know if he was alone or not and my instincts scream to get away from him.

With the poker as a makeshift cane, I start moving.

YANIS

"YOU STILL AROUND?"

We're coming up on the outskirts of Denver.

"I'm here. Wanna meet me at the Columbine Valley station?"

"No. I wanna go straight to the scene."

"Let me give the Jefferson County sheriff a heads-up. They have roads blocked off. How far out are you?"

I look at the sign coming up on the side of the road.

"Next exit is the 470."

"Take it. Follow it until you hit the exit for the 121 South. First right is Deer Creek Canyon Road, stick to it for about eight miles. It'll take you straight to Switzer's Gulch. I'll head out there now."

As soon as I hit the 470, I keep my eyes peeled for a gas station. I'm running on fumes and don't want to waste time stranded dry. The next exit has one so I quickly pull off the highway.

"Last chance to hit the head or grab a coffee," I

tell the guys. "Get some water, granola bars, anything wrapped and easy. I don't plan on breaking for meals until we have Bree."

Near twenty hours she's been gone. It's almost inconceivable. Twenty hours by car could have her halfway across the country. Hell, she could be well across the Mexican border by now. I don't even want to think about a plane, which could have her halfway across the world.

I resist the temptation to take the half tank I've filled so far and get back behind the wheel. I may need every drop of gas I can squeeze in.

By the time I'm done, Hutch is back with coffees and Dimi is coming out of the convenience store attached to the gas station with two full grocery bags. His ass barely hits the passenger seat when I pull away from the pump.

Almost twenty minutes later, I see the roadblock up ahead. A sheriff's deputy stops me and I roll down my window.

"Yanis Mazur for Detective Bill Evans."

The deputy nods and waves us past. I pull into what looks like a rest area on the side of the road and park behind a police cruiser. Evans is already walking up to us when we get out of the Yukon.

"What've you got?" I ask, not wasting time on pleasantries.

Bill doesn't seem to take offense and launches into a briefing.

The crime lab is already working on identifying

a fresh set of tracks leading away from the limo still parked up ahead, as well as fingerprints they lifted from the vehicle. The medical examiner will autopsy the body first thing in the morning, but was able to report he estimated the time of death to be between five and seven yesterday morning.

The driver was identified as fifty-seven-year-old Louis Cirillo. He'd worked for Destination Limo for over twenty years, was married with two adult kids. It was the company that apparently tracked the vehicle down after his wife called in, wondering when he'd be home for dinner.

"Any connection to Bobby Lee Rose? Had he driven her before?"

"Not according to her personal assistant. My colleague spoke with her earlier. At this point there's nothing to indicate this incident has anything to do with Ms. Rose."

It's possible, I guess. The driver could've been the target and Bree an unfortunate bystander, but I doubt it. I'll leave that up to the cops. For now, my only concern is getting Bree back.

"Any signs of a struggle?"

Bill shakes his head.

"Nothing we've found thus far."

"What about security cameras at Bobby Lee's house? Has anyone looked at those?" Hutch chips in.

When Bill looks at him lifting an eyebrow, I realize I haven't made any introductions and quickly correct that.

"Jake Hutchinson and my brother, Dimas Mazur, they work with me."

"Working on it," Bill answers the original question. "We have to go through Boulder Records and haven't been able to contact anyone there."

I already have my phone out. I have Glen Delbert's cell number, Boulder's VP of security.

"I'll call."

"It's fucking four thirty in the morning, asshole," he growls when he answers. "What the hell is so important you call me out of fucking bed? Normal people call—"

"Bree's missing."

I hear rustling at the other end and then a door close.

"Talk to me."

"Yesterday morning around six twenty an airport limo picked her up at Bobby Lee's place. At nine forty-five last night, Destination Limo recovered their missing limo a few miles from the house, driver dead behind the wheel, Bree's stuff still in the back of the vehicle, but no Bree. Estimated time of death of the driver was between five and seven in the morning."

I'm trying hard to keep the emotion out of my voice but I'm not sure I was successful.

"What can I do?" Glen asks immediately.

"I need the video feed from the front of the house. Can you access it?"

"Yes." I hear clicking on a keyboard. "Doing it right now. Want it sent to your phone?"

"Yup."

"Working on it. Anything else? I can round up a few guys."

"Stand by on that. We're gonna need a fucking lead first."

A text notification sounds on my phone and then another one.

"You should have the link to the feed and the password. Keep me updated."

I don't bother acknowledging and end the call, pulling up the video.

"I've got the security feed," I announce.

The small group gathers around me as I fast forward to the six fifteen time stamp. On the small screen I see the gate at the end of the drive is open. At six eighteen the limo pulls in off the street and drives up, rounding the rotunda in front of the house. It's impossible to make out the driver, who remains behind the wheel for a few minutes until the driver's side door opens and he steps out. Dark suit, chauffeur's cap pulled low over his face.

He's at least six feet tall by the look of it, comparing the height of the vehicle to his body.

"That's not the driver," Bill observes. "Our vic is five nine at best."

On the screen we can see Bree walk into view, a ball cap and her signature ponytail visible from this angle. She's wearing dark, casual clothes and running shoes. A vast difference from the way she'd been decked out the night before.

The driver opens the door for her, she climbs in, and he appears to lean into the back seat for a minute. Then he straightens up, closes the back door, and climbs in behind the wheel.

"What was that all about?" Dimi asks.

I rewind and we watch it again.

"Stop. Right there." Hutch points at the guy's hand. "Back up a little and don't watch Bree, look at the guy's hand."

We watch as he opens the door and as Bree walks into view, slips his free hand into his jacket pocket and comes out holding something. I move forward frame by frame.

"Not a knife," Dimi grumbles.

"Small, my guess a syringe. The only way Bree wouldn't have been fighting like hell is if she was incapacitated," Hutch offers.

"Send it to me." This from Bill, who wears a grim expression. "This needs to go to Russel, he's the lead."

When I forward the video, I notice the time on my phone. It's coming up on five. She's been out there for almost twenty-three hours. A dark desperation takes hold of me as I realize the likelihood we'll find her alive diminishes by the hour.

I need to do something.

Abruptly I turn to the Yukon and climb behind the wheel.

"Where are we going?" Dimi says, climbing in the passenger seat.

"Driving. Looking. Anything but fucking standing

around with our fingers up our noses."

Hutch is the last to hop into the SUV as Bill walks up to my window.

"Looks like the other vehicle went west. Not much there but trees and mountains."

I'm about to drive off when someone yells for Bill.

"Found something!"

BREE

THE PAIN IS brutal.

I stuck as close to the road as I dared, putting as much distance between me and the guy I knocked out in case I didn't kill him, which in hindsight, I should've made sure of. At some point I had to rest and found a large toppled tree I could hide underneath. It was only supposed to be for a few minutes, but as soon as I felt safe enough to rest my eyes, I was gone.

Catnapping in odd places and positions isn't new to me. Not in this business. But the waking up has never been this painful.

The earlier adrenaline that propelled me also masked the impact of my injuries, but its benefits are gone. It's hitting me full on now and I need to find some help soon.

I'm no longer able to stand on my right leg, the ankle so swollen I'm afraid of the damage I may have done. I don't even want to look at the long cut on my other leg, I can feel it's probably inflamed with the way it's burning, and I'm sure it won't be pretty. My left hand is a throbbing mess, but at least my right hand is functioning. I'm still holding onto that fire poker like my life depends on it.

I tilt my head when I hear the rumble of an engine. Not a car, something bigger like a semi.

I need to get to the road. Somehow.

CHAPTER 6

YANIS

RUCKER FOUND AN injured woman on the side of High Grade Road.

I floored it before Bill had a chance to finish telling me it's the road Deer Creek turns into. He's behind me now, along with another law enforcement vehicle, both with flashing lights and sirens. I'm breaking every speed limit and if a deer crossed the road right now, we'd be in a heap of trouble.

Dimi is on my phone with Bill.

"He says half a mile up."

I nod my acknowledgment and keep my eyes peeled to the road. I have to slow down for a sharp curve, but as soon as I clear it, I can see the logging truck on the shoulder up ahead. The SUV hasn't come to a complete stop when I slam it in park with a jerk and jump out.

I don't see her at first, just the back of a bulky guy, crouched over something in the ditch. From behind me a flashlight hits the scene.

"Bree!"

I don't even realize I yelled out loud when the large man turns, but my focus is on the white face illuminated by the beam of light.

Unceremoniously shoving the Good Samaritan out of the way, I crouch down beside her.

"Talk to me," I bark at her.

"Silver luxury vehicle, sedan. Colorado plates, CX…that's all I remember. White male, dark cap, dark slicker, about six or six one. Cultured voice and—"

"Don't give a fuck about that. You, Bree, where are you hurt?"

"Right ankle, left thigh, left hand, ribs," she lists off with visible effort.

My hand reaches for her face, where a strand of hair has come loose from her ponytail and is in her eyes. I gently stroke it out of the way before I look down her body, noticing dirt and debris stuck to her hair and clothes.

I wince at the sight of her thumb sticking out at an odd angle from her hand. There's a handcuff still attached to her other wrist. Then my eyes trail down to assess the damage to her legs.

"Trouble breathing?"

Dimi crouches down on the other side of her.

"I'm okay," she mumbles, even managing a fucking smile for him.

"Like hell you are." I look over my shoulder and yell. "Where the fuck is the ambulance?"

"Ten minutes out," a disembodied voice sounds behind me.

"Ms. Graves, can you tell me what happened to you?"

An older guy I assume is the lead detective, Russel, steps up to her head and looks down on her. That pisses me right off.

"Fuck off," I snarl. "Your goddamn questions can wait."

"Mazur. Cool it."

Bill is behind me, putting a warning hand on my shoulder which I immediately shrug off.

"I'm not waiting around," I announce. "I'm taking her to the hospital."

Her skin is almost translucent and her gray eyes look far too big for her face. Before anyone can stop me, I slide my arms underneath her and lift her off the damp ground. She hisses sharply with the movement, but when I ask her softly if she's okay she clenches her jaw and nods.

"EMTs will be here any minute."

"That's a minute too late. You wanna help, clear the way for me. We'll intercept the ambulance," I tell Bill.

"Wait…I dropped a fire poker. It has his DNA on it."

Bree's words are slurred and the next moment her eyes flutter shut.

"Let's fucking go."

Hutch keeps his hand on my back for support as I

carry my load up the embankment to the Yukon. Dimi is already ahead, getting into the driver's seat and Hutch helps me into the back seat with Bree in my arms. I bend down and press a kiss to her forehead.

"Gonna get you help, *Tygrys*," I mumble against her skin.

The endearment slides from my lips effortlessly, even after more than a decade.

I used to call her that: Tiger. She reminded me of the character in the book our grandmother used to read to us. Fearless and full of energy.

Of course, that was before it all went to shit.

"ARE YOU HER husband?"

"No, her boss," I snap at the nurse trying to hold me back when I attempt to follow the stretcher with Bree down the corridor.

"Then you have no right to go in with her," she fires back, unintimidated.

Each of my arms is grabbed and I'm pulled away from the door by Hutch and my brother.

We ran into the ambulance on Deer Creek Road and I hopped in the back with her. I was able to relay her reported injuries to the EMTs, since Bree was still out.

On the way to the hospital while they cut off her shirt and pants—revealing bruising on her ribs, a long nasty cut on her leg, and a bad-looking ankle—I had time to think. Too much time, unfortunately.

The last time I sat in the back of an ambulance with her, she'd been shot in the shoulder during a rescue attempt. We'd been tasked with the protection of the rebellious, seventeen-year-old daughter of a wealthy client and had allowed ourselves to be distracted.

With each other.

It was during a late-night shift change, Bree showed up early for hers with a hot meal for me. I was outside of the home in our surveillance van, watching the monitors. She'd been enthusiastic and both of us were insatiable back then. By the time we came up for air, the meal was no longer hot and the girl had managed to turn off the alarms and sneak out of the house to meet with an online 'boyfriend' without us noticing. The boyfriend turned out to be a forty-two-year-old man who'd been grooming the girl for weeks so he could kidnap her for ransom.

It took us twelve hours to get her back, but not before she'd been severely traumatized. Both Bree and I had been riddled with guilt and too eager to take down her captor, resulting in his death and Bree's injury.

While I was in the back of that ambulance, I came to the decision working together and sleeping together had been a mistake. Thinking I was doing the right thing, I broke it off with Bree, half-expecting her to pack it in.

But then her mother died just three weeks after Bree got shot. She was still on medical leave at the time and requested an additional few months' leave to get her mother's affairs in order. It seemed like a good idea at the time, but when she returned to work three months after the shooting, she had a wedding ring on her finger.

It fucking hurt, and for the longest time I hated that I'd meant so little to her she turned around and married someone else. I knew I had no right to feel that way, since I was the one who broke things off, but it burned for years.

I never met the guy she married. She didn't speak of him, or her life outside of PASS. We found a way to work together. She was too valuable to lose with her special combination of skills. By the time Dimi joined PASS, she no longer wore her ring. I never wanted to know and she never volunteered what happened.

Yet here I am, many years later, sitting once again in a hospital waiting room to hear the extent of her injuries, wanting to know it all.

They say love and hate are two sides of the same coin and over the past years I've started to believe it myself.

After last night I know it to be true.

BREE

SOMEONE IS SHINING a bright light in my eye.

"Brianne? It's Dr. Finley. You're at Littleton Adventist Hospital."

I force my eyes open, blinking a few times to clear my vision.

"Hi."

"Do you remember what day it is?"

"Sunday." I think hard. "No…Monday."

By the time they pulled me out of the back of the ambulance the sun was starting to come up. I'd been gone for almost twenty-four hours.

"I need to talk to the police," I announce, trying to sit up.

A firm hand on my shoulder keeps me in the bed.

"First we take care of your injuries," he says in a tone that leaves no room for argument.

For the next however long, I'm probed and prodded, X-rayed, CT-scanned, poked for blood, cleaned out and stitched up, and my ankle is stabilized. Then Dr. Finley leaves the room, telling me to rest while we wait for results.

I'm missing chunks of time when I was either drugged or out of it, but I remember everything I took an active part in. I recall the log home, the trek through the woods, and flagging down the wrong damn car. I remember how every part of me got hurt. Crawling up the embankment to try and catch the first truck that rumbled by, leaving me despondent. By the time I heard the second one approach, I was able to do little more than wave the poker in the air, hoping someone would spot me.

I also recall everything after that, Yanis's sharp bark but worried eyes. The way he lifted me in his arms, that cruel mouth of his nothing but a thin line, but his touch exquisitely gentle.

I'm so tired, I don't even have the energy to protest and close my eyes.

The next thing I know the doctor is back, this time with Yanis who lingers by the door.

"So, Ms. Graves, looks like you've torn ligaments in your ankle but no fractures. It's a significant injury that'll require rest and—"

"How long?" I interrupt, the prospect of any time off work not a happy one for me.

"It can take anywhere from three to six months to heal. A lot depends on you."

Dr. Finley outlines the treatment plan for my ankle, which is basically sit on my ass with my foot up for the next three to four weeks to start with. After that I have to see a PT, who will tell me when I'm ready to start moving again.

I'll heal.

The cut took twenty-four stitches to close and will leave a mark but is otherwise of no concern. The two broken ribs will heal on their own, as long as I don't sleep lying flat and keep breathing deeply, even though it hurts like a motherfucker.

I'll heal but it's going to be hell.

Rest is not in my vocabulary and the thought of being stuck in my two-bedroom apartment with only a small balcony for a month or God forbid, longer, is almost as terrifying as the past twenty-four hours have been.

I glance over at Yanis, who has been quiet so far.

"Because you've been through quite an ordeal and

were dehydrated when you got here, we're gonna keep you overnight."

Dr. Finley lifts his hand to silence me when I open my mouth to share my opinion on that. Behind him I catch Yanis grinning and I send him a dirty look.

"You're going to need some help at home, though. At least until the swelling is down; I don't want you to put any weight on that ankle."

"She won't."

The first words from Yanis and they're imperious. Figures, he's rarely anything *but* bossy.

Dr. Finley leaves saying he'll stop by in the morning to check in on me, and then I'm left with Yanis still looming by the doorway, staring at me.

I can't make out what the funny expression on his face is supposed to mean. I'd say it's concern, but I don't trust my instincts when it comes to this man. This morning he seemed pissed and started barking at me, but then seconds later he kissed my forehead and called me *Tygrys*.

The last time I heard that was before he dumped me while I was recovering from a gunshot wound in the hospital. I still remember the utter devastation I felt, despite putting on a strong face. I had no choice; I'd just found out my mother was terminally ill, and with no one else to look after her I had to stay standing.

But something died inside me that day and I'm not about to be fooled by his gentle lips and sweet words again.

"What?" I snap, suddenly angry he's even standing

in my room.

He inhales deeply and releases his breath slowly before walking up to the bed.

"Scared the fuck out of me."

See?

Words like that. Words that make me hope perhaps he still cares, when I know damn well I'm just another employee to him. One he can barely seem to tolerate at times.

I'm still trying to come up with a snappy comeback when he adds, "The boys are gonna want to see you before heading back to Grand Junction. That okay?"

Does that mean they're all driving back?

"By all means."

I wave my hand haphazardly, determined not to be disappointed. Yanis frowns, eyeing me curiously for a moment, before turning and disappearing down the hall.

Dimi and Jake don't stay long and keep the visit light and easy, but I don't like it when they leave. I suddenly feel like an outsider.

At some point I'm sure the cops will show up, wanting their pound of flesh, but until they get here I'm going to get some rest.

Not much, as it turns out, when the scraping of a chair wakes me up.

"Aren't you heading back?" I ask Yanis, who takes a seat beside the bed.

"Tomorrow."

He doesn't say *with you*, but it's implied.

There it is again, that pesky bubble of hope, but I quickly squash it before it has a chance to grow. He's being a responsible employer, that's all.

CHAPTER 7

YANIS

A HANDFUL OF hours of restless sleep in three days isn't cutting it.

I woke up on a waiting room couch two doors down from Bree's room. It's as far as I was willing to go after the nurse booted me out. Bree tried to get me to leave for hours, but her threats to kick my ass didn't quite hold their usual punch. Not while lying in a hospital bed, but I'm sure once she recovers, she'll make good on the promise to clean my clock.

She's still sleeping—I poked my head in a few minutes ago—so I'm on the hunt for some coffee. It's barely five in the morning and I'm eager to take her back to Grand Junction.

Yesterday afternoon, Bill Evans showed up with his colleague to get Bree's statement. Good thing Bill was there, otherwise I might've taken a swing at that idiot Russel, who was doing most of the questioning and he wasn't gentle about it either.

The idiot pushed Bree hard with his questions, was

skeptical at all her answers, and all but accused her of making shit up. Unfortunately, when he produced a map, pointing out where she'd been found and asked her to retrace her steps to the house she was held at, she couldn't do it. Never mind that she'd been drugged, injured, and had been trudging through the woods for hours.

Luckily Evans jumped in or I would've. The woman had given them more information than any normal person could have. She was detailed with what she did remember. Even recalled part of a license plate she'd only had a brief glimpse of in the dark.

I eventually walked the detectives out, leaving her to rest. She was exhausted, and Bill promised he'd keep me in the loop on the investigation. I got my phone charger out of the Yukon, grabbed a few of the snacks and a water Dimi bought earlier, and by the time I got back to the room she was sleeping.

This morning there are only two other people in the diner I find around the corner from the hospital. The moment I take a seat, a waitress shows up with a pot of coffee and holds it up in lieu of a question.

"Please, and could I have three eggs over hard, bacon, whole wheat toast, and home fries?"

All I've had to eat since leaving Grand Junction is a donut, two granola bars, and a bag of chips. I need something substantial in my stomach.

"You bet."

She snaps her gum between her teeth, as she fills one of the mugs that was upside down on the table before taking off with my order.

I scan through emails and messages, answering what I can and forwarding the rest to Dimi until breakfast arrives. Business is picking up with another three booths filled in the meantime. My guess, hospital staff either coming off shift or about to start.

I'm shoveling down my meal when a message comes in from Lena asking how Bree is. Instead of messaging back, I call her. There are some things I want her to take care of before we get home.

"Jesus. Do you sleep?" she complains, answering on the third ring.

"Only when unavoidable. Bree is okay, sleeping a lot but we'll be coming back today. How is everything at the office?"

"I called in Shep and spoke with Kai. He won't be back until Thursday but Shep is coming in this morning. I've also adjusted your schedule for the vineyard, Shep will take over your place on the rotation for this week. We can adjust after if needed."

"Good. Did Bree's report on—"

"Yup," she interrupts. "Went to the client yesterday. Also got two inquiries I passed on to Hutch and the order for Finley's Fields came in yesterday afternoon. Dimi and Radar are going to head out there to do the installation. Everything's under control, Boss. You just worry about Bree."

Right, as if I don't already.

"Okay. See if you can get into her apartment? Pack up some of her shit and get it over to my place."

Lena is silent for a beat or two.

"You're kidding, right?"

Fuck, no, I'm not kidding. She has a third-floor apartment in a building without elevators. I have a one-level house with extra bedrooms. It makes sense.

"No. She's not allowed to put any weight on that foot for at least a week and her other leg has twenty-four fucking stitches holding it together."

A slight exaggeration but the point is she shouldn't be hopping around on that leg. She should also be looked after until she's a bit more mobile.

Lena snorts. Apparently, she finds that funny. I don't find it funny at all.

"Your funeral, Boss," she jokes, chuckling. "I'll see what I can do, but my guess is she'll balk. She'll want to be in her own space with her own things. I know I would."

I take a moment to think that over and have to concede she may have a point.

"Fine. Then go to my place, pack up a bag for me, and get it over to her apartment."

I don't wait and hang up before she can launch an objection. One way or another, Bree needs looking after in the short term, and she may not like it, but it'll be me doing it. I know her likes and dislikes, I know she takes her coffee black and needs half an hour of quiet in the morning so she can wake up.

I also know she prefers cream cheese to butter on her toast and will eat any pizza you put in front of her but her favorite is Hawaiian. She bites her bottom lip when she's worried, twirls her ponytail when she disagrees, and smiles way too brightly when she's hurting. She pretends to be tough as nails, but her empathy is one of her best traits. She'll be gentle with others but hard on herself.

I know her too well.

Which is how I also know Lena is right in her thinking. Bree will hate me invading her space and robbing her of her independence. She's not going to make it easy, but that won't stop me from doing what is right.

From what I should've done years ago.

BREE

"How ARE YOU doing?"

His finger lightly brushes the top of my left hand.

With my thumb back in its intended position— which had been almost as easy as dislocating it—I'm tempted to flip my hand palm up and tangle my fingers with his.

With the bleak prospect of the coming weeks, the comfort of his hand might feel good but wouldn't be smart. I remember, not so long ago, taking the liberty of touching Yanis in comfort and it left me with an old wound oozing.

"I'm okay."

I'm actually sore, the seat belt feels restrictive around me, my ankle is throbbing, and we're only halfway home.

Surprising how you can feel fine in a hospital

bed, but something as insignificant as sitting in a car knocks the wind right out of you.

I can feel Yanis's eyes on me.

"Sure you are," he comments dryly, patting my hand before putting his back on the wheel. "Why don't you close your eyes for a bit, unless you need to make a stop?"

A stop? Hell no. I'd rather deal with a full bladder than have him pick me up again like he did, lifting me in the passenger seat. The lack of personal space makes it hard to stick to the colleagues-only relationship we've cultivated all these years. At least it does for me.

"I'm good," I mumble, demonstratively closing my eyes.

I wake up, two hours later, outside my apartment building with Yanis opening the passenger side door.

"I can walk," I start, but he's already sliding his hand underneath my legs.

"Arms around my neck," he instructs. "I'll come back down to grab your stuff later."

Detective Evans showed up this morning with my backpack and phone. Crime techs had looked them over, judging from the smudges of fingerprint powder, but since mine were the only ones found they were able to release them.

He didn't have any news to share, but would contact us if anything popped up or if they had further questions for me.

The man doesn't even break a sweat as he carries

me up three flights of stairs to my floor. My front door is open and to my surprise Lena is waiting in my apartment with Phil, the manager, who looks a little nervous. Both look on with interest as Yanis installs me on the couch, carefully lifting my ankle onto a throw pillow.

"I hope this is okay?" the older man mutters, wringing his hands. "She mentioned you were in an accident."

"It's fine," I quickly put him at ease, despite feeling a little weirded out having people in my normally solitary space.

"Okay, I'll get going then."

I wait until he leaves before turning to a grinning Lena.

"What are you doing here?"

"Dropping off some stuff and making sure you're all right with my own two eyes," she says, throwing Yanis a look I can't quite decipher.

"What stuff? Work?"

Yanis snorts.

"No work, not until you're cleared," he grumbles.

"He was talking about physical work. I can still work on my laptop."

"All he said was no work."

Semantics. Surely there's nothing wrong with doing some work remotely.

"Yes," I agree patiently, "but he clearly implied nothing causing physical strain."

His eyes narrow on me.

"He also said rest. Work does not equal rest."

I let out an annoyed sigh. It's not worth arguing about since he's going to be gone soon enough anyway.

Lena seems to be enjoying our interaction as her eyes dart from me to him.

"Don't you have somewhere to be?" Yanis asks her.

"Are you kidding? And miss all the fun?" she fires back.

I glare at him, which he doesn't seem to notice at all, as he locks into a staredown with Lena.

"Oh fine," she concedes, rolling her eyes at Yanis. "I'll head back to the office. I put your bag in the spare bedroom, by the way."

Wait.

"Uh, I'm sorry, whose bag in what spare bedroom?"

Turning to me with an innocent look on her face, she explains, "Yanis's overnight bag in *your* spare bedroom. Although if you ask me, it's a waste of clean sheets."

My mouth is still hanging open when she walks out of my apartment and pulls the door shut.

"Wait. Why is your bag—"

But when I turn to Yanis, he's on his way to my kitchen. He opens my cupboard, grabs a glass, and fills it from my faucet. Then he brings it to me.

"Need anything else?" he asks, as if I hadn't spoken. "I'll get your stuff from the car and then I'm gonna have a quick shower. Try to get some rest."

He presses the TV remote in my hand and disappears out the door.

What the hell?

I can't have him staying here, and he certainly can't have a shower in my only bathroom. The thought of him…

Nope, that can't happen.

Surely he's not thinking of sticking around and playing nurse? That would be beyond awkward.

I'm wound up when he returns and blast him the moment he walks in the door.

"You can't stay."

"Okay, then we pack you a bag and you come stay with me," he says, cool as a cucumber.

My brows snap together and I imagine steam may be coming from my ears.

"That's an even worse idea," I sputter.

"You're being stubborn. You're in no shape to look after yourself."

Nothing like telling me I'm stubborn and can't look after myself to get my blood boiling.

"I'm not stubborn and I'm perfectly fine."

I push myself up, as I'm lifting my foot off the couch, and accidentally bump it into the edge of the coffee table.

"*Fuck!*" I yell out at the pain.

Immediately Yanis is there, pushing me back down on the couch, and carefully lifting my foot.

"Smart move," he mumbles, making me want to slug him hard. "Gonna grab that shower now," he adds.

Then he leaves me to stew as he disappears toward the bedrooms.

An angry, frustrated tear slips from my eye.

Damn that man.

CHAPTER 8

BREE

"*H*AND ME YOUR cup."

He reaches a hand over my shoulder and I give him my empty coffee mug.

We've been doing this dance now for two days. Yanis, as normal, is man of few words, and I've become silently compliant. He has the ability to make me feel like a recalcitrant child and behave like one too.

I tried doing things myself to prove I didn't need him around, but that didn't go so well. I finally gave in to letting him take care of me. He's been hands-on, cooking, serving me, and even helping me to the bathroom and into bed.

I've done what I can sitting down, but haven't had a shower, and desperately need one. My hair is getting greasy and washing with a washcloth while sitting on the toilet only goes so far.

"Here you go," he says, handing the mug back. "Lena is coming by with some stuff for me to sign, but this afternoon I have a meeting with the new Chief Security Officer of Jelnyk Mining, who is flying in."

He sits back down at my small dining table, which has been reclaimed as a desk for Yanis to work from.

Jelnyk is one of our long-term clients. The company has mines all over Latin America and we provide security frameworks for them. Each mine comes with a different set of challenges: product, environment, political unrest, physical landscape, and requires customized security. Although a lot of it can be planned remotely, we need a man on the ground— sometimes for months—during the design phase, and then to make sure the system works effectively.

"Is there a problem at one of the mines?" I want to know, turning to look at him.

He shakes his head. "No, but they're expanding operations of one of their smaller sites in Peru."

"Oh. Will you be sending one of the guys out?"

"Depends, it sounds like I may have to make a trip out there myself at some point. I'll find out more today."

I nod and turn back to the book I've been trying to read. It's good but a little steamy. Every time things get physical in the story; I become highly aware of Yanis's proximity and stop reading.

Right now, I have a hard time concentrating on the story at all. I really want that shower but I hate asking him for help. Maybe I can ask Lena.

"What time is Lena coming?"

He lifts his head.

"She said she had an errand to run on her lunch break and would pop in on her way. I'm guessing around noon. Why? Did you need her for something?"

Damn.

"It's been three days; I need a shower and was going to—"

He's already up and moving toward me.

"Shoulda said something," he grumbles, plucking my mug and Kindle out of my hands before picking me up off the couch.

"Yanis, really. You've got stuff to do."

"It'll wait."

He sets me down in the bathroom and I swallow my irritation at being carried like baggage everywhere. Surely that's a bit extreme, despite what the doctor said. How do other people do this? Or what if roles were reversed?

"You know you have to stop lugging me around."

He braces his hand on the vanity and leans in close.

"Look, I know you hate this, but the less strain you put on your body right now the faster you'll recover. I want you back to normal and on your feet as much as you do."

My body tenses up.

Right. In other words, he doesn't want to waste any more time with me than necessary. I get it.

He growls and with a finger under my chin lifts my face. He's so close I can see the golden swirls in his blue eyes. They darken when he's angry or when he used to get turned on.

"Whatever you've got running around that mind of yours, stop. You overthink things. Let me look after you."

It's almost a plea and confuses me even more.

"Fine," I mumble ungraciously, eliciting a sigh from him.

"Good. Can you get yourself undressed? I'm just gonna grab a kitchen chair so you can sit down in the shower."

It shouldn't bother me; I share a locker room with the guys back at the office. Those brief flashes of nudity don't bother me. At least they don't under those circumstances. But I feel vulnerable here, in my own bathroom, with him. More exposed and in much closer proximity.

My body has changed in the past decade or so.

Pushing through my discomfort, I quickly strip off my shirt and out of my lounge pants. I haven't bothered with underwear since I got home. It's easier this way.

Yanis returns with one of my plastic utilitarian kitchen chairs and sets it in the tub, turning the faucet on in the shower without even casting me a glance. With the water running he turns to me and sinks down on his knees, startling me when he picks up my bad ankle. With sure movements he takes off the brace.

"Looks a bit better," he comments matter-of-factly, as if I'm not sitting here buck naked.

His complete focus is on my foot which does look better, less swollen. His eyes never venture up. Maybe he's as uncomfortable as I am.

"I don't mean to be a bother. I could've asked Willa to help."

Now he looks up, a rare smile tugging at his lips.

"Willa is at the hospital."

I shake my head, not understanding.

"Hospital?"

"Her baby is in the NICU."

"Baby?"

I sound like a parrot but none of what he says makes sense. I've seen enough of Willa to know she was not pregnant. Besides, Dimi would've howled at the moon. The whole world would've known.

"They adopted a newborn. Told me last weekend."

"I had no idea."

"News to me too," he says with a twist of his lips. "One person's tragedy is another's dream come true."

Then he explains how this opportunity for Dimi and Willa came about as he helps me in the tub.

I try not to notice how his touch feels on my bare skin.

YANIS

I HAVE A hard time concentrating on my client.

Good thing I thought, at the last minute, Radar should be sitting in because knowing him, he'll have detailed notes of everything the man is rattling off.

My mind isn't on work, it's on the woman I left installed on her couch with the TV remote, her phone, a bottle of water, and a box of cookies by her side.

Neither of us mentioned her red-rimmed eyes when I helped her dry off after her shower.

If not for years of experience curbing my baser instincts when it comes to Bree, I would've taken her wet, slick body in my arms. So fucking tempting. She's changed over the years. Fuller, a bit softer, and undeniably more feminine than the tight, athletic body I remember.

I almost kissed her when I noticed the faint scar bisecting her lower belly. I tried not to stare at the unfamiliar sight, thoughts of what the incision might represent swirling around my head. I can't remember a time she was off for longer than maybe a week at a time. Except perhaps the time right after I broke things off between us. The kind of surgeries that leave a scar like that would surely require a longer recovery.

She'd been gone for three-and-a-half months before she came back married. A marriage I wish I'd asked her about at the time.

I sure as hell intend to ask her about it now. Before I take this thing with Bree any further. One thing is clear, the chemistry we once had is still there, in fact, the air was thick with it earlier. The way her breath hitched and goosebumps rose on her skin when I touched her confirmed she felt it too. As soon as I can get through this meeting, I plan to pick up some dinner, head back to her apartment, and clear the air.

One way or another.

"You seemed distracted in there. Everything all right?"

Radar holds the door open to the parking lot as we walk out of the airport where we had the meeting with Jelnyk Mining security.

"Fine. Tell me you made notes?"

"Of course."

"Good. Email them to me. We'll talk tomorrow."

Without waiting for a response, I head toward the Yukon.

"Boss!"

Radar is still standing where I left him.

"Yeah?"

"Bree up for visitors?"

"No." The denial is out before I can think. Fucking Radar smirks. "Call and ask her yourself. Tomorrow," I add before I get behind the wheel.

I stop by the Village Inn to pick up a couple of All-American Cheeseburgers, Bree's favorite, before heading back to her place.

She looks a little rumpled when I walk in, probably napping. She's been doing a lot of that the past few days. I thought it was to avoid conversation with me, but maybe her body needs the extra sleep to heal.

"Is that…"

"Village Inn."

The solemn face I've seen the past few days suddenly brightens up with the smile she shoots me.

"Yesss. I'm starving."

One of the things I've always liked about her is her healthy, unapologetic appetite. The moment I hand her the plate I dumped her fries and burger on she

91

dives in.

We've been eating quietly for a while when Bree speaks up.

"I had a call earlier. Follow-up appointment at St. Mary's for four tomorrow afternoon. I can take a cab or something."

I raise an eyebrow.

"Well, I didn't want to presume," she adds snippily.

I know she hates not being independent—fuck, I'd hate it too—but part of me hoped it might've waned a little. At least with me.

"Haven't spent the past few nights crashing here because your view rocks, Bree. Presumption is expected."

She rolls her eyes but her mouth twitches.

"Fine. Thanks, and thanks for the burger. It's my favorite."

I stuff the last bite of mine in my mouth and mumble, "I know."

While she clears the final few fries from her plate, I decide this is as good a time as any.

"We need to talk."

I read suspicion in her eyes when she turns them on me.

"About?"

"Us."

She has trouble swallowing that final bite and grabs for her water to wash it down.

"What us? There hasn't been an 'us' for just about all of the years we've known each other. Save for maybe a month or two. Any 'us' there may have been has long been washed out by over a decade of simply working together."

Something about the way she formulates her response so readily makes me wonder if she thinks about what we were to each other—however brief—more than she's willing to admit.

"That's a load of bull, and you know it. There's always been more."

I grab our plates, set them on the far end of the coffee table, and turn my body toward her. I'm purposely confrontational. Bree is wired like I am in a lot of ways. She responds to any perceived threat with a full-frontal attack. The best way to get her talking is to poke at her armor.

Her body language screams disbelief even before she speaks.

"Did you hit your head or something? I was married for chrissakes."

She makes a good play for disbelief but I'm not buying it. I never really did, I was just safer with her hidden behind the identity she'd woven, so I could justify what I'd done.

But I'm done giving myself that out, and I'm done accepting hers.

"Were you? I can't remember ever meeting him, or you talking about him much. He was just a name you may have mentioned."

"Ted Dillard, and we *were* married. For seven years, in fact," she spits back. "If you don't believe me, check the album on the bottom shelf."

She points at the low bookcase underneath her TV. I spot the album and get up to grab it. The first page is a wedding picture of Bree wearing a sundress, her hair falling loose over her shoulders, holding a simple bouquet of daisies. With his arm casually around her shoulders stands a tall, blond-haired man with a boyish face, in dress uniform. Both are barefoot standing on the sand as they smile for the camera, a blue ocean in the background.

My gut sours, but then I notice the tension on Bree's face, the tightness of her smile, and the way her shoulders are pulled up almost to her ears.

So maybe she was married, but she wasn't happy about it.

"A military man," I comment, putting the album back in its spot and reclaiming my seat beside her on the couch.

"Armed Forces warrant officer. Helicopter pilot at Fort Carson."

"Fort Carson?" That's in Colorado Springs, a good five-hour drive from here, if you're lucky. "That's quite the commute," I point out, keeping a close eye out for her reaction.

"Worked for us."

If her noncommittal response is intended to satisfy me, she's sorely mistaken. It just makes the whole thing reek more like a marriage of convenience. What convenience though?

Fuck, my years of guilt-induced hands-off when it

came to Bree are coming back to haunt me.

"Not being together?"

The Bree I knew from back then was enthusiastic, attentive, and grabbing every opportunity to get close. I can't see her as satisfied and happy when her man is a fucking five-hour drive away.

Besides, he doesn't look her type. Despite the military background, he looks too soft for her.

"We both had a career path when we went into it," she hurries to explain with a shrug of her shoulders. "Both of our expectations were open and clear."

That last comment is meant as a dig at me and I'll grant her that. I turned like a damn leaf in the wind on her and deserve it.

"Really? That's pretty advanced for someone you can't have known for more than a month or so?"

A triumphant smirk tugs at the corner of her mouth.

"Ted and I have known each other since elementary school. We grew up in the same neighborhood. Went through high school together before we headed off to college." She leans closer and very clearly articulates, "He showed up for my mother's funeral."

Christ. She doesn't pull any punches.

I have no excuse for not showing up. Zero. Thought I had one back then, a new client who kept me pulling double shifts—seeing that we were short-handed at the time—but in the end I was avoiding her. Afraid if I showed up, saw her in pain, I'd lose what little resolve I had. I convinced myself it was better, for Bree, if I stayed away.

"Whatever happened to wanting a family? Or your dream house with a view of the canyons?"

Low blows, and I know it, but it's the only way I know to open up the old wounds so we can get at the truth.

The impact is instant as pain shows in the form of shining eyes and shocked mouth.

"Dreams change." She averts her gaze and speaks so softly I can barely make out the words.

Raw. She sounds raw.

It's exactly what I was aiming for, but now that I'm here I can't bring myself to pull her story from her.

Instead, I cup her face and lean in to brush my lips against her slack ones.

"They don't have to," I whisper back.

CHAPTER 9

BREE

I SHOULD BE shocked at the feel of his mouth on mine.

Yet it's like coming home.

His gentle persuasion at the seam of my lips is still so painfully familiar. How is it possible that in all the years, after what were only a few months of being together, the memory of them is still seared into my being?

His taste and his touch wake a craving I used to be insatiable with, and nothing or no one since has been able to fill that hunger.

Oh, I've tried, but somehow none of the modest number of men, who saw more than one date, were able to erase the memory of this.

My body responds as if it's the most natural thing to open my mouth to his tongue and slip my arms around his neck. His hair is shorter now and I don't have much to grab onto so my nails scratch restlessly over his scalp.

He used to love that, having my fingers in his hair and, apparently, he hasn't forgotten that either as he moans deep in my mouth. I try to shift, wanting to get closer, needing to feel the pressure of his chest against my breasts, eager for his touch.

Instead, he pulls his mouth away and leans his forehead against mine. Already we're both panting like racehorses, and I wonder if he feels as overcome by that same insatiable need we used to share.

"Still my *Tygrys,*" he whispers before lifting his head and looking down at me.

The golden swirls seem to move in the blue of his eyes and I can't avert mine.

"Why?"

I'm not sure where the question comes from or exactly what it is I want to know—maybe all of it—but it hangs between us for endless seconds as he searches my face.

"I thought I was doing the right thing, but I was so wrong."

His voice is raw, tormented, like the look in his eyes I would sometimes catch but quickly dismiss as a figment of my imagination.

With his fingertips he traces my face, eyebrows, cheekbones, down my nose, and to the small groove bisecting my upper lip.

"I'll need more words," I prompt him softly, my mouth moving against his fingers.

I'm mesmerized by his eyes, so open and unguarded, but I don't want to guess and be wrong.

So many years and layers, so much life now between us.

"I was protecting you. We were young, wrapped up in each other. Consumed to the point the rest of the world didn't exist for me when you were around. I missed her coming out of her house. That girl carries the scars with her for the rest of her life because I couldn't look away from you."

"We did. We both carry that responsibility. Not just you," I remind him. "I was there too, Yanis."

He strokes his knuckles over my cheek. Our faces still so close I can feel his breath against my skin. Consumed is a good word for it.

"I know, but it was my promise to keep her safe, my signature on the contract, my handshake sealing it. Just like you are my employee, my responsibility. Then you got shot."

For the first time he closes his eyes, dropping his head to my shoulder. Hiding.

"So much blood, Bree. It's all I could see. Red. I emptied my gun into the guy. Just kept pumping. No control, just pure emotion."

"It was justified." I lean my cheek against his head. "He molested her, shot me, you were justified."

"Call it what you want but it wasn't justice, that was rage. It scared me. You hurt scared me. I thought I was protecting you. Us." He slowly lifts his head. "Then life happened and it seemed I'd made the right choice."

"You chose for both of us."

It's an accusation that has burned a hole in my gut. Maybe my biggest grudge has always been I didn't have a voice. Not in any of it. Not then and not in what happened after. I've never had any say in what happened. Circumstances dictated; events directed me.

"I did."

No guise in his voice or his face.

"So I ask you again, why? Why now? Why?"

The opening of old wounds is painful. You'd think time would have dulled, but it hasn't. Not really. Maybe because we've never had an occasion like this one—never sought one out—a chance to let what for me has admittedly been a festering cut, just under my skin, needing to bleed clean.

"Why care for me now?"

My voice cracks as the words tumble out, revealing not only the deep hurt that is alive in me, but all the other feelings I thought I had locked away in the far recesses of my mind.

"I've never not cared," he says gruffly, sitting back to run a hand through his hair. "As to what brings us here; call it full circle. I ended us when you could've died, it almost ended me this past weekend when I didn't know if you were still alive. Lost and found."

He reaches out and grabs one of my hands with his.

I choke up, needing the connection as much as I want to reject it. I can't dismiss the chasm of time between us. The loss that separates us. The hurt that still exists. The trust that was broken. I've always known Yanis is the one person with the capacity to break me, and I'm afraid if I let him in it might leave me destroyed.

Irrevocably this time.

"It's too late," I whisper.

His hand flexes around mine and I drop my gaze to our joined hands.

"It's not. It's never too late."

"Yanis…" I plead, but he's persistent.

"We're older. We've changed. I'm not asking you to go back where we were then, I'm asking you to start again. From this point forward."

"It's not that easy."

He coughs out a sardonic laugh.

"Tell me about it. We have a lot to clear out of the way, but I'm still asking. Take a chance."

It's his turn to plead, and I glance over to him finding nothing but sincerity in his eyes. The sudden inflation of my little balloon of hope scares me. It would be so easy to lose myself to his draw. It's not just his looks, which have only improved with age, but it's his solid judgment, his strong morals, his effortless leadership, his sense of responsibility to everything and everyone. Ironically, all the things that drove him to break things off with me.

I know that on a cerebral level, but my heart…I'm afraid to risk it.

"What'll happen if I take a chance?"

He lets go of my hand and lifts his to my face, his

touch infinitely gentle as he places his palm against my cheek.

"We go slow. Learn each other again. Be honest about who we are. Talk through roadblocks or baggage that might pop up along the way."

I can't hold back the grin that wants to surface at his words.

"Talk, Yanis? I have to admit, that's probably the newest and most surprising change in you. You were never a talker, you're a doer. I swear I've heard more words from you tonight than I have in all the years I've known you combined."

He shrugs with a self-deprecating smirk on his lips.

"Even old dogs can learn new tricks."

I hope so. God, I hope so.

He curves an arm around my shoulder, pulls me into his body, and reaches for the remote.

"Enough talking for tonight."

I allow myself a smile as I settle back against him.

He finds an episode of *Longmire*, which I normally love. Unfortunately, I'm wiped, emotionally drained, and Yanis's chest is as comfortable as I remember.

We've barely passed the opening credits when my eyes grow heavy.

YANIS

I CAN TELL she's disappointed when we leave her doctor's office.

When I offered to wait in the outer office, she didn't object. It's early yet, I have to exercise patience and give her a chance to get used to the idea of an *us* again.

No, not again. An us, *period*.

Last night was good. I still have a thousand and one questions I want to ask her, but I get the sense I push too hard and she'll retreat. Feeling her body melt into mine was enough for the moment. She also let me kiss her when I carried her to her bed, but I didn't stay.

It would've been too easy to give in to that fire we still seem able to stoke in each other, but I don't want us to burn hot and crash after. I want us to burn hot and make that fire last.

I bend over the back of the wheelchair I'm pushing her in.

"What did he say?"

"Another whole week for the stitches," she grumbles. "No weight on the ankle until all the swelling and bruising is gone. He wants to see me again next week and then we'll talk about physical therapy."

She sounds dejected. It's tough to be helpless, but I'm secretly glad it bought me another week of dependency.

Seven more days of showing her I mean what I say before I lose my leverage.

"Where are we going?" she asks when I push her wheelchair past the exit to the parking lot.

"Talked to Dimi this morning. He asked us to come meet Max."

She twists her head back and glances up with shock on her face.

"They named him after your father?"

I grin back.

"Yeah. It's a surprise for my parents, though. They're arriving this weekend. They're gonna be staying at my place."

"You'll be going home then?"

She tries to make it sound casual, but can't quite hide the hint of disappointment.

"You've met my parents, right? They like roaming around naked."

I mock-shiver.

Actually, not so much 'mock' since I've seen my parents' wrinkled bare attributes one too many times growing up.

Still, it earns me her grin. She has met them. She knows what they're like, she's just never had to be witness to it. They tend to get dressed for company.

"You saw me naked yesterday," she teases. "You didn't seem offended."

"No comparison. *You* I wouldn't mind naked all the time."

I'd love to capitalize on the flash of heat spreading over her face and the slight puff of air leaving her lips slightly open, but we've reached the NICU and Dimi is walking toward us.

I've never seen my brother like this. He softens when he looks at his wife, clearly loves her to distraction, but this... He radiates happiness.

Damn if my heart doesn't squeeze in my chest. My brother, who I've been at odds with more often than not, who came back from his last rotation a shell of the man he was going into the armed forces, who battled through the loss of his leg, and the resulting PTSD, to become one of my most valuable operatives and a fantastic husband to Willa.

I'm proud. So fucking proud of him.

His eyes, the same green color as my mother's, are bright and full of life as he walks right up to Bree and greets her with a hug and a kiss. Then he turns to me, that goofy grin still on his face as he pulls me into a hug.

"I wanted you to be the first to meet him," he relays softly before he lets me go.

"Fucking happy for you, Brother. So fucking happy."

"We can only have one visitor at a time in there," he says apologetically.

I look down at Bree, whose eyes have become suspiciously shiny at the brotherly display.

"You go," I tell her, but she vehemently shakes her head.

"No. You. I can watch from here."

She puts her hands on the wheels and rolls herself to the large viewing window. I follow her and lean down.

"Sure?"

She smiles up at me.

"Yeah, go."

I press a kiss to her forehead and turn to my brother, who is looking at me slack-jawed.

"No shit?"

Then he grins even wider at my casual shrug.

"About fucking time."

Willa is sitting in a rocker when we walk in, a tiny bundle pressed against the skin of her upper chest.

"Meet Max."

His face is a little splotchy, his little fist tucked under his chin, and his mouth open in a sleepy pout. He looks peaceful and comfortable in Willa's arms.

I reach out a tentative finger, but Willa nods her encouragement. My God, so little, so vulnerable, and so soft.

"Let's switch spots and you can hold him."

"Fuck, no. What if I hurt him?"

She chuckles.

"You won't. Now sit your ass down."

She makes room for me and my stomach gets tight when she places that tiny human in my hands. Christ, he could fit in one of them.

"Put him against your chest, he likes listening to a heartbeat," my brother suggests. "Just be careful of that big noggin of his, it tends to wobble."

I curve a hand around the back of his head and carefully lay him down against my chest. The kid doesn't even flinch, just as comfortable as he was with his mother.

My eyes drift to the window where I catch Bree wiping at her eyes. Willa follows my gaze and immediately walks out of the room.

"She okay?" Dimi asks.

Frankly, I don't know, which bothers me a little. I can normally read her pretty well, but I saw that scar on her belly and if it means what I think it does, that might suggest this wasn't such a great idea after all.

Ten minutes later, however, I'm the one behind the window with my brother, watching Willa place the baby in Bree's arms and the smile almost cracks her face wide open.

"When can you bring him home?"

"If he does as well as he has the last twenty-four hours, he can come home tomorrow."

I glance at Dimi.

"Are you ready for him?"

"He's little, his needs are simple. We'll borrow some stuff from Jake and Rosie, and the rest we'll pick up and learn as we go along."

I envy my brother his laid-back attitude. I imagine if I were in his shoes, I'd be running this like a structured operation. Pretty sure my brother's way is better.

Not long after, we're on our way to Bree's place with an everything pizza smelling up my vehicle. As per usual, Bree dives right in as soon as I have her on the couch, eating straight from the box.

"Save some for me," I tease, handing her a paper towel to wipe the tomato sauce off her chin.

I want to ask about her reaction at the hospital but decide to wait until after we eat. She's more receptive on a full stomach.

Unfortunately, I don't get the chance, because the doorbell rings just as I'm clearing away the empty box.

"Oh, I forgot," Bree says. "Radar called, he and Hillary wanted to pop in and say hi."

Great. There go my plans.

The first one through the door when I open it is that unsightly little dog of his, Phil. She pointedly ignores me and waddles straight to the couch on those stumpy legs. Bree bends over and lifts her on her lap, letting the dog lick her face.

"Come in," I try to be gracious.

Either Radar doesn't buy into it, judging from the grin on his face, or maybe he doesn't care. He looks a lot like my brother did earlier.

Giving Hillary a kiss on the cheek, I take her coat. It's been getting cooler at night.

I play host and make sure everyone has a drink, giving them a chance to catch up before I sit down beside Bree. I tuck an arm around her shoulder.

"Told ya," Radar directs at a smiling Hillary.

"So you did. Are you gonna tell them or do you want me to?"

"I will." Radar turns to us and that smile is back on his face.

I have a sneaky suspicion of what is coming and tuck Bree a little closer into my body.

"We wanted you to be the first to know. We're pregnant."

Bree's body startles beside me.

CHAPTER 10

BREE

"OH MY GODDESS, Brianne! What happened to you?"

Mrs. Mazur fawns over me as Yanis carries me inside his house.

He played on my guilt to get me to come. Said his mom would be disappointed if I didn't. I'm not sure how much he's told them about the current situation, but I know he's right about Anna.

Yanis and Dimi's parents are relics from the flower-power days. I swear they haven't even changed wardrobe since then. Big-hearted, peace-loving, pot-smoking, and without boundaries, it's a miracle they managed to raise two badasses like the brothers.

Anna and Max also claim the roles of surrogate parents to anyone they deem worthy. Jake was claimed from a young age, but over the years they've claimed quite a few of us associated with PASS, treating us as their own.

As soon as Yanis sets me down on his sectional,

I'm wrapped in Anna's solid arms, a waft of patchouli and pot hitting my nose. They not only grow the stuff; they use it liberally. In joints, pipes, cookies, brownies. Hence the lingering scent. Something I'd normally pull my nose up at, but on Anna and Max it's a comfortable smell. Familiar and warm.

"Well? Talk to me!"

Anna hangs on to both my hands as she sits on the edge of the couch, her body twisted toward me.

"A little mishap at work."

She pulls up a disbelieving eyebrow.

"That why my boy is carrying you around like precious cargo? A little mishap?"

Then, as if she just reminded herself, she drops my hands and surges up off the couch, flinging herself at Yanis, who braces himself, apparently used to this.

"Hey, Mom."

The much shorter Anna reaches up and claps both her hands on his cheeks.

"How is my boy?"

"Good, Ma."

"I can see that. Finally pulled your head outta your ass?"

"Anna, leave the kid alone," Max, who has been keeping to the background pipes up.

I snicker at the look on Yanis's face. The man is forty-six, for crying out loud, has been more of a parent to his parents in terms of responsibility than the other way around. Likely has for most of his life, that's just who he is. What they give him in return,

114

though, is as invaluable. Love, nurturing, acceptance. All of these with great generosity and completely unconditional.

That's who Max and Anna are, they're givers, albeit a little over the top.

"So are you finally together? Shacked up already? Why not in this beautiful house? I thought you built it for her?"

Anna, as usual, is not deterred by her husband's admonishments and happily plows ahead. Her words bring me pause though.

Wait. He built this for me?

Probably just a fantasy of hers, but when I sneak a glance at Yanis I see a ruddy color appear along his jaw. Usually a tell he's pissed or uncomfortable. It's a toss-up which emotion to blame it on in this case. Could be either.

Notable is the way he avoids looking at me.

"Ma, I'm just crashing in Bree's spare bedroom until she recovers enough to fend for herself."

Poor Anna looks crestfallen. I had no idea she harbored hopes for her son and me.

He's not lying. He's still in the spare bedroom. I half expected him to shove his way into mine on Thursday, but he just made sure I did my bathroom routine and got me into bed.

I was actually grateful; the day had been challenging for me in more ways than one. Then yesterday he had to go into the office early, came back and brought me lunch, and then was off for an afternoon meeting at the new winery.

Hillary ended up popping in after her shift at the shelter and brought the dog—I'm sure as arranged by Yanis, since he was going to be later than he thought—and brought dinner with her. Radar was with Yanis at the vineyard discussing the installation of the upgraded security system.

I don't know her that well, but I like Hillary. She's very matter-of-fact—something I can appreciate—is warm, can be funny, and is fun to hang out with. I think of all the PASS wives, I feel most myself with her.

Don't get me wrong, I like them all. Rosie, Hutch's wife, is an absolute sweetheart, a nurturer. Willa, on the other hand, is so capable in all aspects of her life she intimidates me a little. I've never had a gaggle of female friends, lost touch with the few girls I'd sometimes hung out with in college, but since then I found myself mostly in the company of men.

It's the line of work I'm in, I guess it makes me a bit of an oddball. Maybe less of a woman in the eyes of some, but Hillary has a manner about her that puts me at ease. Doesn't make me feel like I'm lacking some essential component needed to be part of the sisterhood.

Among other things we talked about her pregnancy, which wasn't exactly planned but very welcome, and even that felt good. Normal.

When I started yawning around nine thirty, she offered to give me a hand getting ready for bed. I didn't even hear Yanis come in, I was already out, although I could swear I felt his lips brush my forehead at some point.

Then this morning he announced '*we*' would have to let his parents in at his place.

This is maybe the third time I've been in his house. It's nice, all one level with great views from the wall of windows on the back. Rather sparse in furnishings, but it gives the place an airy, uncluttered feel. Unlike his office back at PASS, which is a paper explosion.

"Boys," Anna calls the men to attention. "Grab those bags from the car while I put on a pot of coffee."

"Ma, grab the coffee from the freezer, please," Yanis calls over his shoulder as he makes his way to the door.

"Brought my own!" she yells back.

"No mushroom crap, Ma. Just make regular."

I grin as Anna winks at me. I think more often than not the woman is just yanking her sons' chains with her weird concoctions. I swear she gets a kick out of perpetuating this image she puts out there of a somewhat ditzy, eccentric hippy. In a way it reminds me of my mom, who loved nothing more than to sing along to pop songs at the top of her lungs, with the windows of the car down, as she drove me to school. It used to mortify me, but now when I think back it puts a smile on my face.

"Do any baking, Anna?" I call out just as Yanis walks in with two large bags.

"Don't encourage her," he grumbles, making me

laugh.

Following right behind him is Max, loaded up with coolers and containers he takes to his wife in the kitchen.

"I brought cardamom date and quinoa muffins. High in protein for the new mom."

"Willa didn't deliver, Ma," Yanis feels compelled to remind her.

"Wanna try one?" Anna asks me with a wink, ignoring her son's comments.

"Love to."

The truth is, Anna's baking tastes great, even if her ingredients tend to be on the weird side. Or maybe it's the green butter she tends to use in her recipes.

YANIS

IT'S SATURDAY AND I had plans.

Instead, I'm sitting at my kitchen island, watching my mother and Bree snickering about something on the couch, while Dad tells me about the new irrigation system he designed and installed on his farm. I use the term loosely, since it's basically a pot grow-op. A highly illegal one, especially in Wyoming, which has some of the strictest cannabis laws in the country.

There have been plenty of times over the years I've had to drive up to get Dad out of some pickle he got himself into. But I think I've disavowed him of his dream to strike it rich selling illegal cannabis products. Thank God I still have a friend or two in local law enforcement and they're willing to turn a blind eye as long as Dad keeps his pot to himself. But this new talk of an irrigation system sounds too much like those grandiose dreams of his have made a resurgence.

If only my parents weren't so attached to the farm. They could move here, to Colorado, pick up a piece of land and Dad could get a license and grow to his heart's content without the kind of repercussions he faces back in Encampment, where they live now.

"Dad," I start, but he already has his hand up.

"I know, I know. Don't worry, I'm just testing it out while we're gone. Don't want my plants to die before I get a chance to harvest them."

"Been out in Palisade a few times, working with a new vineyard. Fertile ground around there, Dad. I can keep my eye out. Wouldn't be such a bad spot."

He gives me a look over his ever-present reading glasses, but to my surprise doesn't say anything.

I drink the dregs of my coffee—no mushrooms, thank fuck—and set my cup in the sink.

"We should get going," I announce, walking into the living room.

"We should?"

Bree looks up with amusement sparkling in her eyes. She knows damn well how taxing I find my parents. I love them, but they do try me.

"Yes. We have things to do."

"What things?" my mother weighs in, and it's all I can do not to roll my eyes heavenward.

Bree's soft snicker drags me back to earth, though.

She looks good. More relaxed as she smiles up at me. I've been holding back, kept things at light touches and no heavy topics, but I think maybe we're ready to resume that talk.

"Just…things. Does it matter? You guys are heading over to Willa and Dimi's shortly anyway."

Luckily Ma is easily distracted with the prospect of the baby.

"That's right, it's almost that time. Max! Maybe you should put a clean shirt on?"

The disgruntled sounds my dad produces make it clear he's not in favor of that, but he still gets up from his stool and shuffles down the hall to the spare bedroom where I dragged their bags.

"Why don't you guys stay here?" Ma proceeds to ask Bree. "It would be so much more fun and I could help look after you when my boy needs to work."

I can't hold back the pained groan at the prospect and Bree glances at me pressing her lips tightly together.

"That's a lovely offer, but you are going to have your hands full with that baby. Besides, I still sleep a lot and do that better in my own bed."

"Of course, Brianna, dear," Ma says, kissing her cheek before turning to me. "I'll expect you both here for dinner tomorrow night. We'll see if Dimi and Willa, plus baby, can make it too. A family dinner."

Fucking shoot me now.

Instead, I nod and bend down to lift Bree off the couch. I'm sure I could support her to hop to the car, but I like this way better, and she hasn't objected to being carried around these past couple of days.

Who knows? Maybe she likes this better too.

On the way to Bree's, I stop at the grocery store and pick up a few things while she waits in the SUV, checking her emails on her phone. I loathe shopping, even for groceries, but it's a necessary evil. In an effort to minimize time and energy wasted, I have the layout of the store memorized when I set out on my mission. I know exactly where and in what aisle to find what I need and strategize my plan of attack, so I can be in and out in ten minutes or less.

The one distraction I hadn't counted on is the small flower stand next to the produce section. It's the sunflowers. They remind me of Bree. Bright, happy, simple, pretty, and yet practical.

I stop my cart and grab a couple of bunches from the bucket. Be nice for her to look at while she's cooped up inside.

I realize my mistake when I'm cashing out in the checkout lane. Megan is pushing her grocery cart toward the exit and spots me with my hands full of flowers. She stops and appears to wait while I grab my bags.

"Hey, stranger," she drawls when I approach the doors.

"Megan."

I nod at her and attempt to step around her with my hands full, but she swiftly moves her cart so we walk out the door side by side. Then she hooks my arm with a hand, pulling me to a stop.

"Hey, wait. I meant to ask you something."

I'm uncomfortably aware of Bree sitting in the passenger seat of my Yukon parked twenty feet away, but I don't want to be even more of an asshole to this woman. It's been only a week since we had dinner at the Tap Room and I dropped her off at home, disappointed because I'd made it clear over burgers I really wasn't interested in pursuing anything further. Despite the impression I might've given her when, like an idiot, called her on impulse.

Yet here I am, fucking stuck in the middle of the parking lot talking to her while Bree's eyes burn holes in my back. I know it because Megan is peeking over my shoulder in the direction of my SUV.

It doesn't surprise me when she steps a little too close and I wish I'd left those damn flowers in the store so I'd have at least one hand free.

"What?" I ask, a little too brusquely.

"There's a Better Business Bureau awards dinner next week. It turns out I've been nominated for the Real Estate and Property Award this year."

"Congratulations. That's quite the accomplishment."

I honestly have no idea—nor do I really care— what it entails to receive an award like that, but she seems happy with it.

"I know." She beams a smile at me. "So I was hoping you'd be available for the dinner."

The smile falls when I start shaking my head.

There was no ambiguity about what I told her last week. I made sure to leave no wiggle room, no chance for her to draw the wrong conclusions, or nurture hopes of any kind. But judging from the look on her face I was wrong.

Jesus.

I tried, but diplomacy didn't work. Maybe the blunt truth will.

"I can't." I start backing up. "Consider me permanently spoken for."

Her eyes immediately slide over my shoulder to where I know Bree is sitting. Her eyebrows lift in what I'm guessing is surprise.

Bree doesn't share Megan's flamboyant looks, hers are more subdued, understated, and yet infinitely more beautiful in my eyes. I imagine a woman like Megan may not see it that way.

"Good luck with the nomination," I tell her, before turning my back and coming face-to-face with two familiar gray eyes.

I pull open the back door and toss the bags and the flowers on the seat.

"You're so sweet. Thank you," Megan says intentionally loud behind me while I have half my body stuck in the car. "And I enjoyed our time together last weekend."

I hit my head on the doorframe as I try to whip it around, but she's already walking toward her vehicle, leaving me to stare after her.

When I get behind the wheel, I glance over at Bree,

who is very pointedly studying her phone until she slowly turns her head in my direction.

"That was…" I shake my head. "I don't even know what that was," I admit.

Bree raises an eyebrow.

"Maybe some of that baggage you mentioned we'd need to deal with?"

"Yeah," I grumble, getting really pissed off my Saturday plans keep getting derailed by other people's agendas. "That was Megan. She was my real estate agent, and we…" *Fuck, why is this so goddamn difficult?* "Would occasionally hook up. It's been months but she'd been calling."

I catch a look from her and I know what she's asking without needing the words.

"Last week when I sent you to Denver, I didn't feel good about it, but by the time I got to the office you were already gone. I was pissed, mostly at myself, and ended up calling her. We got a bite to eat, I told her there'd be no more calls, and that was the end of it."

"She may be hard of hearing," Bree comments dryly, and I almost smile.

"So it would appear."

"She's very pretty."

I have to stop for a traffic light anyway, so I twist toward Bree and tag her behind the neck.

"You're beautiful."

"You're full of shit," she says, but with half a smile as she points at the light that just turned green.

"I bought you flowers," I try in a lame attempt to salvage something.

"I noticed," she whispers, but her smile spreads.

CHAPTER 11

BREE

*I*T'S WEIRD.

I'd almost forgotten this side of Yanis existed. This caring side—attentive, human—was so well-hidden by the rigid, almost cold veneer he shows the world, I'd long convinced myself he'd been a figment of my imagination.

I glance over at the sunflowers he finally jammed in a juice jug since I don't own any vases. Don't think anyone's ever bought me flowers before and it's not like I missed that, not in the kind of life I lead, but I have to admit it's nice. *Special*. It makes me *feel* special, despite the mini disaster that preceded it in the City Market parking lot.

That could've been an ugly scene and I have to admit it was tempting, but Yanis looked miserable enough all by himself. I almost felt sorry for him.

The truth is, neither of us lived as monks for the past fifteen years. Heck, I was married for a chunk of them. This is the baggage we now carry. The stuff we need to find a place for if whatever is happening between us now is going somewhere.

I watch Yanis pace around my kitchen, the phone to his ear. He seems agitated, or maybe annoyed is a better word. So far it looks like this day is not going the way he'd planned and he's not very good at rolling with the punches.

"Fuck."

The sound of his phone smacking the kitchen counter is sharp as he braces himself on both hands, his head hanging down.

"What's up?"

He lifts slowly and his eyes meet mine across the room.

"I have to fly to Peru Monday morning. Jelnyk Mining. They ran into some resistance from local law enforcement over the security framework we designed and need me to come smooth the waters."

"So go," I tell him. "I'll be fine," I add, guessing that's at least part of his concern.

"I hadn't planned for this. Not now."

"You can't plan for emergency calls, Yanis. All you can do is adjust," I impart calmly.

He straightens up and starts moving toward me, sitting down on the edge of the coffee table, his body leaning forward.

"I was supposed to use this week to win you back," he says solemnly. "Earn back your trust, get you to let me in again. So far I'm doing a piss-poor job of it."

I smile to myself. He doesn't even realize, showing

me he's not as unflappable and unaffected as he'd like the world to believe he is does more to gain my trust than sweet words or calculated actions could.

"You got me flowers," I teasingly remind him.

The corner of his mouth twitches.

"I did, didn't I? Do I get bonus points for that?"

"Major bonus points."

His face turns serious and his eyes find my mouth.

"Fair warning," he mumbles as he already leans closer. "I'm about to kiss you."

"Not going anywhere."

I barely get the words past my lips when his mouth captures mine.

Unlike earlier pecks and brushes, this kiss means business. Something my body is on board with the moment his tongue slides inside.

God, how I missed this.

I've kissed men, slept with them, but never without effort. Tentative touches with my mind engaged at all times and a determination to have my body feel. Just Yanis's mouth is enough to envelop me in a surge of sensations that spins my mind out of control and my body into action.

An instinctive response—not hampered by measure or consideration, but driven by sheer need—has me hook my hands around his neck and pull him closer.

Groaning deep in his chest, he drops on his knees beside the couch, our mouths fused and his tongue still plundering, as he presses me back into the pillows. His hands roam, one slipping behind my head where it lodges in my hair, while he strokes down my breastbone with the other, leaving his palm to rest on my thundering heart.

This—letting go and simply feeling—is what I've missed most of all. Knowing wherever the rush of heated blood takes me will be worth my surrender.

My back arcs off the couch when his palm brushes roughly over a breast, grazing my distended nipple.

So lost to sensation, it takes me a moment to realize he's lifted away from the kiss, watching me through heavy eyelids as he plays me with his fingers.

"Don't stop."

I try to lift myself up on an elbow but a sharp stab of pain in my ribs keeps me in place.

Right. Almost forgot about those. I silently condemn my physical limitations.

Something Yanis appears to clue in to as his mouth stretches into a lazy smile.

"Patience," he rumbles, the sound vibrating over my skin, doing nothing to stem my frustration. "Some things don't change."

I remember. He was always the one who would set the pace, while all I could do was hurl myself into the ride. At least that's how it used to be between us.

"Only with you," I admit.

He brushes a finger along my cheek.

"I like that."

"You make it sound like a good thing."

This time his smile is open and almost painful in

the memories it invokes of times where he'd look at me like this, without any reservation or shield.

"Because it is. The reward will be worth the wait."

And a hell of a long wait it's been.

"In the meantime," he starts, getting to his feet as he carefully helps me into a sitting position. "Tell me you've got propane in that tank. I bought us a few steaks for the grill."

"There was last time I used it."

"I'll check."

I watch his ass as he walks toward the balcony where my grill lives. A great view, but watching him move around the kitchen is just gonna get me hotter and more bothered. I need to do something. I'm sick of sitting still.

"Let me help. I'm going nuts here."

Five minutes later I'm installed at the small dining table, my bad ankle elevated on a chair as I cut vegetables for roasting. Yanis is doing some dishes.

"Bree?"

He leans against the counter, drying his hands on a towel, his head tilted to one side as he regards me. Something tells me to brace for what's coming. We've talked, but he's been cautious, avoided asking too many questions, and somehow that restraint only heightened my anxiety around things I've kept to myself so long.

Even now, after already half-committing to testing these new waters with him, I'm not sure I'm ready to share it all.

"When did you get that scar?"

Typical Yanis, straight to the core.

YANIS

"SHORTLY AFTER MY mom died."

She only hesitated for a second before answering but she visible shored up before she did.

Regret is immediate. One more thing to add to my list of fucking mistakes. It's amazing she's even talking to me after all I put her through.

"Stop that," she says sharply. "I know you; you've found something else to flog yourself for, but it's not on you. Just like Mom dying was not on you. It just happened. Shit happens and you deal."

That may well be, but she shouldn't have had to go through one hit after another alone.

"What happened?"

"Ruptured cyst," she says, but her response sounds a little too practiced. Then she lifts her chin almost defiantly. "Wasn't the only cyst. They ended up doing a hysterectomy. They left me the one ovary, but clearly that's not going to do me much good without a uterus."

I can't swallow down the fucking log lodged in my throat, so before I have a chance to respond she's already putting words in my mouth.

"So yeah, no kids. Not an option, and I wouldn't blame you if you—"

I stopped listening and am moving toward her at lightning speed.

"Shut up." I cup her face in my hands and look beyond the layer of bravado to the sadness she's hiding. "Don't even finish that thought."

"You wanted kids," she says softly, searching my eyes.

"Yeah. I remember we talked about it once back then," I recall. "We both did. That was then."

I don't say, *"before I fucked us up and we lost our chance,"* but it's implied, and my silent apology comes in the form of a brush of my mouth.

I watch as her eyes blink a few times and a sigh slips from her lips.

"Whether or not you have a uterus does not define who you are or what you mean to me."

She tilts her head and I'm glad to see humor in her gaze.

"You're a surprise, Mr. Mazur."

"How's that?"

"Your vocabulary has come a long way. You're using a lot of words, and they're good ones," she teases.

"Good to know."

With a light kiss, I head back to the kitchen to get going on dinner. Probably not a bad idea to let this process for a bit before I try to dive into the marriage part and what went wrong there.

The safest way forward is a planned path—it's a rule I've lived by—but I can only do that if I know where the landmines are buried. It's essential to a successful mission and I don't want to do anything that can fuck this up.

We eat inside, talking a little about my parents and work, avoiding anything heavier. It's not until long after dinner, Bree briefly returns to the subject.

"I want you to know I may have been angry with you, hurt by you, but I never blamed you for things that weren't even in my control, let alone yours. So please don't take this on."

I look up from my laptop, where I've been doing a little work in preparation of my trip to the Jelnyk mine, and meet her eyes.

"Perhaps not, but I should've been there for you and I wasn't. That is something I own," I state simply, and she seems to accept that with a nod before she turns back to the TV program she was watching.

By the time I shut down my computer and look up, she's slumped over on the armrest, snoring lightly. When I pick her up to carry her to the bedroom, she mumbles something incoherently before her head drops to my shoulder. I should probably wake her so she can do her bathroom routine.

"Bree, let's get you ready for bed."

A disgruntled groan is all I get.

I carry her through into the bathroom and use my elbow to throw the switch.

"Come on, lazy bones. You can sleep in a minute."

I carefully put her on her feet and, half-asleep, she manages to strip her pants down. She's beyond caring I'm in the bathroom with her and that's fine by me. I help her into the oversized jersey she likes to wear to bed and tuck her in before heading back to the living room. There I shut off the TV, turn off the lights, and walk to the sliding door to make sure it's locked.

A glint of light draws my attention to a row of cars parked on the opposite side of the street. I can't place it and wait for a minute to see if I can spot it again.

Nothing. Probably just the reflection off a sideview mirror or a piece of chrome.

The street is deserted.

I turn my back and head for the bathroom to grab a quick shower.

I need to feel Bree close tonight, breathe in her scent, but there's no fucking way I'm going to climb into bed with my dick still hard.

Apparently, age hasn't diminished the effect she has on me.

For the past days I've been walking around with a semi hard-on, but with that kiss before dinner I shot straight from half-mast to maypole.

I bend my head down under the stream—the image of Bree lying on the couch engraved on my retina—and close my fist firmly around my cock. Relief comes fast and furious.

But when I slip under the covers and curve my bigger body around Bree, she moans, pushing her ass against me.

I'm instantly hard again.

Fuck.

CHAPTER 12

BREE

WELL. I HAVEN'T been bored these past days with Yanis gone.

Anna and Max made sure of that.

The Mazur family is very persuasive, which is how I ended up staying at Yanis's house with his parents. What had me give in was a dry comment Max made. He basically suggested it would save people driving back and forth to my place. The last thing I want is to be a burden and Max—in his nonconfrontational, laid-back manner—used that to bring his point home.

So Sunday night we had dinner with the Mazur family and Monday morning we were back. Yanis had a nine o'clock flight to Lima on Jelnyk's corporate jet and dropped me off at his place. He carried my bag into his bedroom, decreed that's where I'd be staying, and then kissed me soundly in front of his parents before taking off.

It's Thursday already and to my surprise the days have flown by. My ankle has gotten a little more exercise now Yanis isn't here to tote me around, and I feel a lot less helpless already.

I keep Anna company in the kitchen in the mornings while she juices, bakes, and lets me help with dinner prep. I've certainly eaten a lot healthier than my usual on-the-fly meals. Then in the afternoons she heads over to Willa's, giving her a chance to catch up on the sleep little Max deprived her of during the night.

Big Max kept me busy while his wife was tending to the little one, taught me card games to play and talked endlessly about the plans and dreams he still built onto. For a completely self-sustainable farm, with livestock and crops—including of the cannabis variety—and a large communal lodge where people could stay and work the land. A bit like a dude ranch for city folk wanting a taste of living off-the-grid. I didn't have the heart to remind him that well into his seventies that might be too much of a venture to undertake, but he seemed happy just musing about it and I enjoyed listening to him.

I received a few texts from Yanis, and a phone call last night, telling me he was wrapping things up but wasn't sure he'd be back in time for my appointment at the clinic today. Max offered to take Anna to Dimi and Willa's, and pick me up to go to the hospital later.

That's why it's unusually quiet in the house right now. They just left and I'm settled on the couch, flipping through the channels on the large screen TV.

My cell phone starts buzzing in my pocket and I fish it out, expecting it to be Yanis calling. But the number displayed is from the Denver PD.

"Ms. Graves, how are you feeling?"

Bill Evans's jovial voice booms and I have to lift the phone away from my ear.

"Bree, please. I'm doing well. Much better than last week."

He'd stayed in touch, mostly through Yanis, but unfortunately there hadn't been much to report on his end. I'm hoping maybe he has some news.

"Good to know. I've been trying to get hold of Yanis, but he's not answering his phone. Checked with your office but they mentioned he's out of town?"

"Yes, he had to go to Peru for a few days. He should be home today or tomorrow, though. He's just wrapping things up. Was there any news?" I immediately add.

"You could say that. We found a body we think may be related to your case."

His words have me sit up straight.

"A body?"

"Robert Connell, career criminal. Fished him out of the Chatfield Reservoir day before yesterday. Was found weighed down with concrete anchors, not far from the north boat ramp, by a bunch of amateur divers out for a day trip."

Yikes.

"How do you figure he's related to the case?"

"Matched him to a partial print we found on the key fob to the airport limo. Those keys were in the ignition when we discovered the dead driver."

139

Jesus. Two dead.

"You're thinking—"

"That Connell was possibly the one who killed the driver, took you, and the same guy you heard get shot. Single hit to the back of the head. Messy."

I remember how messy it was from the slippery puddle on the floor when I ran. I can only imagine what his head would've looked like.

"Any thoughts on the second guy?"

"Not yet, but a 2016 silver Lexus ES 350, license plate CHV-481, was registered in his name."

"I thought it was CX," I bring up.

"Close enough," Evans states. "Can't find the car though."

"If he was the one who got shot, then he wouldn't have been the one driving it that night. The other guy was," I point out.

"Yeah, we figured. Listen, if it's okay I'd like to send you a picture of our dead victim. See if you recognize him as the guy who picked you up. If you're up to it."

Goodie. A picture of a dead guy who's been floating in the water for over a week. I can't wait. Something to keep me awake at night.

"Sure."

The ding alerts me of an incoming message and I put the phone on speaker while I pull up the image. I can tell they tried to minimize the impact a week in the water as fish food may have had, but the results were still stomach-turning.

"Hard to tell." I try to focus on things like the hairline, the nose, the mouth—or what was left of it. "Could've been him. I remember he gave me the impression of a British actor from the seventies with that cap and those longish sideburns."

"Yeah, we noticed the sideburns too. Good, thanks."

"Was that all?"

I'm suddenly eager to delete that picture, get off the phone, and maybe watch something stupid like *Wheel of Fortune* to get rid of that mental image.

"Yes. We're going down a list of known associates to Connell, but as you can imagine most of those aren't that eager to talk to the cops. Good chance that car is chopped up and sold for parts by now, so I'm not holding my breath on that either, but we'll keep plugging away."

I'm about to say goodbye when a thought occurs to me.

"Wait. Did you ever find that fireplace poker? It can't have been far from where you found me, I was hanging on to that thing for dear life."

"We did."

The silence that follows is deafening.

"And?" I finally prompt.

"It was clean."

"What? Clean? I whacked him hard with that thing, surely there has to be blood or tissue that—"

"No," he interrupts. "There was nothing. No blood, no hair, and no fingerprints."

"That's impossible, I used it as a cane after I twisted my ankle. At least mine have to be there."

"That's just it," Detective Evans says solemnly. "It was wiped *clean.*"

It doesn't make sense at all. I know I didn't wipe it down; I was too concerned about preserving evidence.

"I don't understand."

"Neither do I, Ms. Graves. Neither do I. I'm looking into it." I notice he doesn't say *we* are looking into it. "If you could ask Mazur to give me a ring when he gets in, I'd appreciate it."

"I will."

YANIS

MY YUKON IS still where I left it in long-term parking.

I toss my bag in the back seat, get behind the wheel, and rub my hands over my face. That was a long fucking ten hours with not a wink of sleep, despite the luxury accommodations aboard the jet.

I managed to drag myself out of the Lima corporate office for Jelnyk at one in the morning. A good portion of my three days were spent there, aside from a trip to the site. I was able to get most of the concerns resolved. I subcontracted a local security company—cheaper than sending one of my guys out there for the six months scheduled to get the mine up and running—which went a long way to appeasing law enforcement. They don't trust Americans and there are days I don't blame them.

Yesterday I sat down with my Peruvian counterpart

at seven in the morning and worked through the entire day and night to get him up to speed on the project. I'd initially planned to fly out this morning, which would've meant not getting back to town until tonight, but one of Jelnyk's top engineers had a family emergency back in San Francisco and the plane was fueled and ready to take him home. I was able to hop on.

I glance at the dashboard clock and note that I'm probably too late for Bree's appointment, but maybe I can catch her and my dad at the doctor's office.

Sucking down the coffee I snagged on my way out of the airport, I pull out of my parking spot and hit dial on my hands-free.

"Good morning, PASS Security Services, can you hold?"

"Lena, it's me," I quickly say before she blasts me with the soothing sounds of Yo-Yo Ma while I wait.

The classical music had been her idea. She claimed the old-style rock the system originally played for people on hold was making them agitated and pissy with her by the time she finally got to them. The cello was supposed to calm them and make them less aware of how long they waited. Bree agreed with her, so I let it go. I've had no complaints so I guess it's working.

"Boss. Are you on your way back?"

"I *am* back, but I've got things to do. Just checking in to see if there are any emergencies?"

"Well, we had some excitement at the winery last night," Lena shares and I'm instantly alert.

Things had been quiet there since we had a man in place during the nights. No break-ins or attempts at vandalism. It would've been wishful thinking our mere presence would be enough to thwart whoever is trying to mess with Flynn's Fields.

"What do you mean?"

"Someone cut the power just after midnight. They've got Grand Valley Power out there working on it."

"How?"

"Someone took out a power pole down the road. The one feeding into the property. Felled it like a tree. The vineyard is dead in the water until they get it back up."

"What about the generator?"

They have a massive generator. I saw the damn thing. It's too important; the temperatures are carefully regulated both for the production and storage sides of the winery.

"Didn't kick in. They're looking into it. Jake and Radar are both there troubleshooting. Dimi is here holding down the fort."

I have my thoughts around why a brand-new generator, at what I estimate would've been a hundred-and-fifty grand at least, would not start up at a power outage, but keep them to myself. I suspected before there might be someone on the inside and this would fall into line. I hadn't brought it up with Joe Flynn but it sounds like it's time I voiced my suspicions.

Tomorrow I'll head out there.

"Let Flynn know I'll be there first thing tomorrow," I tell Lena.

"Will do. Go get some rest, you sound exhausted."

I don't bother responding, she doesn't really expect me to.

First things first; getting to Bree's appointment. After that I look forward to an early night snuggled up to her.

Dad is in the waiting room outside the doctor's office and grins when I walk in.

"You've got it bad," he says in way of greeting, as he claps me on the shoulder. "She told me you said you weren't gonna make it but knowing you, I figured you'd try anyway. Glad to know I was right."

"Dad…" I warn him and he lifts his hands defensively.

"I know, I know. I won't go there, I'm confident your mother will push enough for both of us. One thing though," he says in a low voice, leaning close. "That Bree is a fine woman, she can keep up with you. Not many would be good enough for my boy so if you don't seal the deal this time around, I'm gonna seriously consider disowning you."

I almost laugh. They own an illegal pot farm. My parents scrape by at best and I'm far from struggling, but his point is made.

"I've got this."

Another clap on my shoulder.

"Glad to hear it, Son, because you need to get laid. You're getting too uptight in your old age."

I'm suddenly thrown back to my childhood when Ma or Dad would be standing by the door, shoving condoms in our hands, when either Dimi or I went out.

I close my eyes and lift my face to the ceiling.

Fucking hell.

"Well, I'll be off. I'll tell your mother you won't be there for dinner. She'll be thrilled."

The moment he leaves, I take a hard seat and lean my head back against the wall.

I must've dozed off because I startle when I hear her voice.

"How did you get back so soon?"

She's standing in front of me, leaning on a pair of elbow crutches. Her foot is in a rigid walking brace.

Damn. Looks like I just lost my justification for carrying her around.

I stand up, cup her face in my hands, and take her mouth. Not much she can do but stand there, balancing on her crutches.

"Determination," I finally answer her.

A frown appears between her eyebrows as she scans my face.

"Did you sleep at all?"

I shrug. No need to deny or confirm, it's probably all over my face. Besides, she knows me too well.

Instead, I change topic.

"What did the doctor say?"

It's pretty clear from her big grin the news is good.

"I can walk, obviously, have to get physical

therapy, and can return to modified desk work."

I don't tell her desk work was all she was gonna get anyway. At least for the foreseeable future. I'm not sure when I'll be ready to send her out in the field again, but that's an issue for another day.

"Good news."

"Isn't it? Oh, and he took the stitches out. I'm almost good as new."

My smile is involuntary in the face of her enthusiasm. I'm grateful she's happy. She may not be completely dependent on me anymore—something I didn't mind whatsoever—but she's healing up, and that has arguably more interesting implications.

Time to get her home.

"What do you want to eat to celebrate?"

She winces. "Do you think it would be a betrayal to your mother's cooking if I said I'd kill for some good juicy meat? She's a good cook, but my molars are starting to wear down from all the masticating on green food."

"What kinda meat?"

"Wanna swing by Rib City and split a rack of ribs and some beef brisket?"

Her eyes sparkle as she shoots me a cheesy grin, so I have to kiss her again.

"Let's go."

We've barely walked down the hall when she stops in her tracks.

"Wait. Where's Max?"

"Sent him home."

"Yanis…" she admonishes. "I should probably let Anna know we're bringing back dinner."

"Taken care of. Dad knows we're not going back there tonight."

Her eyes grow big.

"We're not?"

"We're staying at yours."

"But all my stuff is—"

"We'll pick it up tomorrow."

The frown is back but this time she looks annoyed.

"Sounds like you have everything figured out," she snaps.

"I wish," I scoff. "Truth is, I've barely started cluing in."

Her eyes narrow.

"What does that mean?"

"*Tygrys*, give me a good night's sleep in your arms, away from my meddling parents, and maybe I'll be able to answer in the morning."

Her expressive face instantly softens.

"Okay."

As easy as that. *Okay*.

Not gonna fuck this up.

CHAPTER 13

YANIS

SO MUCH FOR not fucking this up.

Last thing I remember is relaxing on the couch after wolfing down some barbecue. All I did was close my eyes for a minute to let the food digest.

Now it's the middle of the night and I'm still on the fucking couch, but Bree has disappeared. I whip off the blanket she must've covered me with and notice she's taken off my boots as well. That may not have been a wise idea after being on my feet for thirty-six hours straight.

Smooth, Mazur.

I plant my feet on the floor and rub my hands over my face. Maybe a shower is in order. I smell. Groaning at a stiff knee and sore back—courtesy of advancing age and lack of a proper mattress—I get up and move to the kitchen to grab a glass of water. I'm parched.

Running the faucet until the water is nice and cold, I glance out the window. Bree's view is of the street, but being on the third floor you can also catch sight of the mountains to the north past the airport.

Four o'clock so both the streets and the skies are still quiet. Traffic will start moving around six. It's a clear morning, promising to be a nice day if it holds.

Fall is my favorite season, when the temperatures are comfortable and the nights get cooler. Sometimes I head out to McInnis Canyon for a couple of days for rock climbing or some hiking. Maybe this year— provided her ankle is healed—I can convince Bree to sneak away from the office for a few days.

Thinking of Bree, I finish my water, set the glass in the sink, and turn to head to the bathroom when something catches my eye.

A piece of the grill cover is stuck in the sliding door. The grill is on the balcony, right beside it, underneath the kitchen window. The cover is a little too big, which is why it sometimes gets stuck, so I pay attention to that.

I'm trying to think back to the last time I was out on the balcony, which would've probably been Saturday night when I was cooking steaks. It's possible I was distracted. Hell, I've been distracted a lot lately.

Resolutely I move down the small hallway to the bathroom, ready to get out of these rank clothes.

Ten minutes later, naked as the day I was born, I walk into the bedroom to find Bree lying on her back, sprawled out like a starfish in the middle of the mattress. The sheets are twisted under her body, leaving half of her exposed. I can see the scar on her thigh and take a step closer to the bed, running a careful finger along the bumpy edge.

She's wearing plain panties and her sleep jersey is scrunched up under her breasts, the pale white of her skin stark against the dark fabric. Soft and vulnerable, a look uncommonly associated with this woman. But I see it. I've always seen it.

Sitting on the edge of the mattress, I lean forward and softly brush my lips over the soft swell of her belly, taking in her fragrance as my hand strokes the tender inside of her thigh. She lets out a soft moan as she shifts her leg, instinctively opening up for me.

God, I've missed her. The way her body responds to my touch; free of any artifice, letting pure sensation guide her. No other lover has gifted me with that level of trust.

I lick my tongue around her belly button, dipping the tip inside. Her skin shivers against my mouth as her hand cups the back of my head.

"Yanis…"

Lifting up I find her eyes on me, a soft smile on her lips.

"Tell me to stop."

She actually chuckles, the sound rich and warm.

"You know me better than that."

Yeah, I do.

I hook my fingers into the elastic of her panties and tug them over her hips, while she divests herself of the jersey.

I've tried being a gentleman helping her in and out

of the tub, getting dressed, but there's no need to try now.

"I've missed you," I confess, as my hands and eyes are already busy getting reacquainted with her body.

"You were only gone for a few days."

Her hand easily finds my cock, stroking the hard length of it in her confident hand. She's still the most unencumbered woman I know and it does my heart good she never lost that.

Shifting in the bed, she bends toward my lap, her loose hair brushing my thigh.

"*Tygrys*, I've missed you for fifteen years."

"Yeah…" she whispers.

The soft air zaps every delicate nerve at the tip before she swirls her tongue around the crown.

As with everything, Bree doesn't hold back, sliding me deep in her mouth. I groan at the feel of her heat, but unless I want to come in the next minute or so, I need to get the upper hand.

I twist away, my cock plopping free from her pouting lips. Before she can launch a second assault, I put a knee in the bed, slide my hands under her legs, and lift her butt right off the mattress. Hooking her legs over my shoulders, I hold her steady for my mouth.

"Mmmm," I hum, reveling in the taste of her.

The moment my tongue grazes her clit, she twists in my hold like a live wire.

Fuck, yeah. Just as I remember.

With only her shoulders on the mattress she can't

go far, whimpering as I lash her with bold strokes, followed with barely-there flicks directly on that hard little pearl which drive her wild.

I can feel the muscles in her legs bunch up as I torture her relentlessly, and I know she's either ready to come or kick me out of bed. My eyes are open on her as my lips close on her clit, sucking hard as I hum again.

She's wild, thrashing, until suddenly her entire body arcs as she keens out her release.

I immediately lower her legs to the crook of my elbows, line up my cock, and bury myself into her still-pulsating heat.

My eyes stay on hers the entire time I pump into her and finally find my release with her name on my lips.

Curled together, her bad ankle hitched over my hip so I don't inadvertently hurt her, we catch our breath.

"Good morning to you too," she says, amusement in her eyes.

"Fucking great morning."

She lifts her hand to my face and traces the lines in my forehead with the tips of her fingers.

"I missed you as well, Yanis."

BREE

"IT'S BEAUTIFUL."

I take in the sprawling vineyard, the fields bordered by a peach orchard. Guaranteed it's even more beautiful when the fruit trees bloom in early spring.

It's coming toward the end of the harvest season for the fruit, so I'll have to get Yanis to stop at one of the many fruit stands Palisade is known for before we head back.

"Yeah."

His hand covers mine on my lap as he shoots me a grin. He's so damn handsome it turns my insides to mush. I'm still a little apprehensive about opening myself up to heartbreak again, although you couldn't tell from the way I responded to him this morning.

Jesus Murphy, that was some wake-up call.

Sex with Yanis was even better than I remembered. I prefer thinking that to the possibility he may have picked up a trick or two over the years. I was like a limp noodle for a long time after, until Yanis finally left the bed to give Bill Evans a shout. I'd told him about the detective's call last night over dinner, but Yanis was asleep just minutes after and I didn't have the heart to wake him up. He'd looked exhausted.

While he was on the phone, I took a quick shower and by the time I got myself dressed and followed the smell of coffee into the kitchen, he was already cracking eggs in a pan.

When I mentioned I wanted to go to Palisade with him, he balked at first, wanting me to wait until after the weekend. A gentle reminder our early morning romp was more exercise than sitting in a vehicle or a chair somewhere convinced him. Not that I would've stayed home anyway, but this way is easier. I know him, he can be a bear when he doesn't get his way.

It's going to feel so good being useful again.

The plan is for me to sit and observe while Yanis talks with any of the employees who have or had access to the generator. I'll be looking for tells; signs of deceit, guilt, or even discomfort. Everybody has a tell, no matter how stoic their poker face is.

Our bodies easily betray us with small signs of stress. Even the complete absence of movement is a stress signal. People naturally get nervous or restless when questioned, even when they've done nothing wrong. When you encounter someone who remains perfectly still, chances are they're trying to hide something.

When we pull into a spot in front of the large log structure of the winery, two men walk out of the front door.

"That's Joe Flynn," Yanis says.

I peg the blond-haired, casually dressed man as the vintner, since he looks most like he belongs in these surroundings. The other guy looks too sleek, too *city*. Power suit, slicked-back black hair, expensive sunglasses, and a smile that put some dentist's kids through college, I'm sure.

Practicing my observational skills, I focus on the second man. There is something in the way he shakes the owner's hand, grabbing the wrist with his other. It looks friendly enough, but is often a subtle attempt at dominance, same with the jovial clap on the shoulder that follows after. Ironically, Joe's reaction—which is almost dismissive—is far more powerful.

By the time Yanis helps me out of the car and hands me my crutches, the suit is walking toward a dark gray Mercedes-Benz GT. Oh, yeah, clearly out to impress. Too bad no one seems to be as Joe is already greeting my boss.

Yanis is making introductions when an engine is turned over and revved loudly. Joe lightly shakes his head while still holding my hand, as we collectively look at the Mercedes speeding past us out of the parking lot.

"Asshole," Joe mumbles.

"Friend?" I inquire with a smirk.

"Used to be a college buddy, but I think acquaintance is a more accurate description these days."

He finally lets go of my hand and looks down at my walking boot.

"If it were winter, I'd wonder if you tried your hand at skiing."

"Nothing as adventurous as that." I flit a quick glance at Yanis, who almost imperceptibly gives his head a shake. "I missed the last step at my apartment building, went through my ankle. Not very dramatic I'm afraid."

"Still, you should probably keep the weight off that foot," he says, putting a hand in my back and gesturing toward the massive, solid-wood front doors.

I can almost hear Yanis's molars grinding, but he's too much of a professional to start a pissing contest with a PASS client. That doesn't stop him from glaring at me, though.

After Joe shows us into a tasting room, already occupied by Radar and two computers, Yanis asks him to give us fifteen minutes before showing in the security guard who was on duty last night. He's at the top of our list.

"DMV check," he says to Radar. "Colorado vanity plate, DRKNGL."

I look at him surprised.

"Where'd you get that? The guy?"

"Don't trust him. He was looking at you," he bites off.

Radar stifles a chuckle, ducking his head behind his screen. I have to bite my lip myself. This morning's good mood appears to have disappeared as Yanis dares me with his eyes.

Oh boy, if he's going to do a background check on anyone of the male persuasion unfortunate enough to glance in my direction, we're going to have a problem. I wonder how he managed all these years.

"Angelo Sarrazin," Radar interrupts our stare down. "Thirty-three, address on the license is in Cherry Hills Village."

I whistle. *Wow.* Cherry Hills is probably the most affluent city per capita in the greater Denver area. Massive houses on gated properties, well over the million mark.

"Now this is interesting," Radar adds, looking at his screen. "Guess who else is listed to that same address?"

"Wouldn't be Guiseppe Albero, now would it?"

I'm shocked to hear that name. Albero is head of one of Colorado's largest crime families. No wonder Flynn was quick to dissociate himself from the guy.

"Got it in one."

"So who's Sarrazin?" I ask, now intrigued.

"Heir to the kingdom," Radar is the one to respond. "Maiden name of Albero's wife, Elena is Sarrazin."

I have no clue where he digs up all this information in minutes, but that's Radar, he can find out anything online.

"Give me everything you can find on Sarrazin."

CHAPTER 14

YANIS

*F*UCKING ALBERO.

I knew the moment I heard the name Sarrazin that we were dealing with the Albero family. I'd paid attention to that family for the past twenty years.

The plane crash was one of the first calls I went on after transferring to the Grand Junction PD. A private jet flying into the airport from Denver went down, just two miles north of the airfield, in a huge ball of fire. All that was left by the time I got there were unrecognizable bits of fuselage and charred body parts.

I saw the explosion and was first on the scene.

The jet was owned by the Albero family and Guiseppe's wife and two children had been on board. There'd been no survivors, they were killed along with the three crew members. To this day I have the image of a blackened teddy bear lying in the barren landscape of the high mesa seared in my mind.

Grand Junction was overrun with federal agents of

every ilk and I remember being questioned by just about every one of them. Then one night there'd been a knock at my apartment door and the crime lord, along with two henchmen, stood on my doorstep. I recall almost drawing my weapon, but the devastated man only wanted to know one thing. Did his family suffer? Given the midair explosion, I was able to assure him they never knew it was coming.

That was my only encounter with Guiseppe, but I did pay attention to any mention of him in the news. Including his marriage—a year after the crash—to one of his employees, a single mother to a then thirteen-year-old boy, Angelo Sarrazin.

Now Albero's stepson and heir to the family throne.

I'd love to know what the hell he was doing here at Flynn's Fields Winery.

"Ready for the last one?"

Joe Flynn sticks his head in the door of the room.

"Give us five."

We've talked to everyone from security guards, to maintenance personnel and groundskeepers, working our way down a list of staff with reasonable access to the large storage structure at the back of the main building. It houses not only the generator but tools, cleaning supplies, maintenance and grounds equipment, and a host of other things, which means more than just a few people had access.

Last up are two of the cleaning crew who were in yesterday.

"So far, any top contenders?" I ask, turning to

Bree, who has quietly been taking notes.

"Nothing raising a huge red flag, no, although the maintenance guy," she checks her notepad, "Brian Whistler, is hiding something. But, judging from the red-rimmed eyes and slight tremor to his fingers, I'm guessing it's a bottle and not a nefarious plan to sabotage his employer."

I nod. I got a bit of an off-feeling from the guy, but she's probably right.

"Put a mark by his name anyway."

The moment the first of the cleaning crew walks in, I get a vibe and glance over at Bree to see if she picked up on it as well. The guy is almost cocky, a smirk on his face and a defiant look in his eyes, as he practically saunters into the room.

Dan McNeely, twenty-nine, drives the obnoxious old Camaro parked in the employee lot. The way he takes a seat without invitation—slouching down with one arm draped over the back of his chair—tells me he and I won't get along. This is one who doesn't deal well with authority. I wonder how he got the job.

I give him the spiel I gave everyone else, telling him we're hoping someone saw something suspicious. Ask for help instead of whereabouts. Bree actually taught me that one. Psychology one-o-one.

"When you were in the storage room at any time yesterday, did you see anyone else in there?"

"I didn't see nothin'."

"No one going in or out?" I keep my voice casual, even though the guy is grating on me. From the corner of my eye, I see Bree noting something down. "It seems a lot of people need to be in that space. I'm trying to get a timeline together."

I reach over and turn Bree's notepad in my direction so I can read what she wrote down.

GOTCHA!

"Right here, Matt in groundskeeping stated he was in storage around 4:00 p.m., parking his ATV, and mentioned seeing you having a smoke outside?"

I watch him fidget, sitting up a little straighter, a bit more alert.

"Yeah, so? Ain't no law against that."

"Of course not, I'm just asking because you would've seen anyone coming or going. Would you say you were there for five minutes? Longer?"

We should've pushed on having cameras in all employee-only areas but Joe felt it would be too invasive. I'm thinking he'll be on board now, since it would've saved us from getting information this way.

The cops were focusing on the damage to the power pole, not convinced the generator was actually messed with and willing to wait for the service guy to come out and make a determination first. But the vineyard's maintenance man, who was in here earlier, made a point of telling us he'd just done a test run of the generator last week, which is something he's scheduled to do monthly to make sure it's working properly. Last week it was, last night it wasn't.

"Maybe fifteen? I dunno," McNeely says with a shrug. "I was on break," he adds defensively.

"Did you see Matt?"

"Yeah, I saw him leave."

"Was there anyone else in there at the time? Either coming or going?"

"Didn't see no one."

Fifteen minutes later, I shut the door behind him and turn to Radar.

"What've you got?"

"Spent two years in juvie for break and enter. Couple of arrests as an adult, petty theft, possession, one assault, but nothing seems to have stuck. Only one previous employer, a scrapyard in Colorado Springs for the past seven years."

"Why the sudden move clear across the state to Palisade?" Bree points out.

"Find out how long the guy has been at his current address?" I ask Radar. "I want to know if his coming here coincides with the opening of the winery. Also, find out who owns the scrapyard. I'm pretty sure this is our guy, but I want to find out why before presenting him to law enforcement."

"You don't trust them?" Bree asks me.

I shrug.

"They don't seem to think what goes on here is of much urgency, they've made that clear to Joe. So rather than hand over a name and have them put him on a back burner, I'd prefer to hand them over a viable suspect with some solid, albeit circumstantial, evidence."

"I can get in touch with my contact at the station here. Find out what is buzzing when I bring up the name of the winery?"

That's what makes Bree invaluable to PASS, her ability to make connections—particularly in law enforcement—and maintain them. Her psychology degree comes in useful more often than not, as she's just proven again.

"By all means, but first let's you and me go grab some lunch."

BREE

TALBOTT FARMS.

It's been many years since I've been here. A little late in the season but they harvest until almost the last week of September, and I'm able to snag a tray of nice-looking peaches. I figure Anna may like some as well.

We grab some food and order a couple of ciders we take out on the covered porch, picking a lone table in the corner.

"How is it?" Yanis asks when I take the first bite of a decadent bacon burger.

"Good."

It comes out muffled on account of my full mouth. Yanis grins and I wink back.

Despite the intensity of the morning, I feel surprisingly lighthearted. I like this—nice day, gorgeous view, great company—and he seems to relax as well.

I'm not eager to bring up what might be a sensitive subject, but I've been itching to know.

"So what's the plan?" I ask after swallowing down my bite.

"Plan for what? The winery? I've got twenty-four-hour coverage now, Joe has agreed for us to install more cameras, and Radar is digging into McNeely's background. See if he can come up with a motive."

Not exactly what I was referring to.

"I mean for when we get back. I know I won't be able to drive until the boot is off, but I can Uber it into the office for a few weeks. And I'm getting pretty handy with these crutches."

His food is halfway to his mouth and his eyebrows are drawn together.

"What are you saying?"

"I'm not saying anything, I'm asking; what is the plan? Or better, what is *your* plan?"

He puts his burger in the basket and wipes his hands methodically on the napkin. Then his eyes lock on mine and I can see a storm brewing.

"I was inside you for the first time in fifteen years just this morning and you ask me that?"

Yup, he's pissed. Although the tight set of his jaw would've told me that. Frankly, I don't care if my question makes him angry and I have no problem explaining it to him.

"Yes, I'm asking, because I made assumptions once before and turned out to be completely off."

"You don't trust me."

I shake my head; I could've predicted that response as well.

"It's not about trust, it's about clarity. But more than that, it's about self-preservation. I don't mean to beat you over the head with history, but the truth is, it changed me. Made me more cautious."

I take a quick sip of cider and keep an eye on him from under my lashes. I can see him thinking.

"All I'm asking for is some parameters so I know what to expect," I add.

He breaks the stare, drops his head, and for a moment I wonder if I'm the one fucking things up by asking him to state his intentions.

"I want you," he finally says, and I let out the air I was holding. "If it were up to me, we'd wake up every damn morning like today, and I don't give the last fuck where that ends up being."

I reach across the table and cover his hand with mine. He turns it palm up and curls his fingers around my wrist. His blue eyes burn into mine.

"Yanis..." Before I can conjure up the right words to share, he continues talking.

"That's what I want, but I get that's jumping ahead, so I was waiting to take my cues from you. You tell me to go home, I'll go. Won't like it, and I'll probably be back on your doorstep tomorrow, but I'll go. However long it takes for me to convince you."

"Ask me out."

My question clearly startles him.

"Out?"

"On a date."

"Isn't that a little like tying the horse behind the cart?"

I start pulling my hand from his but his fingers tighten on my wrist, so I lean forward instead.

"You're the one who suggested we go slow, learn each other again moving forward. What happened this morning seems unavoidable between us—natural—but that doesn't mean we shouldn't—"

I can't get another word out before he leans across the table and covers my mouth with his, swallowing the rest of my words. By the time he releases me, a family sitting a few tables away is staring at us.

"Have a preference?" he asks.

"Sorry?"

He smiles and I melt a little.

"For our first official date, any preference?"

I grin back. Looks like I'm getting what I want. When we were younger, I was in as much of a hurry as he was. Any time we spent together we were mostly naked or on our way there. This time around I want to put the effort in, but more importantly, I want him to put the effort in. I'm not saying we won't get naked—now that genie is out of the bottle, I don't see it going back—but I also want to know we can connect on other levels. Ones that don't involve work or sex.

"Surprise me."

I'm pretty sure I'm taking a big risk, judging by the lazy smirk on his face, but it'll be a good test.

"Deal. Now eat up. Your food's getting cold."

He lets go of my wrist and picks up his burger, but twenty minutes later, when we get into his SUV, his hand seeks out mine and he holds on until we pull up to the office.

"Good to get another few hours of work in?" he asks.

"Yup."

Beats sitting at home watching reruns on TV.

I watch as he gets out, walks around the hood to my side, and opens my door. But instead of helping me down he leans in, kissing me again. Doesn't look like we're keeping things on the down low, we're parked right outside Lena's window.

"Word of warning," he says in a low voice. "I don't plan on holding back out here or in there, and I'm staying at yours for the weekend. We'll reassess on Monday."

My heart and head do battle but when he mouths, "*Please*," my head waves the white flag.

"Okay."

Then I roll my eyes at his responding grin.

CHAPTER 15

BREE

"WE'RE LEAVING AT three this afternoon."

Yanis doesn't take his eyes off the road but a little smile plays on his lips.

"For?" I want to know.

"Our date," he clarifies, this time glancing at me.

We just said goodbye to his parents yesterday, who are heading back to Wyoming this morning. Another Sunday family dinner with the Mazurs and some wonderful baby snuggles with Max last night.

I'm surprised to admit I'll miss them after spending some time in their company this past week. Anna would've liked to have stayed but Max reminded her his crops would need harvesting soon. They were hoping to come for another visit toward the end of October.

As he warned me he would, Yanis stayed at my place the entire weekend. The only time he left was Saturday to get some work done at the office. I could've gone in with him, but since I hadn't done a stitch of laundry in the past two weeks, I opted to stay home and take care of that instead.

I feel more like myself, the crutches are a bit annoying but at least I can move independently, even if I'm not able to drive yet.

"That early?"

I was half expecting him to take me out Saturday night, but we ended up cooking together and watching a movie. That was a date in itself, something we'd never really done as a couple.

"I have a few last-minute arrangements to make. I'll drop you off at home so you can get ready and pick you up at four thirty."

I'm intrigued at the early hour and am trying to guess where he might be taking me, but nothing comes to mind.

"Where are we going?" I finally give in.

"Didn't you ask for a surprise?" he teases and I shoot him a glare.

"Yes, but I need to know what to wear."

Like I really care. I'm pretty sure Yanis knows enough about me to realize I don't do dresses. The best he can get out of me would be a pair of black slacks or dark jeans and one of my fancy tops, which usually live in the very back of my closet.

"You're just fishing for information and you know it," he accuses me. "But fine, I'll throw you a bone. Don't wear anything that requires dry-cleaning and bring a sweater."

I feel my mouth spreading into a smile. Whatever

we're doing, it's going to be outdoors. I'm already liking it.

"Morning!" Lena chirps when we walk into the office a few minutes later.

She's been all smiles since Friday afternoon when she clearly saw us in a lip-lock in the parking lot. Guess the suppressed tension between Yanis and I had not gone unnoticed after all. The fact we are now 'an item'—something Yanis likes to make sure everyone knows—is not causing a single person to react in surprise. A relieved sigh or a muttered, *"It's about fucking time,"* but not a single look of confusion.

"Morning," I return.

"Calls?" Yanis snaps at the same time.

His normal, crusty, all-business attitude. It doesn't intimidate anyone, least of all Lena.

"Yes, a guy from Boulder Records." She ruffles through her message pad. "Glen Delbert." She tears off the message and hands it to Yanis. "Sounded urgent."

"Everyone here?" he asks, pressing a kiss to the side of my head.

"Shep is at the vineyard and Dimi should be in shortly, but other than that, yeah."

"Let me know when he gets here. Staff meeting as soon as he does. Don't let anyone leave."

"Aye, aye, Boss."

"And get Delbert on the line."

She mock-salutes him, but he doesn't even notice, he's already moving toward his office. I toss Lena a wink and hobble over to my desk.

Half an hour later, we're all in the conference room—hustled in by Lena—when Yanis walks in, slamming the door shut.

"Just got off the phone with the VP of Security at Boulder Records and my buddy, Bill Evans, with the Denver PD. Effective immediately our standby contract with Boulder Records is terminated."

"What? Why would they do that?"

Yanis turns to me, anger etched on his face.

"They didn't. I did."

"What?"

I can't believe he'd pull the plug on a lucrative contract like that. Sure, their talent is a pain in everyone's ass, but you can't argue the pay. Hell, we even get a nice check just to be on standby in case they need to pad their own security detail with ours.

Dimi calmly stares at his brother.

"Maybe you should start from the beginning."

For a moment it looks like Yanis might take a bite out of his brother, but then he collects himself and nods sharply.

"Delbert left an urgent message for me to call. Reason for the urgency was to try and get to me before the Denver PD did or the first news story hit." His nostrils flare as he takes in a deep breath. "For the past three years, Bobby Lee Rose has been receiving increasingly alarming anonymous gifts and messages Delbert opted not to tell us about."

"Fucking great."

This from Jake.

"That's ridiculous, why would they keep that kind of information from us?" I want to know.

I'm shocked, trying to process what this means.

"Apparently, not even Bobby Lee herself knew about it until recently. They have that woman wrapped so tight; the admirer's offerings didn't even make it to her."

"Sue Paxton?" I mention the personal assistant and he nods.

"Among others. Her personal security detail, her publicist, her manager. They shield her from everything. Don't want to upset her delicate creative spirit or some such bullshit. They don't want the press to find out for the same reason."

"So I'm guessing she's not at a rehab center?" Radar pipes up.

"Last message they received included pictures of her in her dressing rooms at different concert venues. That had them whisk her off into hiding."

I feel Jake's eyes on me at the same time my mind leaps ahead. He's faster with the conclusion, though.

"Let me guess; they used Bree as bait."

Yanis slams his fist on the conference table so hard it has me jump in my seat.

"Fucking prick said they saw an opportunity to take care of business without risking this going public."

"Except they didn't," Dimi points out.

"Wait a minute." I hold up my hand trying to get the full picture. "Sam…I don't remember his last name, he's part of her regular detail...he helped me out of my corset in the limo, gave me his shirt to cover up, and then had the driver go across town so I could have a burger." The realization the friendly security guard had used me hits me like a fist in the gut. "He was stalling...waiting for someone to make a move, but no one did."

"Not until the next morning," Radar supplies.

No wonder I haven't heard a thing from Boulder Records or Sue Paxton. No, *"Glad you're okay,"* or *"How are ya?"* from any of them. Now I know why and I know I shouldn't give a flying fuck, but betrayal is always a bitter pill.

"Why come forward now?" I want to know.

"Evans." Yanis, who's stayed standing suddenly sits down heavily, turning his troubled eyes on me. "He's been following up with some of the witnesses and went to speak to Sue Paxton to clarify a few things yesterday. Found out from her, Bobby Lee was found dead this morning at a mountain retreat near Aspen."

"Dead?"

It slips out in shock.

"Looks like an OD—pills and booze—Delbert says her agent will be issuing a press release later this morning. I called Evans who shared that Sue was so upset, she came clean about the stalker, and he immediately called the record label. He's on his way to meet with the bigwigs now. Autopsy is scheduled for later today."

"Jesus," someone says.

I don't know who, I'm still trying to process all this information. Bobby Lee, dead. Holy hell, that's going to stir up a media frenzy. No wonder Delbert is scrambling.

Then another thought occurs to me just as Dimi calmly voices it.

"What if it isn't suicide?"

Exactly.

YANIS

TRUST MY BROTHER to zoom in on what has had my stomach in knots since I got off the phone with Bill.

Whoever is obsessed with Bobby Lee must have been pissed at that little stunt her security team tried to pull with Bree as their bait. What if he found the singer's whereabouts and acted his anger out on her? Wouldn't be the first time a stalker kills his obsession. Hell, even if it does turn out a suicide or accidental overdose, the guy is gonna be off the rails either way.

I look at Bree, who is chewing her bottom lip with her teeth. She's worried too. Good. That'll keep her alert. Who knows if a nutcase like that may not decide to come after her?

Fuck. So much for the relaxing date I had planned.

"We'll have to wait for the autopsy outcome on that," I finally respond to Dimi. "Regardless, this guy could be a loose cannon out there. Bree…" I turn to her. "I need you to put together a profile on him. Evans said he'd shoot over pictures of the notes and gifts Delbert handed over to him last night. Use those, and your personal knowledge of the guy to give us some idea who is out there."

I spend another twenty minutes giving the guys a briefing on the floater in the reservoir, the missing blood and fingerprints on the fire poker, and Evans' unspoken but implicated intent to look into his own department for some answers.

Then I firmly steer the meeting to work that actually pays bills. The Jelnyk mine, the vineyard, other smaller contracts, and new business. I'm handling Peru, Dimi and Radar are collaborating on Flynn's Fields, and Jake is taking care of smaller contracts with Kai's help.

I feel moderately better when I walk back into my office after the meeting.

"Are you okay?"

I swing around to find Bree followed me.

"Fine. Why?"

"You got a little tense in there."

I resist the knee-jerk reaction to blow her off and instead grab her upper arm and pull her inside, shutting the door behind her. Then I cup her face, tilt it up, and take her mouth in a deep kiss.

The little whimper escaping her lips when I let her come up for air sends a ripple down my spine. Damn, I better watch myself before I strip her naked and have my way with her on my desk, in the middle of a workday, with the entire office within hearing.

I rest my forehead against hers.

"All relaxed now."

She chuckles and shakes her head lightly.

"It's that easy, huh?"

"With you it is."

She lifts a hand, placing it in the center of my chest where I know she'll find my heart racing. All she has to do is look down at my crotch to find me hard as a rock as well, but I'm sure she already knows that. She has that effect on me.

"Look, if you wanna cancel—"

"No," I interrupt her. "I don't. And unless there is some major crisis that can't do without us for a night, I won't."

She lifts her chin and purses her lips. I gladly accept the invitation.

"I'd better get to work then," she says, smiling warmly.

I don't know how many times I've fantasized about this exact scenario. The two of us in my office, door closed, and her smiling up at me like that. So much time wasted.

"You'd better. I hear your boss is a hard-ass."

The smile turns into a smirk as she shrugs and turns to the door.

"Oh, I don't know, turns out he's a bit of a softie underneath all that snarling."

Despite the fucked-up way this workweek started, I'm smiling when I sit down behind my desk.

BREE

"ARE YOU SERIOUS?"

I notice the trailer with the Rimrock Adventures logo on the side right away. A young kid, maybe early twenties, is hauling a raft down and carrying it to the bank of the Colorado River.

Yanis still wouldn't say where we were going when he picked me up twenty minutes ago. All he did was scan me from head to toe and nod his head approvingly.

We're in Fruita, just west of Grand Junction, at a small boat launch. I'm not sure what he's thinking, because in another hour and a half that sun is going to go down, but it looks like whatever it is involves a raft.

"Hey, are you Yanis?" the kid calls out when I'm helped out of the vehicle.

"Yup. You Kevin?"

The young man nods before looking at my crutches with some concern.

"Is she going? I'm not sure if that's a good idea."

I open my mouth to speak but Yanis beats me to it as we approach the trailer.

"Kevin, I'd be careful. This one could wipe the floor with you blindfolded on a bum leg with one arm tied behind her back. Don't piss her off, she's got a nasty disposition."

I stifle a grin at the man-child's facial expression.

"Babe, be nice to the man while I get the rest of the stuff, okay?"

Instead of getting my nose bent out of joint for being called 'Babe,' I double over laughing instead.

Christ, it's been a long time since I've laughed like this. Turns out there is a side to Yanis I didn't know about. Like a sense of humor. Where the hell has he been hiding that?

Kevin busies himself with life vests and paddles, taking his sweet time until he sees Yanis walking up. He's carrying two coolers he takes right over to the raft, strapping them down between the two seats.

"If that's all, I'll see you in a couple of hours."

He waves and climbs into the van towing the trailer.

"You gonna stand there all night?"

I look back at Yanis who is waiting by the raft, grinning wide.

Oh boy. I can feel my heart giving that extra little pump, the one that releases all the emotions.

I have to hand it to him, when I asked him to surprise me with the date, this is not what I had envisioned. My eyes burn as I walk up to him and instead of climbing in, I toss my crutches in the float and lift my arms around his neck.

"You are *good*," I admit before showing him exactly what I think of our date so far.

"Fuck, you're gonna kill me," he mumbles when we come up for air. "We should get out there or we'll miss it."

"Miss it?"

"The sunset over McInnis Canyon. We can watch it from a flat rock in the middle of the river right below the Pollock Bench Trailhead."

I get in the raft, mostly because I don't want to let on I'm getting emotional. As soon as I'm seated, he shoves me and the raft the rest of the way into the river before jumping in at the last second.

"You okay?"

I smile for him.

"Perfect."

"Good. Want to lounge back in the front? You can keep your leg elevated on the seat or do you want to get in on the action?"

There isn't much more than an occasional ripple in this part of the river, but I'm afraid I'll be a sniveling mess if I don't have something to distract me.

"What do you think? Action, of course. You said we're cutting it short."

Turns out, even with the river flowing at a decent clip, it takes both of us paddling briskly for a good hour to get to our destination. Yanis manages to jump on the rock without getting wet and pulls the raft partially out of the water before helping me out.

Then he has me rest on the edge while he brings out the coolers, taking a folded blanket out of one and a few pillar candles out of the other. He throws the life vests down as pillows before turning to me.

"Are you crying?" he asks, catching me rubbing my eye.

"Nope. Just some dirt," I lie as he helps me sit down. "By the way, how are we getting back?"

If I were with anyone else, I would've made sure I knew what the plan was, but I guess I trusted Yanis to have things in hand.

"Kevin. He'll pick us up over there." He points to the far shore on the north side where I can just make out a small clearing.

I watch as he starts unpacking, amazed he's thought of everything. One of the coolers holds cold beers and the other a smorgasbord of Mexican food from Aztecas, another favorite restaurant of mine.

We talk about random things—none of them work-related—as I gorge myself on dinner and we keep an eye on the horizon where the sun is sliding behind McInnis. When it's almost down, and the deep reds and golds spread through the sky, Yanis braces himself against a rock and pulls me closer so my back is resting against his chest.

We stay like that, only occasionally talking in hushed voices, until the first stars appear in the sky.

Bar none, best date ever.

CHAPTER 16

YANIS

*I*T'S STILL DARK so the employee parking lot only holds three cars when we pull in.

Dimi and Radar followed me in the PASS van, stocked with tools and the additional security equipment Radar picked up yesterday.

We're hoping to install the bulk of the cameras before staff comes in, which is why we're here at this ungodly hour.

I left Bree in bed at my place, where we've stayed since my parents left on Monday. If it were up to me, she'd give up her apartment and just move in—she belongs in my house—but I know she still has some reservations and I'm trying hard not to press.

Yesterday I was about to make arrangements for Lena to swing by and pick her up at my place on her way to the office, but Bree's scathing look stopped me. She was brewing the rest of the day and I got an earful when we got back home.

She reminded me, just because she couldn't

operate a car didn't mean her brain was out of commission as well, and she wasn't exactly helpless. Then she mentioned maybe it was time for her to head back to her own apartment. It was abundantly clear I'd overstepped, which was a damn shame since I'd scored some serious points on our date the night before. Two steps forward, one step back.

She ended up staying the night anyway, but I have no doubt she'll be at her apartment tonight. I'll give her that space, not because I want to, but because I think she needs it. Heck, maybe we both do.

As a result of circumstances, things have moved fast these past weeks. Don't get me wrong, I know what I want the outcome to be and keep my eye on the prize, but perhaps a small step back is the smarter move for the long run. And I want our run to never end.

A sharp knock on my window shakes me from my headspace.

"You gonna sit there all fucking day?"

My brother wasn't too keen on getting his ass out of bed early. Probably because he's as sleep deprived as his wife is since the arrival of Max. If things weren't as crazy and Bree wasn't on limited duty, I would've told him to take a damn month off, but circumstances suck at the moment so that's not really an option. He knows.

Joe is waiting when we walk in.

"No need for you to be here this early," I tell him.

We spoke yesterday and discussed where the added

cameras were going to go. There really is no reason for him to get out of bed.

"I never left," he clarifies. "Couch in my office is comfortable and until this shit is sorted out, I plan to stay close."

"You can't be married," Dimi suggests, making the other man grin.

"Nope. Dodged that bullet once, not walking into that battle again."

"Amen to that," Shep—who just comes walking into the lobby—agrees.

He's been a good addition to the team. A good guy overall. He also has the ex from hell and two little girls he doesn't get to see much, courtesy of their mother. Until I offered him full time with benefits, he'd been juggling three jobs just to keep up with child support and alimony, and have something left to live off, which wasn't much.

I send the three of them off to start with the installations and accept Joe's invitation for coffee in his office. This is a good opportunity to get him up to speed on some of the stuff Radar was able to uncover on Dan McNeely. I haven't mentioned his name to Joe yet because I didn't want to run the risk he'd do or say something that would raise McNeely's suspicion and cause him to bolt.

He motions to a chair and pours a coffee from the pot sitting on his filing cabinet.

"Thanks," I tell him, when he hands me the cup and wait until he takes a seat before I dive in. "What do you know about Dan McNeely?" When he looks a little confused, I add, "On your cleaning crew."

That seems to flip a trigger and he swings his chair around, pulls open a drawer in the filing cabinet, and pulls out a folder.

"Dan McNeely. Twenty-nine, worked at Falcone Scrap and Metal before starting here back in July. Nothing notable in his file." He looks up. "Why? What about him?"

"Just clearing up some stuff. Did you put out an ad for that position? I'm trying to figure what made him stand out from other candidates."

He looks back at the file and pulls out a note torn off a yellow legal pad.

"No. I remember now, he walked in one day. We weren't open to the public yet but had a sign out front indicating we had several positions open and to call to inquire, but he chose to come right on in. Showed moxie. I didn't interview him, my manager did." He appears to study the notes. "Says here his references checked out." Then he looks up. "I assume there's a reason for your interest in him?"

There's an edge to him I can't quite place. I wish I had Bree with me, she'd be better at reading him.

"There is," I confirm but don't elaborate. Instead, I ask him another question hoping to shake something loose. "What if I told you Falcone Scrap and Metal was a subsidiary of Patria Holdings?"

I note the recognition in the way he stiffens in his seat, his face suddenly like a carved mask. Oh, yeah, he knows what it means. Question is, will he admit to it?

Almost as fast as the mask appeared, he forces his expression into something that probably should pass as confusion or surprise.

"I did not know that." That much is probably true, judging by his reaction. "I don't think I've heard of... Patria, you said?"

And there is the lie.

Patria Holdings is the Albero family umbrella covering about two-thirds of their business ventures. Most of those are legit, or at the very least appear to be. Patria had been in the news about ten or twelve years ago, when Guiseppe Albero had been charged with money laundering. He ended up walking away scot-free on some stupid technicalities, after a lengthy trial.

There is no way in hell if you knew anyone associated with the family that you could've missed it. Which tells me Joe is not comfortable being associated with the man we saw leave here in a cloud of dust on Monday.

Interesting, and if I weren't in a hurry to get this resolved, I might've left him with the illusion he's getting away with the denial. As it is—and as I'm sure he's already figured out—his connection to the Albero family may well be at the root of the disruptions at the winery.

"Cut the bull. Don't forget I stood right there when Angelo Sarrazin peeled out of your parking lot. Do you want this problem solved or what?"

"*Fuck*!" He hauls back his arm and pelts his coffee mug across the room, where it shatters against the wall. "That fucking asshole."

Well, that escalated quickly.

BREE

"CAN YOU TALK?"

"Hang on." I hear rustling on the other end and wait for Bill Evans to get back on the line. "Go ahead."

I spoke to Bill earlier today as well. He'd called for Yanis but Lena told him he was out and passed him on to me instead. The autopsy report was in and he'd managed to obtain a copy. There was no ambivalence around the cause of death—overdose—but the ME was hesitant to label Bobby Lee's manner of death as *accident*, *suicide*, or *homicide* and instead had gone with the more obscure *undetermined*.

As it turns out, not everyone had been happy with the report. He mentioned getting called into his chief's office and told to back off Bobby Lee's case since it was out of his jurisdiction. He was asked to hand over his file and the evidence Delbert had handed to him on the spot. Bill concluded someone high up in the Aspen PD must've called his boss, and that made him very suspicious.

It did me too, especially when Bobby Lee's domicile was very much in his jurisdiction and so was my abduction and the dead body found in the reservoir. Besides, even though Bobby Lee was found dead in Aspen, you'd expect the police departments to collaborate.

"I just wanted to make sure you got my email with the attachments," I ask him.

He mentioned this morning putting together a file of his own with what he could remember and was looking for the pictures of the notes and gifts he sent on Monday.

"I did. I also got that profile you did. Very helpful. Won't be able to do anything with it until I get home. I'll send you guys copies of my notes then too. Can't risk it now. I have a feeling there are eyes on me."

Jesus. I wouldn't want to be in his shoes. We just dealt with some corruption here in the Grand Junction PD we helped uncover, but at least the chief is a stand-up guy.

If you put everything together and add the missing evidence from that fire poker I hung on to for dear life, things are starting to stink to high heaven. Somebody would have to have a lot of power to be able to exert that kind of influence.

"Anything we can do?" I ask him.

He scoffs.

"Any openings for a seasoned detective in Grand Junction? It would have to be without a reference because I have a feeling I won't get a good one."

He makes it sound like a joke but I'd bet my right hand he's dead serious. Heck, if I were him, I'd want to get the hell out of Dodge too.

"They just did an entire revamp of the department,

so you're about six months late, but I have other connections I can tap into." The name of a former Denver commander of major crimes I had some dealings with in the past pops in my head. He's now chief of police in Durango and last I heard they were looking. "Actually," I quickly add. "Did you ever work with Benedetti?"

"Benedetti? On occasion. Why?"

"He's chief of police in Durango. I heard they were looking. I can put in a call for you if you're serious?"

"Fuck, I might take you up on that, once I get to the bottom of what's going on."

"Be careful out there."

Bill's chuckle sounds bitter.

"Yeah. Thanks, don't be too worried though, I'm pretty tough."

"No doubt," I appease him.

"Mazur is a lucky bastard," he mumbles before ending the call.

Another reason to like the guy, but I'm genuinely worried. Hope Yanis is back soon because I get the sense his friend is in over his head.

I DON'T ACTUALLY see Yanis until I'm outside the office, sitting on the step, waiting for Uber to come pick me up, when his Yukon turns onto the parking lot.

We only talked briefly on the phone earlier but

I could tell he was in the middle of something and figured I could fill him in on the situation with Bill later.

"What are you doing out here?" he asks when he gets out of his vehicle.

"Waiting for an Ubhmph…"

He swallows the rest of my words when he pulls me to my feet and swoops down for a kiss.

"Give me a few minutes and I'll drive ya."

"The Uber driver's already on his way."

"So? Cancel your order." He hands me his keys. "I won't be long. I just want to check in with Lena and grab my laptop. We've had quite a few developments at the vineyard."

He disappears inside. Sounds like we've both had informative days.

I unlock the Yukon, get in the passenger seat, and pull out my phone to cancel the ride. Then I try to figure out what to do for dinner, but before I can decide whether I want to pull something from my freezer or pick something up, Yanis gets behind the wheel.

"Wanna hit the diner? We can find a quiet booth and eat and talk at the same time," he suggests as he starts the engine.

"Sure."

I wouldn't mind a baked mac and cheese with meatloaf. It's been a while.

Fifteen minutes later, we're in the booth closest to the kitchen, mostly because no one ever seems to want to sit in that section.

"Had a little talk with Flynn this morning," he starts as soon as we put our order in. "Dropped Patria Holdings on him and he tried to play off like he'd never heard of it, so then I ended up calling him out about his buddy, Angelo Sarrazin. Turns out those two had a beef years ago, Joe thought it was smoothed over, but it looks like maybe our mob prince still has some hard feelings."

The waitress shows up with our beers so he waits until she moves on to another booth before he leans over the table.

"Sarrazin is the one who introduced McNeely. Claimed one of his guys at the scrapyard had a sister in Palisade who was ill, and did Joe maybe have a job for him at the winery. Joe thought he was doing a good thing."

"So you figure McNeely is Sarrazin's plant? What is this, some kind of revenge thing? What was the beef?"

Yanis sits back and shakes his head.

"Won't tell me more than it was over a woman."

"Interesting. Looking at them, you wouldn't guess they'd have the same taste."

"I wouldn't know, I've only ever been interested in one woman."

He gives me a smarmy grin and a wink. He sure is in a chipper mood, although I'm not so sure that'll last, once I tell him my news.

"Smooth, Mazur. Nice tricks you've got."

I grin and shake my head.

"Glad you approve. I'm working on expanding my repertoire."

Again with the jokes. Who is this man?

"So did you get the cameras set up?"

"Yup. All installed. Shep and Radar are both staying the night there, in case something goes down it'll be good to have the backup. We still don't have conclusive proof McNeely was responsible."

"Even more important now the freaking mob may be involved," I conclude.

"Bingo. And one more interesting tidbit Joe mentioned. He said McNeely wasn't the only recommendation Sarrazin made. Apparently, he's the one who suggested PASS."

"What? We've never done work for them, have we?"

"Fuck no. I have no clue how that came about, but I do find it interesting."

"I'd say."

The waitress is back and slides our food in front of us. One million calories in that little oven dish but it's so worth it. Best mac and cheese I've ever had.

"Quit making those sounds," Yanis grumbles as he digs into his own.

"I can't help it, it's so fucking good. You won't mind if I pack on a few pounds, right? I could eat this stuff by the vat."

I shove another bite in my mouth and hum my bliss.

"Why don't you tell me how your day was?" he

asks, a little annoyed at me.

Yeah, that'll be a sure way to get his mind off my humming.

"Something's dirty in Bill's department."

His fork stops halfway to his mouth.

"You're kidding."

"Not even a little."

CHAPTER 17

YANIS

*I*T'S BEEN A crazy week.

We've collectively been juggling a heavy workload and by Friday night the strain is showing.

Lena left ten minutes ago and gave Bree a ride home. As eager as she'd been to get back into the swing, she was plum worn out and I had to put my foot down when she started nodding off at her desk.

The guys and I are in the conference room, trying to sort out coverage for the weekend, and Dimi and Radar just got into it. I'm not even sure over what exactly, one minute we're trying to divvy up the schedule and the next those two are nose to nose. I wasn't kidding when I said it's been a crazy week.

Ironically, these are two of my more levelheaded guys and don't often get their noses out of joint, but there must be something in the air tonight.

"Knock it off!"

I cranked up the volume and both heads turn my way.

"What the fuck is with you two?"

Radar is the first to pipe up.

"Been home a net total of two fucking nights in the past seven days."

Dimi scoffs.

"At least you got to sleep two nights. Haven't fucking slept in weeks."

"All right, enough," I cut them off before they get into it again.

Last thing I need is my guys at each other's throats when I need everyone on top of their game.

"Jake, Kai…are you good to cover Saturday and Sunday night? I'll take tonight's shift at the winery." I point my finger at the other two. "You two take the weekend off and fucking rest up. We don't need this shit right now."

"What about Bree?" Dimi wants to know. "Who's gonna keep an eye on her?"

"Bree," I answer, sounding more confident than I feel.

A month ago, I wouldn't have thought twice about it, but it eats at me now. Guess this is my first challenge to see if I can be both her man and her boss. Trust, she said…well, guess it's time I put my money where my mouth is.

"She's a trained professional. Let's not forget that."

"She's hurt," Dimi fires back.

"And you're missing a leg," I lob back, getting pissed on Bree's behalf. "Yet you don't see any of us doubt *your* abilities."

That shuts him up.

"Bree can look after herself," Jake confirms, and with that the discussion is done.

"Go home," I direct at my brother and Radar. "Don't wanna see you back until Monday."

Twenty minutes later, I lock up the office and as soon as I get behind the wheel, I dial Shep's number.

"I'm coming in to relieve you. You good hanging in until nine?"

"Got nothing planned but my bed, Boss. It'll hold."

"Good."

Then I drive straight to Bree's apartment, she doesn't even look surprised when I let myself in.

She's in the kitchen, hobbling around without her crutches, which are leaning against the couch. Something smells good.

"Whatever that is, got enough for two?" I ask.

I poke my head over her shoulder and slide my hand around to her belly.

"Stir-fry and yes, there's enough."

She twists her neck to look at me and I use the opportunity to plant a kiss on her mouth.

"I thought you were going to be late at the office tonight?"

"Mmm. I was, but plans have changed."

I let my lips graze a strip of bare skin on her shoulder before I step back and lean a hip against the counter so I can look at her.

"How so?"

"Dimi and Radar both need a break so I'm heading

to Palisade tonight. Kai and Hutch are taking the next two nights. Shep's gonna need a break soon too."

"I can take a shift at the winery," she offers, her face hopeful.

I resist the knee-jerk temptation to shut her down and pretend to give it some thought.

"It may come to that if this drags on any longer, but mobility is gonna be an issue. You catch anything on the monitors you'd have a hard time chasing someone down on crutches."

I hate seeing her face fall.

"Yeah, good point. Fuck, I hate feeling useless."

"You're far from useless." I brush a strand of hair behind her ear. "With the rest of us in and out, I need someone with their wits about them at the office. I'd like to scratch one item off our plate, but things seem to keep adding on. It helps to know you've got things covered there."

Her face turns my way, a smirk on her lips and an amused sparkle in her eyes.

"Smooth, Mazur. Positive reinforcement. Making me feel essential. You're getting good at this psych stuff."

I grin back.

"I learned from the best."

"Don't overdo it," she cautions with a smile, before turning back to her wok. "Grab some bowls, will you? I don't want to overcook this."

Quality time has been hard to come by this past week, and since it looks like the weekend is just going to be more of the same, I don't want to waste the hour—at most—we have together with work talk or anything particularly heavy. It sucks, because I'd hoped maybe she'd relax enough this weekend to open up about some of that baggage accumulating the past fifteen years, but it looks like that'll have to wait.

The food is great and I tell her so, which seems to please her. She doesn't complain when I clear the dinner dishes and quickly wash them up and is content to watch from her kitchen table.

I'm gonna have to hustle if I'm to relieve Shep at nine.

"Any chance I can get you to crash at my place?" I ask, wiping my hands on a towel.

Her eyebrows snap together in a puzzled frown.

"Why?"

Good question, one I don't really have a proper answer for, other than it would make me feel better about leaving.

"I don't know. Maybe I like the idea of you in my bed, even if I'm not there."

"Mmm," she hums, smiling as she gets up and hobbles over. "That's kinda sweet, Yanis. You keep surprising me."

She slides her arms around my neck and fits her body against mine. My arms close around her, one hand slipping down the curve of her ass.

"I surprise myself," I admit, which makes her laugh.

I love it when she laughs, her head back and slender

neck exposed. Her eyes close, the lines around them a little more prominent. Her mouth stretches wide, offering a glimpse of those small white teeth, and the sound escaping comes from the gut.

Bree laughs with conviction. It doesn't happen often but when she does, it's as if the world stills around her.

Then she reaches up as she pulls my head down for a kiss.

"Maybe another night. I have some things I want to do around here."

Not an unexpected answer and I'm not going to argue it now, I'm already going to be late.

"Sure."

I go in for another lip touch and then reluctantly let her go.

"Lock up behind me, okay?"

She throws me a mock-salute.

"Will do, Boss," she tosses back.

She's wrong, this is not me bossing her, this is me loving her.

BREE

"BENEDETTI."

I couldn't settle down after Yanis left, so I'm finally following through on the conversation I had with Bill Evans earlier this week.

We've only spoken a few times since Joe Benedetti left the Denver force for Durango, but I make it a point to check in from time to time with all my law enforcement contacts. It makes it much easier when and if a case pops up where we need their support or input.

"Joe. It's Bree Graves. Sorry to call you at home."

"You actually caught me in the office. Bree Graves, how are you?"

"I'm good. Burning the candle at both ends again? Don't you have a wife waiting at home?"

Benedetti lost his first wife not long before he left Denver, but was lucky to find love a second time around.

"Ha. She's off at some horticultural conference in Salt Lake for the weekend, and I have a desk piled so high I can't even see the door anymore."

"Still short-handed?"

"Yeah. One of my officers recently took the detective's exam, but even with him added, the schedule's tight. Seems to be an ongoing struggle to keep this department staffed."

"That's actually what I was hoping to touch base about," I capitalize on the opening I finagled. "Do you remember a detective by the name of Bill Evans from your time in Denver?"

"Evans? Wasn't he in Littleton? Or Englewood?"

"Littleton," I confirm. "It's possible he's looking. Ran into a bit of a fishy situation."

"Fishy, how?"

I spend the next half hour filling Benedetti in on what happened to me in Denver. I brush off his concern and share what I know about the situation

Evans finds himself in.

"I haven't personally spoken to him since Wednesday, but I know he's not feeling too comfortable where he is now. He spoke with my boss."

"Don't blame him," Benedetti agrees and then falls silent.

I decide to wait him out, give him a chance to process. It doesn't take long.

"Got his personal number?"

Quickly putting him on speaker I find Evan's name in my contacts and message it to Joe.

"Incoming. What are you thinking?"

"I'm thinking I may have a talk with him. I'd like to know where his head's at. I've dealt with most of the top brass in the Denver area. On both sides of the law," he clarifies. "Might be able to offer some insight, but I also have good connections with the local feds here. You never know when that may come in handy."

"I appreciate it, Joe. Especially given how busy you already are."

"Hey, if it nets me another detective, I'm gonna owe you one."

A seriously decent guy. Glad to know he hasn't lost his sense of justice, even in a job I know is rife with politics.

"That happens you can buy me dinner if I'm ever in town."

"Deal. I'll hold off 'til tomorrow before I give him a call, in case you wanna give him the heads-up."

"Probably not a bad idea."

As soon as I get off the phone with him, I shoot Bill a text rather than call him.

Talked to Benedetti. Expect a call.

Barely a second later I get a responding message with a thumbs-up emoji.

With that off my list, I get up, flick off the lights, and head to the bathroom to draw a bath. My body is aching. Despite being stuck behind a desk all week, I probably should've eased into things a little more. The bath will hopefully relax me enough so I can sleep.

While the tub fills, I pull up an audiobook on my phone. I normally listen when I'm driving, which I haven't done in weeks. I don't like using headphones unless I'm working out in the gym at the office, so I prop up my phone on the vanity and press play. Then I take off my walking boot, strip down, and toss my dirty clothes in the hamper, and with a groan of pleasure get into the tub.

The male narrator's voice—he reminds me of Yanis—is of a nice rumbly quality and I close my eyes, letting myself sink into the story.

The water is cool when I startle awake. The audio is still playing but I must've been dozing for a bit because I'm not sure what's going on in the story. For a moment I consider heating up the water but it's probably better to get out and in bed. I'm already pruned.

I pause my book—I'll have to remember to backtrack the chunk I missed—and note to my surprise it's after midnight. Jesus, I didn't just doze off for a bit, I slept solidly for almost two hours. No wonder my fingertips look like raisins.

I strap on my walking boot and slip into the kimono I have hanging on the back of the door. Then I head for the kitchen to grab a glass of water for the night. It feels chilly in here, but that's probably because I was in cold water for a while. I'll get warm soon enough under my fluffy comforter.

The apartment is dark, but the sparse light coming in from outside is just enough for me to find a clean pair of underwear and a fresh night shirt. I quickly change and turn to the bed when all the air is sucked from my lungs.

There something lying in the middle of my bed.

Not wanting to take my eyes off the object, my hand searches blindly for the light switch. With the stark overhead light on, I see what it is.

A fire poker.

I react, diving for my gun in the top drawer of my nightstand. Then I press my back into the corner and visually scan every inch of my room, starting with the window, which appears untouched. I ease slowly toward the door I left open, leading with my gun.

When I hit the doorpost, I take a deep breath in, count to three as I exhale, and swing around, stepping into the doorway. I do a quick scan of the hallway, make sure the bathroom is clear, and flick on every light as I go.

Nothing. There's no one in my apartment, but there definitely was someone at some point, because that poker didn't leave itself here. The front door is locked and deadbolted, the windows look solid, and the latch on the sliding door is still in place.

I retrieve my phone from the bathroom counter where I left it and dial.

CHAPTER 18

YANIS

TIME IS CRAWLING.

I brought my laptop and have been able to do some work, but my eyes are getting gritty from staring at either my laptop screen or the two bigger ones, showing a grid of all sixteen cameras we have tracking movement all over the winery.

I've been following the movements of the vineyard's night security guard doing his routine rounds, something I suggested to Flynn should continue as normal to avoid raising suspicion with staff. The older man is aware I'm here and was in here earlier to fill up the travel mug he carries around.

Between the two of us, one coffee pot is gone and a second one is brewing in hopes it'll infuse some energy, because mine is fast wearing out. There was a time I could pull all-nighters, sometimes two in a row, and not think twice about it. Guess my forty-six years are starting to show, because I've barely done three hours of this shift and already I'm struggling.

The coffee machine stops gurgling so I get up to get a fresh cup and stretch my legs. When I turn back, something catches my eye on one of the big monitors. Movement behind the large wine storage facility where the fermentation tanks are kept.

A quick glance confirms the night watchman is still inside that same building, checking every nook and cranny, so the shadow I just saw darting across the small video window is definitely not him.

On full alert now, I click on the exterior camera feed to pull it up full screen.

There, just inside the first row of vines, I see movement. I quickly enlarge a different angle on the second monitor, coming from a camera we mounted on one of the high floodlights used during harvesting. Zooming in as close as the camera allows, I notice the figure is not empty-handed.

Fuck.

I grab the two-way radio, shove my phone in my pocket, and dart out of the tasting room. The agreement had been to observe, record, and wait for law enforcement if anything happened, but if I don't step in now, it could spell disaster for the vineyard.

"Steve, come in..." I use the radio while I'm running out the back door.

I wince at the loud crackle coming through and hope the sound doesn't carry. I don't want to announce my approach, I want to catch the fucker in the act.

"...Steve here..."

"Got a prowler, I'm heading your way. Call 911.

Police and fire. Stay put."

"…ten-four…"

Glad the man doesn't ask unnecessary questions; I turn off the radio. Making sure to stay in the shadows, I make my way over the storage barn, keeping my back to the wall as I inch my way along to the corner. There I drop the radio and unholster my gun before sticking my head around the edge.

It's about twenty yards to the first row of vines from the back of the building, to allow room for equipment and vehicles. Only a matter of seconds to dash across the open space to the cover of the vines, but it's still seconds of exposure.

If I go full out, he'll hear me, if I make a careful approach, he may see me. Six of one, half a dozen of the other, and given that my best sprinting days are behind me, I stand a better chance of catching him with stealth.

I crouch as low as I can manage and make my way into the vines, trying not to make a sound. I don't hear anything, but the closer I get to the vines, the stronger the smell of gasoline becomes.

Son of a bitch, if I don't catch him before he throws a match there'll be no way I'm fast enough to get out of here ahead of the flames.

Sneaking a peek over the vines, I see him about three rows down and moving away from the winery to the far end of the field. I duck back down and move as fast as I dare up this row to get level with him. Then I slip between the vines to get over a row and hold still until I'm sure he hasn't heard me.

On the next quick glance, I see he's stopped in his tracks and I hold my breath as he slowly swivels his head around.

Then I hear it too—sirens.

Before the guy can make the decision to run, I dive out of my hiding spot and run full tilt at him. Hoping to startle him long enough so I can reach him.

But he's fast. I watch him flick on a Zippo lighter and helplessly follow the arc of the flame as he tosses it behind him in the row of vines before taking off.

I'm now not just running to catch him; I'm running to get out of the path of the sudden whoosh of flames.

No longer concerned about stealth, he runs full speed toward the creek that borders that side of the property. I'm having a hard time keeping up but at least I'm clear of the fire. The next thing I know a shot is fired, I feel the brush of something pass by my head, just before I hit the dirt.

He's fucking shooting at me.

I tentatively lift my head and catch him taking off again. I jump to my feet, raise my gun to eye level, and take aim.

My legs may not be fast enough to catch up, but no one can outrun the speed of a well-aimed bullet.

Almost before I register the sound of the gunshot, I watch the guy's body spin before going down. I break into a run and hope to fuck I get to him before he gets back up.

I reach him just as he scrambles to his feet and

launch myself at him. He falls facedown in the dirt, which makes it easier to restrain him long enough to slap a pair of zip ties on him. Ignoring his yelp of pain, I haul him in a sitting position and yank off the balaclava he's wearing.

Dan McNeely.

It doesn't surprise me, but it still feels good to have suspicions confirmed.

"You shot me, you asshole," he complains.

I look at his left arm. The sleeve of the black hoodie he's wearing glistens with blood. He's lucky it's just his arm.

I was aiming for his torso.

Grabbing his right arm, I haul him to his feet and turn him toward the winery, only now noticing the emergency vehicles pulling up to the fire destroying the section of vines we left behind us. Suddenly the floodlights come on—Steve must've thrown the switch—and shouting voices can be heard.

Keeping a firm hold on McNeely's good arm, I march him to the two cops coming toward us.

"Mazur?" one of them asks as I hand the punk over to the other.

"That's me."

"I'm gonna need your gun."

I fish it out of its holster and hand it over by the barrel.

"You'll find his back there. He dropped it."

"Was it discharged?"

I look the young officer straight in the eye.

"Yes, or I wouldn't have returned fire."

He pauses a moment before nodding.

"Show me where."

As I retrace my steps with the officer right beside me, I hear a phone ringing in the distance. Recognizing the ringtone my hand immediately goes for my back pocket, which no longer holds my phone. I must've lost it when he shot at me.

"Hey, where are you going?" the cop asks when I make a sharp left toward the fire, following the sound.

"I went down when he shot at me. Must've dropped my phone," I call over my shoulder. "The gun should be in front of you somewhere. Can't be far."

The ringing has already stopped when I find my phone, so close to the fire I can feel the heat.

A quick glance at the screen shows a missed call from my brother and an uneasy feeling crawls up my spine.

There'd have to be a good reason for him to call me in the middle of the night.

BREE

I'VE BARELY MOVED from my spot in the middle of the apartment when a sharp knock sounds at the front door.

"Bree! It's me. I'm here with the cops. Open the door."

Jake.

I called him. It made sense because he's closest to me.

Forcing my feet to move, I walk to the door and throw the locks back, but it isn't until Jake steps inside and quietly removes the gun I'm still holding, I feel I can breathe.

"You good?" he asks, as two officers who stepped in behind him slip around us into my apartment.

I nod.

"Yup."

"Good." He grabs my crutches and hands them to me. "Use these. Your ankle is hurting."

Now that he mentions it, I can feel it throbbing.

"Ms. Graves, why don't you have a seat?"

Turning, I find one of the police officers standing by the couch. I look for the second one but she must've gone into my bedroom.

It takes me a while to fill them in on what happened tonight and what the fire poker represents. The one officer takes notes, but after listening to my story calls in a detective. Detective Bissette shows up ten minutes later.

I remember her, she was one of the detectives working a murder case we were involved with earlier this year. She clearly remembers me too.

"Do you mind if I have a quick look around?" she asks and I shake my head.

"Go right ahead."

She does a perfunctory scan of the living room and kitchen before disappearing down the hall.

Ignoring the remaining officer and Jake, who is hovering in the kitchen, I elevate my leg, sink back in the couch, and suddenly exhausted, I close my eyes.

"Ms. Graves, you had a bath?" Bissette calls from the hallway. "There are damp footprints on your carpet."

"It's Bree, and yes, that was me," I confirm.

I hear her talking, probably to the female officer, but can't make out what she's saying. My eyes drift to Jake, who mouths, *"Coffee?"* Knowing chances are slim I'll get any decent sleep tonight anyway, I nod.

Footsteps come down the hall and Bissette walks in, taking a seat in one of my club chairs, while the officer darts out the door.

"She's just getting a camera. We're gonna take some pictures before we take the evidence with us."

"Best dust for fingerprints now," I tell her. "Last fire poker that was taken into evidence got miraculously clean before anyone had a chance to look at it."

She raises a single eyebrow, but turns to the other uniformed officer.

"Go grab the kit."

"Thanks," I mumble.

"Tell me from the start?" she asks, pulling out a voice recorder.

I sigh and go over the entire thing again.

"No idea how they may have come in?" she wants to know when I'm done.

"Windows look untouched, front door was still on the deadbolt, and the sliding door is latched."

She's about to say something when there's a loud commotion on the gallery outside and Yanis storms in, followed by the young officers. Yanis looks like hell.

"The fuck, Bree?" he barks, advancing on the couch. "I had to hear from Dimi?"

I guess word got around. Not surprising.

Jake stalks in from the kitchen, I'm sure to run interference, but I can take care of myself.

"Hello to you too. You look like hell and you smell like you spent the night in a smokehouse," I fire back.

"You call Jake and not me?"

Sick of him hovering over me, I get to my feet. Not that it helps a lot, I'm still looking up at him.

"You were twenty minutes away and working a security detail. Jake was home and only five minutes away. Which was the better call?"

He opens his mouth and quickly closes it again. I figured logic would win out, although he doesn't look too happy about it. He focuses on Bissette.

"How did they get in?"

"Nothing obvious," she answers.

Yanis walks to the sliding door and suddenly swings around, his eyes on me.

"Did you go out on the balcony at all the past few days?"

"No. Last one out there was you."

I notice Detective Bissette following the interplay carefully.

"Then they got in through here."

"How do you know?" she asks moving toward Yanis.

"Second time I've seen the barbecue cover stuck in the door. Last time I closed that door I made sure it wasn't caught."

"How is that possible? It's locked from inside," I question.

"Does it lock from the outside as well?"

Bissette shoves Yanis out of the way as she pulls a pair of latex gloves from her pocket and slips them on.

"If it does, I don't have a key," I comment, grabbing my crutches and hobbling toward them.

The detective already has the door open and steps onto the balcony.

"There's a lock."

I give Yanis—who is leaning through the opening—a little shove and stick my own head outside to take a look.

"Which apartment is the manager's?" Bissette asks over my head.

"One-ten. First floor, south corner."

I straighten and back up so she can step inside.

"Richards. Go wake him up," she instructs the officer before turning to Yanis. "You said the cover was stuck once before? How long ago was that?"

"Little over a week ago."

"Anything indicating someone came in then?"

Yanis shakes his head and then looks at me.

"Do you remember anything out of place?"

I try to think back but nothing comes to mind.

"I don't."

Yanis turns to Jake.

"Do you have a signal detector in your kit?"

A chill runs down my spine.

Jake looks at me, his face a mask, before nodding.

"Let me go grab it."

"What are you thinking?" Bissette asks Yanis when Jake is gone.

"I'm thinking no one risks breaking in unless they want to take something." His eyes find mine. "Or leave something behind."

He must've noticed the shiver rippling over my skin because in two steps he's in front of me, pulling me against his chest.

"Bree hasn't been alone at night in this apartment since we got home from Denver," he further clarifies. "Not until tonight."

The detective clues in quickly, as is clear from her next words.

"Someone's been watching."

CHAPTER 19

YANIS

"*H*OW COME YOU smell like a campfire?"

This time I had no problem convincing Bree to come home with me. I think what shocked her more than knowing someone had been in her apartment was the discovery of two wireless cameras in her house. Her bedroom and bathroom specifically.

"Had an interesting night. McNeely made a move tonight," I share as I turn left onto my street.

"What?"

Bree twists in her seat and I catch her look of surprise from the corner of my eye.

"Caught him on one of the cameras heading into the vines."

I tell her about the fire and the shooting, the phone call from Dimi, and the frustrating half hour I was stuck answering questions from local cops before they reluctantly let me go. I had to leave my weapon with them and commit to coming into the station in the morning, but I planned to do that anyway. I want to hear what that punk I shot has to say.

I opt not to share I blew through every speed limit to get to her.

"Quite the coincidence," she comments when I pull into my driveway.

Putting the car in park and shutting off the engine, I turn to face her.

"Is it?" I pose the question that's been plaguing me since we found those cameras. "What if it's not? If someone's been watching, they would've noticed my comings and goings as well. What if the two are connected?"

"But why? The cameras were in my bedroom and bathroom for crying out loud. That implies an interest that definitely can be labeled as personal. How does that fit in with the vineyard?"

"Don't know yet," I admit, opening my door.

The sky's already getting a little lighter and we need to get a few hours of shut-eye. Looks like we'll need to grab it while we can. Something tells me things are heating up on all fronts.

I help Bree down and let her go ahead to open the door, while I grab the stuff we packed up at her place from the back seat. She's already punching the code in the alarm. My house is outfitted with a numbered door lock and a state-of-the-art alarm. The first for convenience—no keys to worry about—and the second is for security. My neighbors are at a fair distance and I have expensive equipment in the house. Add that to my long hours and frequent traveling and my place is a prime target for thieves.

I carry her stuff straight to the master bedroom and she follows me on her crutches.

"What do the two cases have in common?" she asks from behind me, as I put her things on the bench at the foot of my bed.

Turning, I lift a hand to her face etched with fatigue.

"*Tygrys*, we need to get some sleep."

"I know, but humor me for a minute."

"Fine," I grumble, but the question does make me think. "PASS is involved with both, but other than that I can't see a connection."

"Maybe there is," she suggests, stifling a yawn. "We know someone of some influence is involved in the business in Denver. Someone who isn't afraid to use power or money, or both, to get to all levels in the department. Those were some high-tech gadgets they found in my apartment, Yanis. They've gotta cost a whack."

I grunt in acknowledgement and wait for her to make her point.

"Someone with money, who wields power, is also behind the sabotage at the winery."

"You're talking about Sarrazin? What would he have to do with Bobby Lee or the attack on you?"

"Remember Robert Connell? The floater whose prints were linked to the limo? Evans said he was a known criminal with connections."

"You're thinking the Albero family?"

She shrugs.

"Worth checking into. Maybe give Evans a call, drop Sarrazin's name and see what he comes up with."

I tighten my arms around her. This is one of the things that makes her such a valuable agent; the ability to think outside of the box. Her great mind is fucking sexy as hell too.

"Radar can look into any possible connections between Bobby Lee and anyone in the Albero family," I suggest.

"Has Flynn ever revealed the details of the beef between him and Sarrazin?"

He hadn't, other than to say it was about a woman, and yet he'd taken the other man's recommendations in hiring McNeely and PASS, which seems odd if they're supposed to be enemies. They hadn't looked particularly acrimonious when Bree and I saw him with Sarrazin. Annoyed, maybe, but not much more than that.

Since I have to head back to Palisade later anyway, I'll stop by the vineyard and sit him down.

"I'm coming with you," Bree announces when I tell her of my plans.

I won't argue with that. I'd rather have her where I can keep an eye on her myself.

"Fine. Now can we get some sleep?"

"Yeah."

She snuggles into me and I press a kiss to the top of her head.

"You still smell like smoke," she mumbles in my chest.

"Then let me go so I can grab a quick shower."

She lifts her head, the expression on her face one that has me want to confess my feelings. Vulnerable and trusting. Instead, I drop a hard kiss on her mouth and head for the bathroom. She's here under my roof and plans to stick close, that's enough for now. Last thing I want to do is make her feel pressured if I tell her I love her. Plenty of time for that.

By the time I walk back into the bedroom she's already under the covers, fast asleep. I carefully get in, trying not to wake her, but the moment I stretch out, she turns and snuggles up against me.

My last thought before I drift off myself is how perfectly she fits me.

BREE

IT'S ALREADY AFTERNOON by the time we drive into Palisade.

Yanis wants to hit the police station first and hopes I can act as liaison in getting him in to see McNeely. I'm not sure if I'll be able to—I've only established a connection with one of the two police sergeants on the force recently—but I'll give it my best shot.

The police department is right beside the fire station. An unassuming, one-floor brick building with little more adornment than a flag pole and a bench at the entrance. Plenty of parking around the side and back, though. It doesn't look particularly busy with just a few cruisers and a couple of regular vehicles parked in the slots.

"I was hoping to speak with Sergeant Fillmore if she's available?"

I take the lead when we walk up to the front desk.

"And your name is?" the woman who looks past retirement age asks briskly.

"Bree Graves. I'm with PASS Security? She and I spoke a few weeks ago."

"Have a seat."

Without looking, she waves at a few chairs on the opposite side of the lobby.

The moment we're seated—well out of hearing distance—I notice she picks up her phone, glancing our way briefly. A few minutes later, a tall woman around my age, dressed conservatively in a pantsuit, walks into the lobby, her eyes aimed my way. Yanis is already on his feet by the time she reaches us.

"Linda Fillmore."

Her introduction is followed by a firm handshake before she turns to Yanis.

"This is my boss, Yanis Mazur. He owns PASS Security."

They shake as well and she narrows her eyes on him.

"I know. You were at Flynn's Fields last night," she shares. "I was just reading the report. Your name stood out."

"It's actually the reason we're here," I volunteer.

"I figured as much. Follow me."

She turns on her heel and walks ahead of us down a hallway and through the bullpen to a small office at the far end.

"Mazur!"

Both Yanis and I turn around to one of the officers standing up behind his desk.

"Wait your turn, Scottie," Linda tells the young officer sharply before waving us into her office, closing the door behind us.

"Chris Underwood's a friend of mine." She's looking in my direction. "I had a word with him after you called a few weeks ago. It won't come as a surprise he has nothing but good things to say about your outfit."

Christopher Underwood is Grand Junction's Chief of Police. He hired us last year to help clean up his department, which had come under scrutiny. Good to know the sergeant is tight with him, maybe that'll give us a foot in the door with her.

"Good to know," Yanis mumbles, drawing her attention.

"I'm sure," she comments dryly. "However, that doesn't mean I won't be looking closely into the events of last night. There are a few things that raise questions."

"Like?"

"Your involvement with Flynn's Fields, for one."

I haven't had a chance to speak yet. I get the feeling these two have forgotten I'm even here, the way they glare at each other. I wish I could give Yanis a cautionary kick to the heels, but he's sitting on the wrong side of me.

In the few minutes I've observed Sergeant Fillmore, I can tell her rank did not come easy. Not surprising, in a small force like this you're less likely to see diversity in the ranks than in larger departments.

A man like Yanis—who exudes testosterone without even trying—might get her back up, and he in turn will see it as a challenge.

"Told the officer everything last night. I'm sure it's in his report."

This conversation is definitely not going in the right direction, judging from Yanis's tone. Linda Fillmore leaning forward, her elbows on her desk as she glares at him, confirms it.

"Tell me anyway," she says in a low voice.

The moment I notice Yanis moving forward in his seat, I clamp a firm hand on his arm. Linda notices and raises an eyebrow. I meet his sharp look and give my head a little shake and his nostrils flare.

Chances of Yanis getting to talk to McNeely are diminishing by the second.

"Joe Flynn hired my company to install security after several incidents of sabotage occurred at the vineyard. He felt it necessary since there was no satisfactory response from your department. I agree with his assessment."

I close my eyes and slap my hand to my forehead. That just sealed it. We may as well pack it in.

But the next moment my head jerks up in surprise at Linda's words.

"So do I," she says, easing back in her chair with a

satisfied look on her face. "Which is why the door to my office is closed. I'm in an awkward position here and wanted to be sure where your loyalties lie."

"I'm not sure I'm clear on what is happening here," I finally interject.

Yanis is the one who responds.

"Unless I'm way off base, Sergeant Fillmore has some concerns about her department."

"A few," she confirms. "I don't want to go into too much detail, but suffice it to say your visit isn't the only surprise I had today. I was told this morning it would serve me well to fast-track this case."

"Fast-track, how?" Yanis asks.

"Process Mr. McNeely with a minimum of questions."

"Or else?" I ask, since I assume there was an *or else* added to that request.

Linda glances at me.

"Or else my position within the department would be on shaky ground. I was told to be a *team player*, to prove I'm *one of the boys*." She lifts her chin defiantly. "You should know I was just about to sit down with Mr. McNeely and have a comprehensive and in-depth discussion with him."

I look over at Yanis, who nods approvingly. Clearly Sergeant Fillmore does not intend to bow to pressure. Good on her.

"Maybe we should share what happened in Denver," I suggest to Yanis. "Sounds like Linda and Bill may have something in common."

"Who's Bill?"

We spend the next twenty minutes sharing our suspicions with the unexpected ally we found in Sergeant Fillmore.

"I'm going to give you my cell number," she tells me. "If you wouldn't mind passing it on to Detective Evans. I'll leave it to him if he wants to talk to me."

I'm handed a card with a phone number scribbled on the back.

"Now…" She turns her attention to Yanis. "How would you feel about sitting in on my interview with Mr. McNeely? Wouldn't hurt to have a second person in the room, and who knows? Your presence may encourage him to open up."

IT'S CLOSE TO four in the afternoon by the time we're on our way to the vineyard.

While Yanis and Linda were interviewing Dan McNeely, I used the time to follow up with Bill Evans, Detective Bissette, and Lena at the office.

Bill didn't answer his phone but texted me ten minutes after I left him a message, apologizing for not answering but he was in the middle of something, and could I please shoot over the sergeant's number, which I did.

Detective Bissette shared the department's lab was looking at the cameras to see if they could determine the source. Apparently, there weren't any prints found in my apartment that were unaccounted for, so the cameras are the only tangible lead she has. She assured me she had officers on the street ringing doorbells and checking for security cameras on buildings up and down my street, and was confident something would surface.

"So I told her to get in touch with Radar if her techs are not successful. I figure if anyone can get information from those cameras, it would be him," I continue filling Yanis in. "Then I checked in with Lena to see if there was anything urgent. She says it's been quiet there."

"Good."

I glance over and notice his jaw is still as tight as when he marched out of the interview room.

"Your turn," I prompt him. "Although I'm guessing it didn't go so well."

He snorts.

"Fucking punk," he shares with fire. "Two hours we tried and the little shit said nothing. Finally, when Sergeant Fillmore told him he'd be charged with attempted murder he asked to speak to his lawyer. Two fucking hours wasted on that piece of crap and nothing." Frustrated, he slams the heel of his hand against the steering wheel. "I need a connection to Sarrazin."

"You know there are other ways, right?" I carefully suggest. "Radar can pull phone records, look at his bank acc—"

"Not ready to make that call. Wouldn't be

admissible in court," he cuts me off. "Let's talk to Flynn and see what he can tell us."

We caught Joe on his way out the door at the winery. He mostly repeated he and Sarrazin were nothing but old college buddies, who happened to fall for the same girl, and occasionally ran into each other. When asked if it surprised him Sarrazin might be involved with the trouble at the vineyard, he made the comment he wouldn't put anything past his former friend.

Half an hour later we're on our way back to Grand Junction, not much wiser, and Yanis's mood hasn't improved.

"Fucking call Radar."

Aye, aye, Boss.

CHAPTER 20

BREE

"YOU DON'T HAVE to come in, I can take a cab back to the office."

As he's done regularly these past couple of days, he ignores my suggestion and walks me into the hospital.

Grumpy bear.

I have a follow-up appointment I hope will have me walking out of here without this damn plastic boot. The swelling is gone, there's no sign of bruising left, and the few times I've tested the ankle it feels pretty stable. I don't mind doing some PT to get it back to full strength, especially if I can start driving myself. My poor Jeep has been parked in the office parking lot this entire time.

I have a feeling Yanis doesn't share my hope.

The only time he leaves my side since someone broke into my apartment is during office hours, when one or more of my teammates are around. I know he still struggles with the fact he wasn't there right away, but he's going to have to let up at some point. As endearing—however unnecessary—his protectiveness is, it's starting to feel claustrophobic.

We walk up to the desk and I tell the receptionist I have an appointment.

"You can go right in, Ms. Graves. Number three. The doctor will be right in."

When Yanis starts following me to the small hallway with treatment rooms I stop and turn, putting my flat hand on his chest.

"I'm good," I tell him.

He seems surprised at first, but then his jaw clenches and he gives me a sharp nod. I don't miss the flash of hurt in his eyes, but he doesn't say a word before turning back to the waiting area.

Great. Now I feel guilty for setting some boundaries.

It's not that I don't want him to come in—I have nothing to hide—but I'm tired of being treated like a child who needs monitoring twenty-four seven.

When I walk back into the waiting area half an hour later—still with crutches—but without the walking cast, he's on the phone facing me. His eyes immediately drop to my feet.

"Gotta go," he says to whoever he has on the line before ending the call. Then he gets to his feet. "Ready to go?"

I nod and we're quiet as we make our way back to his SUV, but when he's about to pull out of the parking spot I put a hand on his arm.

"Wait." I twist in my seat so I can look at him.

"Talk to me."

"About what?"

He doesn't know me well if he thinks he can put me off with feigned ignorance.

"About what has been eating at you." His frown lines deepen and his mouth sets in a rigid line, but I'm not about to let that deter me. "Are you angry at me?"

"Angry?"

He seems genuinely surprised at that.

"Yeah. You barely talk to me, and you bark at everyone else. You don't even ask what the doctor said."

"Was that me inside you this morning?"

I shouldn't be surprised he comes back with that. He's right, in that respect nothing's changed. We're good together, we always were. But he's shown me another side to him recently as well. That of a man willing to put in the effort for more than a physical connection. I liked that side of him—a lot—but now he treats me like he did before and that doesn't sit well.

"I was there, Yanis," I respond, working on keeping my calm. "And that's not the part I'm talking about. Something is wrong and it bothers me you won't just tell me what it is. Why not share?"

He barks out a harsh laugh.

"Share? Sure, I've had shit on my mind. It sucked not to be able to get to you when you needed me. *Again,*" he emphasizes, before his shoulders slump and his next words sound defeated. "And every day that passes without getting closer to solving this case is a slap in my face."

Talk about taking the wind out of my sails.

I'm suddenly not pissed anymore. I get it—I get *him*.

The past days have been frustrating for everyone with no real new leads developing. The only contact we've had with Bill has been occasional texts, he's impossible to get on the phone. We haven't had an update from Linda in Palisade. Detective Bissette is hitting dead ends with my building manager, who claims he never had a key to the door, and the cameras they recovered are still with the lab. To top it all off, Radar has his hands full with his pregnant wife, Hillary. Debilitating morning sickness left her severely dehydrated over the weekend and he had to take her into the hospital for IV fluids.

It's like hitting your head against a brick wall and I'm sure no one does that harder than Yanis. On the best of days, he carries the weight of the world on his shoulders, and these past days were definitely not the best.

"Yanis…" I lift my hand to his face but he abruptly turns away, shifts the vehicle in drive, and pulls out of the parking lot. Determined not to take it as a rejection I forge on. "Why didn't you just tell me? I understand."

He's silent for a while, maneuvering his vehicle through city traffic until he finally speaks.

"You say it bothers you I don't share. Sharing goes

both ways, you know?" He darts me a quick look but it's enough to recognize he's not angry, he's somber, and that's almost worse. "You expect me to trust you, yet you keep yourself guarded. I've had it on my lips to tell you I fucking love you, but held back because I don't even know if you want to hear it."

An invisible hand reaches into my chest and squeezes my heart. A sudden lump plugs my throat and my nose tingles as tears burn my eyes.

He's right. There are things I know he wants to understand, but he's been patiently waiting me out and I haven't given him anything. Trust goes both ways and as much as I've wanted him to earn mine, I've done nothing to earn his.

"I do. I want to hear it," I finally manage, my voice raw.

YANIS

"AND I'M SORRY I've kept a wall up."

Fuck, she's killing me.

I open my mouth to tell her it's all right, but she's already speaking.

"I told you I grew up with Ted. We were neighbors, our mothers were friends, and so were we; just friends. After graduation he went straight into the military while I headed out for college. We stayed in touch, mostly through our mothers."

I can see tears streaking down her face, and it's all I can do not to pull over and take her in my arms. Instead, I drive the Yukon past the office and head toward home.

"He showed up at Mom's funeral with his mother. I was in a bad place. He showed up at my mom's place the day after the funeral and offered to help sort through her things." She wipes impatiently at her wet cheeks. "We talked quite a bit over the next couple of days, got to know each other again. Shared our problems. We were both dealing with a lot. He suggested maybe marriage would be a solution. For both of us."

I grind my teeth as I pull into my driveway.

"Maybe I need a drink for this," I admit as I get out.

What I really want to do is find the bastard who took advantage of Bree in a weak moment and introduce him to my fist. Instead, I grind my teeth and help her out of the vehicle.

Once inside I head straight for the cupboard over the stove and grab the rye.

"You?" I hold the bottle up for her and she nods.

"Mine with ginger ale, please."

I fix us drinks and join her on the couch, taking a fortifying sip before I shift to face her.

"Go on," I prompt, bracing myself. "Why was marrying him a solution?"

"Ted needed something to lend him credibility."

"Credibility?"

"He was already passed over for a promotion once and up for a second try. The US Army practices the 'move up or move out' policy, meaning—"

"Yeah, I know, get turned down twice and you're on your way out the door. How does marrying you play into that?"

"He was always very private but suspected his commander had cottoned in on his orientation. Ted is gay."

If you hit me in the head with a sledgehammer it wouldn't have the impact her words do.

"What?"

"Ted is gay," she repeats, playing with the hem of her shirt. "He always dreamed of a military career and felt if he had a wife his chances would improve."

Her marriage was a sham?

It takes me a minute to process the information, and then I have only one question.

"What was in it for you?"

"Security," she answers far too easily—like it's been practiced over and over.

She's got to know that response won't fly with me. Bree didn't and doesn't need anyone to provide her with security.

"You forget, I know you better than that," I point out.

"I needed health insurance," she confesses, purposely not looking at me.

I feel that one in my gut. PASS was in its infancy and at the time I couldn't afford health insurance for myself or my staff. That has long since changed and PASS offers a comprehensive package now, but there was nothing like that back then.

"You mentioned a ruptured cyst. I would've helped you if you'd come to me."

The look in her eyes is part hurt and part sympathy. Something tells me I'm not going to like what she says next.

"There was no cyst," she admits. "I was pregnant."

Suddenly I'm breathing too fast, feeling light-headed—dizzy—and I bend over to drop my head between my knees.

Pregnant?

Holy fuck, do I have a child out there?

I know Bree, so I know the answer, but I have to ask.

"Mine?"

She doesn't answer so I lift my head and glance over. She's crying. Silent tears stream down her face.

"I'm so sorry," she finally whispers.

"Where…I'm…" I stammer and shake my head to clear it. "Where's the baby?"

What am I saying? Baby? Christ, that was fifteen years ago.

This is what shock feels like. As if someone turned you inside out and you can barely remember to breathe.

"I lost it. Ectopic pregnancy." I throw her a confused look and she quickly clarifies. "It's when the egg nestles and grows in a fallopian tube instead of the uterus. I was fourteen weeks when it ruptured." Her gaze drifts, looking at nothing in particular. "There was quite a bit of damage and a lot of bleeding. They were able to leave the other tube, but had to take the uterus."

"Jesus."

Because, what else is there to say?

I get to my feet and walk to the kitchen door, sliding it open.

"Where are you going?" I hear her ask.

"I need some air."

Without looking back, I walk across the deck and down the steps. Thoughts are spinning in my head at a frightening speed and I feel pressure building inside me.

Bree, pregnant with my baby.

Had she known when I sent her away?

I don't stop until I'm at the edge of my property, where I bend down, bracing my hands on my knees until I feel like I can breathe again. Then I straighten up and stare out at the mesa, willing my mind to slow down its churning.

The one thought that keeps circling back is if she'd carried that baby to term, would I ever have known it was mine?

I need to know.

Taking in a deep breath, I turn on my heel and find her standing at the bottom of the steps, her hand clasped to her chest. At a brisk pace I walk back, but before I have a chance to ask, she gives me my answer.

"I was going to tell you. I just needed some time to…get over the hurt."

I forgot. She knows me well too.

"Bree, I—"

The shrill tone of my phone ringing cuts me off and I pull it from my pocket.

"Dimi, now is not a good time."

"That's where you're wrong," he fires back smugly. "I found something."

CHAPTER 21

BREE

"HEY, WHERE'S YOUR boot?"

Lena leans over her desk to look at my feet.

"Don't need it anymore."

Yanis brushes past me and heads for the bullpen. I notice Lena looking after him with an eyebrow raised.

"Not even his usual grunted greeting? What crawled up his butt?"

I shrug at her and rush after him.

The five-minute drive to the office had taken place in loaded silence. I'm well aware I dropped a bombshell, but I wish he'd had a chance to finish what he was going to say when Dimi called. The uncertainty is killing me.

If I'd thought there was even the slightest chance of us rekindling anything at some point, I would've told him. Probably. He'd never given any indication until he did a full one-eighty last month. There'd been no reason to open that can of worms.

Cowardly, I know.

Then suddenly I had it back—had *him* back—and I knew I should come clean, but I didn't want to lose what I found again. The first time it almost broke me. But when he mentioned loving me, I knew it wasn't fair to keep him in the dark. I had to come clean about the past or there could be no future.

The truth is, I still love him too. I never stopped. Working together, seeing each other on a daily basis, had kept that hopeless flame alive. Except, as it turns out, it wasn't hopeless. It's just…complicated.

Yanis is a proud and principled man, and I'm afraid he'll see keeping my secrets for so long as a betrayal.

"Radar had me going over these phone records he pulled on McNeely."

Dimas is in Radar's office, showing his brother something on the monitor on the desk and I sidle up on his other side to get a look.

"I highlighted one number. Look at the dates and times of the calls."

Yanis sees it before me.

"They correspond with the events at the winery."

Sure enough, the same number appears for each of the dates. In fact, this past Friday there's a series of incoming calls from that number between about eight thirty and midnight.

I point at the first call logged at twenty-seven minutes past eight.

"That's right after you left my apartment," I point out to Yanis.

"Tell me you know who that number belongs to,"

he says to his brother.

"It looks to be a burner number. Radar thinks he can trace it. He said he'd be in shortly." He minimizes the screen and pulls up another. This one looks like a PayPal account. "McNeely's bank account showed his income from the winery, but also money drawn from a PayPal account. Radar was able to hack into it and found a bi-weekly payment coming in from one Moira Kennedy."

"Who is?" Yanis prompts.

"Executive assistant at Falcone Scrap and Metal in Colorado Springs," Dimi says with a triumphant smirk as he looks up at us. "Now tell me, why would Falcone continue to pay McNeely regularly when he hasn't worked there in over six months?"

Great information, solidifying the ongoing link between the Albero family and McNeely but not enough by itself. I'm sure the reason this Moira Kennedy is using her own account to forward the payments is to create another level of separation, and I'm sure the family wouldn't hesitate to throw this woman under the bus to save their own ass.

Now, if we can link that phone number directly to Sarrazin, that would have a lot more clout, although, I'm not sure if there will be any legal way to make the information we find stick.

"Good," Radar says when he walks in. "You're here."

"What've you got?" Yanis asks, as Radar shoves Dimi out of his chair.

"Give me a second to pull it up."

"How is Hillary?" I ask, since no one else seems to.

Radar throws me a quick grin.

"Much better now. They've put her on something for the nausea. They did an ultrasound, according to the OBGYN the baby's doing good. Strong heartbeat."

I smile back at him. Even after all these years, it's still a bit of a bittersweet experience, but this is my family, how can I be anything but happy for them?

"Can we get back to this?" Yanis barks, pointing at the screen.

"Yeah, sure," Radar quickly says, looking surprised.

Dimi gives his brother the stink eye, but neither of them get what a raw topic it is for Yanis. I wish I felt confident enough to put my hand on his back to signal my understanding, but I'm afraid he'll snap, he's strung so tight.

"Okay, so I was able to triangulate the movements of the burner phone." Radar points at the screen where a map of Colorado is visible. "I marked them out on the map. At the time of the first call to McNeely's phone, the burner pinged off this tower here."

He indicates a red dot on the map.

"That's right here," I notice.

"Yup. Right under our noses. Watch how it moves east, pinging different towers. Then suddenly it turns back, making a few detours before it returned to where it started."

The location he points to is within a four-block radius of my apartment. My heart starts beating faster.

Then he enlarges a second map so they're visible side by side. "And this one is Sarrazin's registered cell phone account."

The path showing up on that map is identical to the first one. Including the detours and of course the tower four blocks from my apartment.

I know I floated the idea that everything might be connected, but to have it confirmed still makes me a little ill.

"We've got him," Dimi says excitedly.

"We have confirmation it's him, but we can't take this to the cops," Yanis says with a dose of reality. "What we can do is find out where the hell he's been staying in town, and see if we can find out where he stopped that night. That's the kind of information we can hand over to Bissette."

"I also think maybe we should go have a talk with my building manager," I suggest, my focus on Yanis. "If he can wield power over law enforcement brass, it's not a stretch to imagine he could've bribed or threatened the manager into giving him a key to my balcony door. Because this sure looks like it was Sarrazin in my apartment that night."

He nods once before putting a hand on Radar's shoulder.

"You guys start calling hotels, short-term rentals, and find out where he might've stopped that night. Oh, and start looking for any connection between

Sarrazin and Bobby Lee." Then he turns to me. "Let's go find your manager."

As we walk out of the office, Yanis says, "Try Evans again. Tell him it's imperative we talk to him. I don't like you being in the crosshairs of a fucking mafia thug. We also need to touch base with Sergeant Fillmore."

I'm not too hot on that factoid myself, but I'm not sure what we can do about it if they have law enforcement in their pocket.

"Have you thought about going to the CBI or the feds with this?" I ask when we're driving away from the office. "I'm getting a little worried."

"Not yet," he grinds out, his jaw tight and his eyes locked on the road.

"We're vulnerable, Yanis. I'm not just talking about me; I'm talking about PASS."

That earns me a sideways glance and a pat on my knee.

"I know, Bree. But let's build our case first. Get something concrete in our hands before we make any moves."

I guess that makes sense, but we better find something soon. I have a bad feeling.

"Sure."

He stops in front of a red light and turns his head toward me.

"Not gonna let anything else happen to you. I promise."

I nod, wishing I could feel as confident as he

sounds.

"Okay."

YANIS

"LET ME DO the talking."

Bree nudges me out of the way.

I just knocked on the door of apartment one-ten. The nameplate on the door says; *Matthew Billings, Manager.*

Heavy footsteps sound on the other side and the door opens a crack. Red-rimmed eyes in a face that looks older than it probably should, peer at me suspiciously before settling on Bree.

"Hi, Matthew? It's Bree, from three-fifteen? I just need a quick word."

The door opens a little wider.

"What can I do for you?"

He glances my way suspiciously.

"Oh sorry, this is my boyfriend, Yanis. Could we come in for a second? I promise it won't take long."

I force myself to relax and even try to throw in a friendly smile to put the man at ease. It takes him a moment to make up his mind but he finally eases the door open, stepping out of the way to let us in.

Bree leads the way into a small front room that is set up as an office. She's clearly been here before. The cramped space is cluttered with a desk, a bookcase, and a filing cabinet, as well as two uncomfortable looking visitor chairs. An ancient computer and stacks of files litter the desk and a layer of dust covers every visible surface. It doesn't look like Matthew spends a lot of time in here.

He sits down in the squeaky office chair behind the desk and Bree and I take seats as well.

"I was wondering if you could help me," Bree starts. "I know you already spoke with the police and I understand that can be intimidating."

I notice the man's eyes dart over our shoulders to the door, his only exit.

"I have nothing to add," he says quickly, getting to his feet.

"Mr. Billings," I take over before he sends us packing, and I'm taking a risk. "We know Angelo Sarrazin was here." If I needed any confirmation, the terrified look in his eyes is enough. "We also know he forced you into handing over the key to the balcony door of three-fifteen."

"I don't know what you're—" he starts denying, but Bree interrupts him.

"Matthew, this man kidnapped me, chased me through the woods. He's responsible for at least two killings, one of which I was witness to."

All the blood drains from his face.

"Then you understand why I can't help you," he whispers, sounding breathless.

"I get you think you're keeping yourself safe, but you're wrong. You're not safe, that man won't think twice about hurting someone—me, *or* you."

"He said you had something that belonged to him. Threatened to get me fired for drinking on the job."

He lowers himself in his seat and lifts his watery eyes. "I sometimes have a sip or two during the day. Got me in a spot of trouble at my previous job. This is the only job I could get. If I lose it, I'll be on the street."

I'm thinking a bottle is closer to the truth than the sip or two he mentions. His blue-tinged nose tells me he's well beyond an occasional drinker.

"We'll help you," Bree offers, giving me a quick warning glance.

Bleeding heart.

―――――

HALF AN HOUR later, we're on our way to the airport with Matthew and his suitcase in the back seat. He has to leave town in a hurry for a family emergency.

At least that's the story we're going with.

Detective Bissette is meeting him at the airport to take his official statement before he flies off to see his brother in Ohio. She'd been surprised at the turn of events. A little put out, but when I promised her full disclosure if she'd come to the PASS office tomorrow morning, she said she'd be there.

She's waiting just inside the automatic doors when I pull up along the curb.

I help the building manager out of the car and walk him inside.

"We're gonna talk tomorrow," she says, a warning in her eyes.

She's crusty as hell, this woman, but she's also

shown herself to be smart. I like her.

"You bet." I clap Billings on the back. "You have a safe trip. We'll be in touch."

He left Bree with numbers to reach him.

Back in the Yukon, the silence suddenly becomes oppressive again and I figure it'll only get worse the longer I delay.

So I dive right in as I pull away from the airport.

"You should've told me," I tell her.

She's silent for a moment, probably changing gears.

"When?" she tosses back. "I found out in the hospital when I got shot. I was still reeling from the news when you walked in and told me we were over. Should I have told you I was pregnant then? That would've gone over like a lead balloon."

"I would've…" I start before I realize I don't really know what I would've done.

At the time, I truly felt I was doing the right thing. I'd like to think I would've done right by the baby as well, but all of that is water under the bridge now.

"See? You don't even know how that would've gone. It doesn't matter anyway, because I was still coming to terms with the reality of it all when Mom suddenly died, and then that consumed me. I'm sorry, but the truth is I didn't have it in me to consider you at that time, I was too busy trying to put one foot in front of the other."

No matter how hard I try, I can't find fault with what she's saying.

"I get it."

I sense rather than see her eyes on me when I turn into my driveway and pull up in front of the garage. Then I face her.

"Do you? Because my world looked pretty fucking bleak at the time. I was terrified, Ted was there and offered a solution, and I jumped at it. By the time I had enough of my wits about me to inform you, it was already too late. After the hysterectomy, I figured what was the point?"

Before I can react, she's got her door open and is getting out of the vehicle.

I'm still thinking about what she said when she disappears inside the house. My earlier anger wanes as I consider what she must've gone through. The many what-ifs I've asked myself since finding out don't serve anyone. Not like we can go back and change what happened.

I can hear her rummaging around in my kitchen when I finally walk in and close the door behind me.

"Bree…"

She turns at the sound of my voice, looking suddenly exhausted. I didn't think about what dredging all of it up would take out of her. I imagine it was probably as painful as it was for me to hear it.

I cross the distance between us and curve an arm around her waist, pulling her flush against me. She doesn't resist but her face is still a mask.

"*Tygrys*," I mumble, and watch tears well up in her eyes.

When the first one escapes, I bend my head and kiss her gently.

"Hold me," she whispers, tucking her head under my chin.

I can do that. I can do that as long as she'll let me.

CHAPTER 22

BREE

"BABY..." I moan long and deep as his fingers and mouth work me to a delicious, lazy climax.

"Good morning," he rumbles, lifting his head from between my legs.

"You can say that again," I concur slightly breathless.

He wipes his mouth with the back of his hand, a satisfied grin spreading on his handsome face. Then he crawls up my body, the bristly hair on his chest brushing against my already sensitized skin. I hiss when his hips drop between my legs, the crown of his cock sliding along my crease.

"How do you want it?"

He's already poised at my entrance and I notice the tendons in his neck straining. He's holding back for me.

"Any way you wanna give it."

My voice is husky as I reach a hand down to grab

onto his ass.

"Knees high, *Tygrys*."

I do as he asks as he pushes up on his arms and powers to the root inside me.

His strokes are deep and forceful and I have to brace myself against the headboard. His eyes never leave mine, even when he loses his rhythm. His mouth falls open as he grunts his way to release, which comes in long, hot spurts.

We're still connected as he sinks through his arms. I relish his weight on me and wrap my limbs around him so he can't go anywhere.

"I'm too heavy."

"No, I like you right here."

I feel his lips smile against my skin.

At some point I wonder if he's dozed off and I try to inch out from underneath him. Nature calls.

"Bree?"

"Need to go to the bathroom."

He rolls off me so I can swing my legs over the side, but he grabs for my hand when I stand up. I turn back to grin at him when I see his face is dead serious.

"I know it'll never be enough, but I'm so fucking sorry."

I lean down to kiss him.

"Enough of that," I mumble against his lips. "We're done looking back."

We talked last night about regrets. It was good to clear the air, but had been exhausting and I'm done rehashing what we can't change. Getting hung up on the past is not going to help us move forward.

DETECTIVE BISSETTE ARRIVES twenty minutes after we get to the office.

Lena shows her into the conference room where I've been busy marking up the large whiteboard.

I've put together a timeline with Sarrazin's name at the top and arrows linking him to each of the incidents in Palisade, Denver, Grand Junction, and one with a question mark to Aspen, where Bobby Lee was found dead.

"Wow," she says, staring at the board. "I assume you found something tangible to link that name to all of those events?"

"Yes, but I'll let Radar explain as soon as everybody gets here."

"Fair enough."

"In the meantime, help yourself to some coffee."

Lena put a tray on the table with a large carafe and mugs, and Dimi was going to pick up some donuts on his way in. It's bound to be a long morning.

"So how did you get your building manager to talk?" she asks, pouring herself a mug and taking a seat.

"We told him we knew Sarrazin had been by to see him. He clammed up at first, but then I mentioned what happened to me in Denver and his resolve started crumbling. It still took some convincing, but with a plan in place to ensure his safety he finally caved."

At that moment Lena walks in with Sergeant Fillmore in tow. I start making introductions, but as it turns out the two women already know each other. Not long after the rest of the crew is assembled.

Yanis is the last one in and immediately takes control of the room.

"Right off the bat, I need to be clear that some of the evidence we've unearthed was not legally obtained." He looks at each of the women in turn. "You may take issue with that, but I ask you reserve judgment until you've had a chance to get the full scope."

Fillmore and Bissette exchange a glance.

"I have no issue," Bissette is the first to react.

In all fairness, she knows us. We collaborated on a case not that long ago along with the FBI.

Fillmore is slower with her response.

"I'll reserve judgment."

"Good. I don't know if either of you knows Detective Bill Evans? He worked with the Denver PD but is now in Littleton." Both law enforcement officers shake their heads. "He was looking into Bree's abduction and two murders that seem to be related, but was taken off the case when he started digging too deep."

"Sounds familiar," Fillmore volunteers and then turns to the other detective. "You?"

"We had our share of problems in the past, but those have been mostly weeded out by these guys."

The accolade from Bissette is a bit of a surprise.

She wasn't too receptive of our involvement in police business last time around.

"I was hoping to have Evans here as well, but I haven't been able to reach him. I just checked in with his department and apparently he's taken a leave of absence."

That's a surprise to me, and concerning.

"He has?"

Yanis glances at me and from the look on his face it's clear he's concerned about it too.

"Starting last week apparently." He turns back to the rest of the room. "I'm going to hand this over to Radar, who's going to show you what he's discovered, and then we need to have a talk about the possibility of calling in the feds on this."

Both Bissette and Fillmore sit up straighter in their chairs. Understandable, calling in the FBI usually means handing over the case, but this one is bigger than any of the individual departments can tackle on their own.

Radar pulls down the video screen and shows the cell phone evidence he uncovered, as well as the financial link between the Albero family and Dan McNeely.

"I've uncovered something else this morning, which is why I was a little late."

Then he drops a bombshell when he pulls up a few images of what looks to be some cocktail party.

"Fuck me," Dimi mumbles, staring at the screen. "Is that Bobby Lee?"

"It is. Found these through one of her online fan platforms," Radar explains. "The poster works for a catering company."

The pictures we're looking at are candid shots of the singer surrounded by an interesting collection of characters.

In the background you can make out a campaign banner with a partial name visible.

Holy shit.

YANIS

"ACCORDING TO THE poster, this was a campaign launch for Delmer Beauregard."

I didn't need Radar to confirm we're looking at the recently elected Colorado Attorney General smiling broadly at a laughing Bobby Lee.

Nor do I need any help identifying the older man with his hand on the Attorney General's shoulder. It's a face I recognize well. After all, almost two decades ago he showed up uninvited at my apartment.

Guiseppe Albero.

"Well, that explains a few things," Linda Fillmore comments dryly.

Yeah, it does. If you're looking for reasons why several different police departments might experience pressure not to look too closely at anything the Albero family might be involved in, the Attorney General's influence would be at the top of the list.

"Is that Sarrazin?" Bissette asks, getting up and walking to the screen, pointing at one of the other images.

I recognize Bobby Lee from behind, a man's arm visible around her, his hand on her ass. The rest of him is off camera, but the detective is not pointing at him. She indicates a smaller group to the left of the singer, one individual turned to face the camera, a dark scowl on his face.

"It is," I confirm his identity. "And he doesn't look happy."

There is no mistaking where his glare is directed. This may well be the link we've been looking for.

"Yanis," Bree calls my attention and I look over at her. "I'm thinking we should skip the CBI and go straight for the feds."

"I agree," Bissette agrees, the first time she's spoken up. "We need to call in the FBI."

"I can give SAC Sanders a call," Bree offers.

Sanders is the relatively new special agent in charge of our small local FBI satellite office. We worked with him once before and although we had a rocky start, he turned out to be an okay guy. Still, I'm not sure he's the right guy to call in for this. It's too big for him to handle.

"I think we need to contact the Denver office," I suggest. "Anyone have any contacts? Bree?"

"Actually, what about Matt Dunlop?" Radar offers. "He was the tech from the Denver office who helped out in the Lock&Load case? We exchange messages occasionally. I can give him a call."

"Do it."

Twenty minutes later, I get off the phone with James Aiken, Special Agent in Charge of the Denver Bureau, who was very interested to hear what I had to say. So interested, I barely started to explain my reason for calling before he cut me off with the announcement he's flying in this afternoon. Something tells me he's not entirely unaware of recent events.

Walking back into the boardroom, I interrupt a discussion around Dan McNeely.

"What about him?"

I look at Sergeant Fillmore, who turns to me with an angry expression.

"Released on bail this morning," she bites off, holding up her phone. "Just got notification five minutes ago."

"I have a contact at the Mesa County District Court," Bissette shares. "I just texted her and she was able to tell me the Assistant District Attorney suggested bail set at fifty thousand."

"What?" Bree pipes up. "That's ridiculous. For the amount of damage he's done? Not to mention shooting at Yanis."

If not for the serious situation, I might've smiled at her disgruntlement on my behalf.

"You're right," Fillmore agrees. "If there is any clearer indication someone is flexing some mighty muscles, I don't know what is. Not only is it fishy the ADA asked for what is probably one tenth of what bail should've been, but you'd expect the magistrate would've called him out on it."

"It gets better," the detective announces after her phone pings with another message. "Guess who took over as Mr. McNeely's lawyer? The same snake who got Albero out of that money-laundering trial that made headlines some years back."

"Any guesses as to who is footing that bill?" Dimi comments, getting up from the table. "Anyway, I should head out. Jake is at the vineyard waiting for me to relieve him."

Our coverage at Flynn's Fields hasn't changed much, despite McNeely getting caught. We can't know for sure if there won't be another attempt at sabotage, so Joe agreed we'll stick to the twenty-four-hour coverage. It puts a strain on my team, but Shep, Jake, and my brother have worked out a schedule between them. One that thankfully doesn't require me to jump in.

Between Radar, Bree, Kai, and myself we can keep up with the bulk of the other contracts.

"I should probably go too," Linda announces. "I don't want to raise any suspicions back at the station by being away from the office too long."

"Understood. Let me show you out."

I walk her through the lobby to the front door.

"Keep me in the loop? You have my personal cell, right?"

"I do," I confirm. "And I will."

"Tell Agent Aiden if he needs to talk to me, I'm happy to meet with him but it'll have to be after hours."

"I will. Stay safe out there."

She smiles, but it doesn't quite reach her eyes.

She's seasoned law enforcement, I'm sure it doesn't escape her what a potentially explosive and dangerous situation we find ourselves in. Something that undoubtedly weighs on everyone's mind.

It makes me even more worried about Bill Evans's whereabouts.

"Boss, call on line one. Says his name is Bill?"

Speak of the devil.

I walk to the nearest desk and pick up the phone.

"You're not answering my messages," I grumble.

"I was a little busy and my phone is compromised," he says, his voice low. "I'm on a pay phone at a gas station."

"Jesus, what the hell have you been up to?"

"Tailing our friend. Or at least I was until someone started taking potshots at my car. It's out of commission."

I notice Bree following Dimas and the detective out of the conference room and I wave her over.

"Where are you?" I ask him before putting my hand over the receiver and mouthing, "Bill," to Bree.

Behind her I notice my brother opening the door for Bissette.

"Outskirts of Rifle. Sinclair on Hwy 6."

Fuck, that's an hour each way.

"Hang tight. I'm gonna come get you."

"Yeah, that'd be good. Heads-up, though, I think he's on his way…*fuck*."

"Bill?"

I hear a few clanging sounds and footsteps running away. Then a soft click as someone hangs up the phone.

"What's going on?"

Concern is etched on Bree's face.

"If I'm not back before Aiken comes in, tell him I'm heading out to Sinclair Gas on Hwy 6 in Rifle. Bill is in trouble."

I rush into my office to grab my sidearm.

"Wait. You can't go alone."

Bree steps in front of me when I walk out. The look on her face stops me in my tracks and I tuck my gun away before cupping her face in my hands.

"I'll take Radar."

"But I—"

"Baby, I need you to stay here and coordinate. Lock up behind us. Bill started saying something about someone being on his way, but he never got to finish who or where to. Could be here, could be the vineyard. Either way, call Kai, get him in, and give Dimi a heads-up. He just left."

"Okay."

I kiss her hard before letting her go.

"Radar! You're with me!" I yell, and he instantly comes tearing out of the conference room.

I'm almost at the door when I hear Bree call out.

"Be safe!"

I turn and throw her a wink.

Then I rush out the door, Radar on my heels.

CHAPTER 23

BREE

I REGRET STAYING behind almost as soon as he drives off the parking lot.

"What's going on?" Lena asks, poking her head over my shoulder.

That jumpstarts me into action and I flip the locks on the front door.

"Call Kai and tell him we need him here," I tell her over my shoulder as I start walking toward the back. "Oh, and drop the blackout blinds on the front windows."

The lobby, hallway, and bullpen, as well as Yanis's office are all facing the parking lot. The entire front of the building is large windows that are usually only covered with a sun screen, but you can still see shapes moving around inside. I'd feel better if we blocked any view.

I walk through the locker room to the large combined storage, workout room, and garage space in the back. That's the only other access to the office, through the two rolling garage doors or the small service entrance beside them. All three appear securely locked.

Then I unlock the small armory. Basically, a steel cage the size of a walk-in closet which holds some weapons, ammunition, surveillance and security electronics, and other expensive or dangerous equipment. Aside from the sidearm I always carry when working, I select a small ankle holster that holds the Sig P238 that fits my hand nicely. I also grab a blade and sheath that clip horizontally to my waistband in the small of my back, pulling my shirt down over top.

Probably overkill, but it makes me feel a little better, knowing who we're dealing with.

On my way back to the office, I dial Dimi to give him the heads-up. He says he'll call Jake.

"What's going on?" Lena repeats.

Her face now worried as I walk to the panel by the front entrance and set the alarm.

"Could be nothing, but we may have some trouble incoming. Did you get hold of Kai?"

"Yes. He's on his way in. Should I be worried?"

Part of me wants to tell her no, that everything is under control, but that's something the guys would probably do to shield her. She may not be a trained member of this team, but she's still a member. She deserves to know.

"I'd prefer to say careful. Things are starting to heat up and since we're dealing with an organized crime family, we'd be stupid not to take every precaution."

She nods once, opens a drawer in her desk, and pulls out a Taser and a can of mace.

"You know I can't stand guns, but these'll do in a pinch."

"Better than nothing," I conclude. "Still, for now I think you should move away from the windows as well. Why don't you set yourself up in the conference room? We can hang there until Yanis figures out what is going on."

If anyone out there gets any wild ideas about coming in, that room would be the safest one, stuck between the locker room and the kitchen, and far away from windows.

Lena doesn't question me and simply picks up her monitor, lugging it across the hallway. I head for my desk to grab a few things of my own when the alarm suddenly starts blaring.

Yanis

"Bissette."

"Detective, it's Yanis Mazur."

"If we're gonna be this thick, you might as well call me Crystal. I just left your office."

Radar chuckles beside me, but I'm wired too tight to crack a grin.

"Crystal. We may have a situation." I quickly brief her on Evans's call. "May wanna watch your back. He's shooting at cops now."

"Once they cross that bridge," she states and she's dead on. "Need anything from me?"

"Just keep in touch."

"Will do."

I already spoke with Fillmore, so she's aware as well and is going to keep an eye on the vineyard. Evans was referring to Sarrazin when he mentioned *our friend*, but it's unclear where he's supposed to be heading. It's anyone's guess.

The farther away we get from Grand Junction, the more I wish I had Bree with me. It had been a sound strategic decision taking Radar into an unknown and dangerous situation, given that Bree is still not fully mobile. Leaving her in charge of the office made more sense. The professional in me trusts her capabilities, but the protector in me wants her close.

"Next exit."

Radar points at the turnoff to Highway 6.

"Give me an idea of the layout," I ask him as I veer off the highway.

"Main building and parking straight ahead at the rear of the property, pumps and scale on the right with large propane tanks behind those. Not a lot of room to park or hide at the back of the building and it's fenced off. Looks like chain-link. Beyond that a road and open land."

"We'll go in the front. See if we can locate his car, we'll take it from there."

"What does he drive?"

"I think it's a Buick. LaCrosse, maybe? Burgundy."

To be honest I wasn't paying much attention when I saw him in Denver last month. I'd been a little preoccupied with Bree.

Radar points to the sign for the gas station ahead and I hit my signal and move to the median. I have to wait for a large truck to turn out of the entrance before pulling in.

"There," Radar indicates. "Far side of the building, by the bathrooms."

The rear of the car is visible, wedged between a fence separating the industrial warehouse to the left and a cube van on the right. It's out of sight from the pumps and most of the traffic and I suspect he parked it there for that express purpose. It's not until I pull up into the slot on the other side of the van and get out, I notice the pay phone between the *his* and *hers* doors to the washrooms. I reach into the Yukon to snatch a ball cap to keep the sun out of my eyes and tug it on my head before moving toward the Buick.

"Shot out the window," Radar says, as he slips between the van and the car.

Sure enough, the side window is gone, shattered glass littering the passenger seat.

Ballsy, shooting at a driving car in broad daylight, which is worrisome all by itself since doing so without drawing attention would require a silencer. To add another layer of concern there is blood on the center console and some on the driver's seat.

Evans didn't mention he got hit. *Fuck.*

I pivot around to the pay phone and look at the ground underneath. More blood. Not exactly a puddle, but enough to know it can't be just a graze. Drops lead away from the phone to the side of the building and the narrow passage between it and the fence.

"It leads to the back," Radar comments, already starting in that direction.

Toward that service road behind the gas station, and the open land beyond.

"Hold up," I call out. "Take the car around."

I toss him my keys and follow the trail of blood to the rear of the property.

Looking around I can't see any good places he may be hiding, except for the cluster of large propane tanks on the other side. No one in their right mind would risk shooting at those, but that's not to say someone might not have other tools in their arsenal. Especially since their target is already injured.

But the trail isn't leading there, it's leading straight to the chain-link fence, which is about eight feet tall. Not an easy feat to scale for someone who is injured, but desperation and adrenaline can make people do impossible things.

A splash of red visible in the dry grass on the other side confirms Bill got over. I take a few steps back to get a running start and plant my right foot as high as I can against the fence, launching off the left as my hands reach for the top. As I pull myself up with sheer upper body strength, I swing my left leg up and over, and carefully drop down on the other side.

With my eyes focused on the ground in front of me, I follow the thinning trail down a ditch and up to the road. There isn't a lot of traffic and I'm able to cross over to the other side, where I lose the track.

My own adrenaline has been fueling me but I'm forced to stop and take a deep breath. There's a lot of land out there. Dry mesa going up a rocky ridge with only an occasional cluster of brush that wouldn't exactly provide secure coverage. The rocks would, if he was able to get that far.

I hear a car door slam behind me and swing around to find Radar approaching, carrying the rifle I have clipped behind the passenger seat for easy reach.

"Which direction?"

"I don't know. Lost the track, but my guess is that rocky ridge over there." I'm pointing to an area that isn't quite as sheer as the rest, with plenty of loose boulders to hide behind. "Let's split up. I'll head right, you start from the left. We'll meet in the middle. Call out if you find anything."

Radar nods and starts off in the direction I pointed him at while I go the other way.

The terrain is fairly level at first but gets rougher the closer I get, with smaller boulders and deep gullies formed by centuries of winter runoff. I keep my eyes peeled for any tracks but don't find anything until I come up to a cluster of rocks and brush.

There's what looks like a stain of blood at shoulder level on a large boulder. As if someone was leaning or brushing against it. When I touch it with my finger it seems to be dry. It's been there a while.

I wish I would've thought to bring radios, but had been in a hurry. It would've been safer than calling out since I don't know who is out here, or what we're heading into. Still, I need to let Radar know.

"Found something!"

The next moment shards of rock explode inches from my face.

I'm already dropping to the ground when the suppressed sound of a shot registers. I'd bet my life that was a rifle and not a shotgun. From my vantage point I don't have a good view, so I crawl to the other side of the rock—where I hope I have a little more coverage—and lift my upper body.

One of the drawbacks for me is that there's no visible barrel flash with a suppressor of any kind, but maybe someone is stupid enough to stick their head up.

I'm sure Radar heard the shot which was still audible, just not quite as sharp. He's the one with the rifle and therefore the better range, so if I can just draw some more fire, he may be able to spot something from his vantage point.

I give him a minute or two to get closer and then lift the ball cap off my head, sticking it into view. The impact of a bullet rips it right out of my hand.

Radar's shot is not silenced and loudly reverberates against the rocks. A second one sounds and I get to my feet with my gun drawn, knowing whoever was shooting will be distracted. Then I hear a volley of muffled gunfire coming from the top of the ridge. I can see a shooter and fire off a few rounds in his direction, but it's the well-aimed loud crack from Radar's rifle that appears to bring the man down.

"Status!" I call out.

"One down. I'm coming in from your ten!"

"Mazur!"

I wasn't expecting to hear the faint sound of Bill's voice.

"I'm coming!"

I start to step out from behind the rock and scan the direction I think his voice came from when another salvo kicks up the dirt at my feet. This shooter is closer and slightly farther to the left than the other.

"There's two!"

"Good to fucking know," I yell back, as I crawl on my elbows to the cover of the next rock. "Radar?"

"Got a bead. Hang tight," he returns right away.

I hate waiting for someone else to do the hard work, but I trust Radar as I do every other member of my team. Besides, it sounded like he's up a little higher on the ridge and has the better vantage point. I'm a bit of a sitting duck in the gulley.

I would've expected to hear sirens—for sure we've drawn some attention—but other than the distant rumble of traffic the mesa is silent.

And that, more than anything else, makes me uneasy.

CHAPTER 24

BREE

"STAY IN THERE."

Lena sticks her head out of the conference room but I wave her back.

The noise is coming from the back, but I still do a visual check of the front lobby as I make my way to the locker room. Nothing is moving and the entrance door is closed. It's not unusual for our guys to come in the back, but with the alarm on you'd only hear a short beep when the alarm is disarmed.

With my sidearm in hand, I move through the locker room. The door to the back is closed and I ease it open a crack, scanning what I can of the space beyond. Unfortunately, I can't see the service door from here—the surveillance van is blocking my view—so I gingerly make my way to the other side of the vehicle, using it as cover while I check my surroundings.

When I round the rear of the van I lead with my gun, prepared to shoot first and ask questions later.

Kai is lying facedown on the floor underneath the alarm panel by the closed service door.

"Kai?"

He tries to lift his head but seems unable, moaning softly.

I approach cautiously, sweeping the space with my gun from side to side, but other than Kai nothing is moving. I note the cover for the alarm panel is flipped up.

What if he had a medical emergency? Came in, started entering the code and collapsed? I can't see any blood, there are no injuries visible, and the bay looks otherwise empty.

Kneeling down beside him I put a hand on his back.

"Kai? What happened?"

He mumbles something incoherently.

Grabbing his shoulder, I try to roll him on his back but he's heavy. He needs medical attention. Putting the gun down, I use both hands to turn him over.

"My songbird..."

Before my ears can register the whispered words, I feel a sting in my back and my body explodes with unbearable pain.

My muscles jerking and no longer in my control, I fall forward over Kai's prone body, unable to do anything to protect myself. I can't stop him tying my wrists with what feels like zip ties.

I'm aware of a hand grabbing my arm, flipping me over, and then I see him.

"Hello again."

His smile is more disturbing than the Taser he's holding in his hand.

Angelo Sarrazin.

I try to move my fingers but other than a few twitches, they're useless like the rest of me. Kai moans again.

"What did you do to him?"

The words are slurred, my mouth not cooperating.

He ignores them—tucking the Taser in his pocket with the leads still attached—and reaches down for me.

The sound of a gunshot reverberates through the cavernous space and Sarrazin collapses on top of me. I try to move to roll him off but although the pain is gone, my body is like rubber.

"Did I kill him?"

Lena comes into view, her face white as a sheet, and a weapon clutched in her hand.

"Can you point that somewhere else?"

She looks down at her hand as if she didn't even realize the gun was there. She promptly drops it on the concrete floor, just as the back door swings open.

"FBI!"

YANIS

"RADAR!"

I've been waiting to hear something—anything—for the past ten minutes, but other than the distant traffic noises things have been quiet. Surprisingly so.

"Looks all clear, Boss."

He sounds much closer than before.

I cautiously get to my feet and see him standing on the ridge where I saw one of them go down. I start moving in that direction.

"What've you got?"

"Think I just winged him. Just a few shells and some blood. Looks like they took off."

Damn. I was hoping we could catch at least one of them.

As I reach the rocks underneath the ledge, I hear my name called. The voice is coming from my left where a large boulder partially obscures a crevice in the rock wall.

"Evans?"

I move closer and notice there's a slight widening near the bottom of where the boulder rests against the ridge, barely large enough for someone to fit through. I go down on my haunches.

"Bill? Are you in there?"

"What the fuck took you so long?" his disgruntled voice comes back.

"You hurt? Can you get yourself out of there?" I ask, ignoring his comment.

"Bullet in my right shoulder. My fucking arm is useless." As he talks, I can hear movement from behind the rock. "Couldn't even get my gun from my shoulder holster. I was too busy fucking running," he complains as his feet appear.

"Need a hand?"

"Be much fucking obliged. Been stuck in that damn hole for an hour waiting for those damn vultures to piss off."

I bite off a grin, glad to know he's at least well enough to be angry. I wrap my hands around his ankles and pull. When I get his body clear, he's using his left hand to hold the other arm in place. His eyes are closed and his face looks kind of gray. The shoulder looks a mess.

"Need a hand, Radar!" I call out, leaving Bill lying on the ground to catch his breath.

It's gonna take both of us to help walk him back to the road.

"Be right there."

A few minutes later I hear small rocks roll down the ledge as he climbs down. When his feet touch the ground, he holds up a sandwich baggie with some dirt and the glisten of a couple of shell casings.

"You carry plastic baggies?"

He grins.

"Hillary baked muffins this morning. I grabbed one for a snack."

"Fuckin' Boy Scouts," Bill grumbles, his eyes now squinting against the bright sun.

"Let's get him up and stabilize that arm," I tell Radar before turning to Evans. "Can you walk?"

"Well, I didn't fucking get here clicking my goddamn heels."

I'm guessing he's in pain since the F-bombs are flying, but he doesn't say a word when Radar and I maneuver him into a sitting position, leaning his back against the rock. We quickly turn the sleeve of his light jacket into a makeshift sling and help him to his feet. He's not looking too good.

"Let's get you to a hospital."

"This Podunk town have any?"

"Our best bet is Grand Junction," Radar contributes. "Unless you want to stop at a clinic, but I have a feeling you'll need more than a Band-Aid."

It takes ten minutes—Evans isn't moving too fast—to get back to the side of the road where the Yukon is still parked where Radar left it. We get him in the back seat but the moment I slide behind the wheel my phone rings.

"Mazur."

"Yeah, James Aiken here. Where the hell are you?"

"Rifle, about an hour east of town. Bringing in Evans. He's been shot," I fill him in.

"*Shit*. We've got some injuries here at your office as well." I'm already hitting my ignition button and put the call on speakerphone. "Front door was locked with an alarm going off, so we went around to the rear just as local PD showed up. Walked in the back door and found three down. Sarrazin and two of your crew."

Jesus, Bree…

"What fucking injuries?"

I'm already peeling away from the road shoulder.

"Sarrazin was shot in the back. He's alive but critical. EMTs are working on him."

"Don't give a fuck about him, what about my crew? Bree?"

"She's just sore. Got hit with a Taser. Your man got hit too, but in addition he appears to have been drugged with something as well. The other woman who shot Sarrazin is just a little shook up, but otherwise fine."

"Other woman?"

"Yeah, your admin assistant, Lena."

"Lena?" Radar repeats incredulously.

I'm as surprised as he is, the woman is not a fan of guns, period. The idea of her holding one, let alone shooting it, is ridiculous.

"Look, I've gotta go," Aiken announces. "See you when you get here."

When he hangs up, I immediately dial Dimi, who's closer, and tell him to grab Jake and haul ass to the office. With Sarrazin down I don't think there's a risk to the vineyard, but just in case I order Shep to stay put.

Funny, it took only a second for fear to grab hold with that phone call, but it takes until we reach the streets of Grand Junction for my stomach to settle back in place.

"Stay with Evans until you hear from me," I tell Radar. "I'll drive up to the ER and drop you off. And check to see if they brought Kai here." I glance in the rearview mirror. Bill has been silent for most of the drive and looks like fucking death warmed over. "Hey, buddy, you hanging in there?"

His eyes open to slits.

"Yeah."

"Did you hear me tell Radar—"

"Yeah."

As if he just expended the last of his energy on talking, his eyes fall shut and his head slumps to one side.

I hear Radar already on the phone to the hospital to give them a heads-up for an incoming GSW.

"I'll come check on you," I tell Bill when medical staff load him on a stretcher seconds after we pull up to the emergency entrance.

"Go."

He motions with his good hand as he's being wheeled inside.

I'm torn about leaving him when he's in such bad shape, but the need to see for myself Bree is okay propels me back behind the wheel.

Ten minutes later I pull into the parking lot, which is still teeming with police vehicles. A police officer is guarding the front door. It takes a minute or two and a lot of patience to talk my way past him.

"Bree!" I call out the moment I step through the door, but the first person I see is a very pale Lena.

She's sitting in the bullpen with Bissette when she turns to look at me. Her face crumples instantly and she's already out of her chair when I get to her and pull her into my arms.

"I'm sorry," she mumbles in my shirt. Then she tilts her head back. "Were you at the hospital? Is Kai okay?"

"Radar will check on him," I assure her, patting her on the back. "And you have nothing to be sorry for."

"Bree told me to stay in the conference room, but I couldn't let her go in there alone. So I took the gun from your desk drawer and went in after her, but he already had her down, and Kai..." She takes in a shaky breath. "I watched him bend over Bree and I thought he was gonna hurt her. I just reacted."

"You did good."

She promptly bursts into tears.

"I don't even know h-how to sh-shoot, I just pointed. What if I'd m-missed?"

She faceplants in my shirt again and I look over her shoulder at Bissette, who raises an eyebrow.

I take Lena by the shoulders and set her back a step before bending so we're eye to eye.

"But you didn't. If not for you, God knows what might've happened."

BREE

I'M TRYING TO ignore the blood on the front of my shirt as I stand off to the side while James Aiken directs the GJPD's forensics unit around the garage.

Both bay doors are rolled up for easier access and I'm grateful for the fresh air. It helps me get rid of my shaky legs.

"Bree..."

I turn my head to see Yanis stalking in my direction, his eyes scanning me top to bottom before they lock on the stain on my shirt.

"It's his," I quickly explain, as I'm almost hauled off my feet and in his arms.

Ignoring the milling crowd of people, he takes my mouth in a bruising kiss, his hold on me painfully tight, but *this* pain I welcome.

"Fuck, *Tygrys*. Fuck," he mumbles, his eyes closed and his forehead touching mine. "That was too close."

"I know, but it's all over now," I soothe him.

He lifts his head and I don't like the look in his eyes.

"I wish it were, but we still have two shooters on the loose. Evans was shot."

Goosebumps rise on my skin.

"Is he…"

"He'll be okay. I think," he quickly adds.

"You don't think it's over with Sarrazin out of commission?"

He shakes his head.

"I don't. I think something more is going on. These guys were committed enough to hole up and wait for Bill to show himself so they could end him. Shots were exchanged, Bree. A fuckload of them. And we were close enough to the road to hear traffic."

From the corner of my eye, I see Aiken walk up and clap Yanis on the shoulder, but his eyes stay on mine as he finishes his thought.

"Not a single emergency vehicle showed."

CHAPTER 25

YANIS

"FOR A YEAR?"

The FBI agent glances at me and nods.

"Give or take," he confirms.

As it turns out, the Denver office has an active investigation into Albero and some of his investments.

"The Attorney General..." Bree mumbles beside me.

We just finished getting the Denver SAC up to speed with an outline of events we believe to be connected. Including Radar's somewhat illegal discoveries, which earned him a stern look from the agent but nothing more.

We're congregated in the conference room, packed in like sardines. Aiken, his local counterpart, SAC Sanders, Bissette and her partner, Garcia, and us. Missing is Sergeant Fillmore and obviously Bill Evans, who by last report is undergoing surgery at St. Mary's.

Also at the hospital is Sarrazin, who is currently

under the knife, with two of Aiken's agents guarding him.

I asked Jake to take a shaken Lena to the hospital to check on Kai, who is being monitored for the effects of the ketamine injection he was jabbed with.

"Very astute, Ms. Graves," Aiken says appreciatively, and I tighten my arm around her as much as our side-by-side chairs will allow.

I haven't let go of her since I got here and Bree hasn't objected to my hovering, and I don't give a flying fuck what anyone else thinks.

"Yes," he continues. "Among other things we've been looking into the substantial contributions made to Delmer Beauregard's campaign. Interesting to note that their connection goes back quite a few years to when Beauregard was the ADA on a money-laundering case against Albero."

"At opposite sides of the courtroom. Curious they seem to be on the same side now?" Bissette observes with an eyebrow raised.

"We suspect Albero has something he's lording over the AG's head," Aiken explains. "Given some of the things we've uncovered, it's likely damaging enough to get Beauregard to put pressure on law enforcement to lay off the mafia boss."

There are nods around the table. Nobody's going to argue that, we all know corruption runs up to the highest levels. Still, it's unnerving to know everything truly has a price.

"So how does a mafia kingpin benefit from the

abduction of one of my agents, the death of a country singer, or the sabotage of a vineyard?"

I pose the question to the entire room, but it's Aiken who answers.

"He may not…" He pauses and I'm about to ask for clarification when he follows it up with, "At least not directly." He gets up from his chair and starts pacing the room. "The old man had a reported falling out with his stepson last year. Sarrazin was kicked off the board of Patria Holdings, Albero's shelter company, and limited to managing the day-to-day operations of only one of its subsidiaries in Colorado Springs."

"Falcone Scrap and Metal," Radar pipes up.

Aiken looks surprised.

"Yes. How did you know?"

Radar explains the connection between Falcone and McNeely, the guy responsible for damage to the vineyard, in greater detail.

James nods. "Makes sense. Now, I don't have any pertinent information regarding the wedge between Albero and his stepson, but I suspect Sarrazin's obsession with the singer played a part in it. The old man wouldn't have wanted that kind of attention drawn to his family."

"Do you think it's possible she knew who her stalker was?" Bree asks him.

"Likely."

They were at the same campaign party. She must've at least been introduced to the two men and realized the power they held.

"In that case, she may have been afraid to point her finger," Bree proposes, nodding her head. "And when she disappeared it probably made them nervous. They would've looked for her."

"And found her," I confirm.

"So then Sarrazin's obsession turned to you."

Crystal Bissette looks at Bree.

"I think Ms. Graves hit his radar when he mistakenly abducted her," Aiken thinks out loud. "But yeah, after Bobby Lee was found dead, he may have directed his obsession your way."

"Which would explain the cameras in your apartment," the detective concludes.

"But it doesn't explain the fire poker left on my bed."

Good point. The fire poker is still unexplained, as is the sabotage at the vineyard.

Radar checked into the story Joe and Sarrazin knew each other from college, which appears to be true enough—they were roommates in fact—but the motivation behind the vandalism is still a question mark.

The meeting is abruptly ended when Aiken receives a phone call from one of his guys at the hospital, telling him Sarrazin is out of surgery. The agent rushes over there in hopes of questioning him.

Shortly after that the GJPD contingent heads out, leaving only us sitting in the conference room.

"Thoughts?" I prompt.

"Bree might still be in danger," Radar supplies.

"She can identify Sarrazin was the one behind her abduction."

"True," Bree adds. "Calling me 'Songbird' like he did then confirmed it for me."

I glance at her and note the deep frown between her eyebrows. She doesn't seem that convinced. Before I can question her on it, Dimi comes forward with a good point.

"We need to put someone on Lena. She's the one who shot Sarrazin. That may well have put a target on her back as well."

Fuck me.

I mentally go over any current or pending contracts. Looks like we're going to be busy protecting our own. At least until the FBI finalizes their investigation and exercises some arrest warrants.

In the meantime, Albero is circling the wagons.

BREE

I FEEL LIKE I've run a marathon.

I only wish it was something that noble instead of getting zapped with fifty-thousand volts. *Damn.*

"How about we swing by Aztecas on the way home?" I suggest, glancing at Yanis.

It's about eight in the evening, I haven't had a bite to eat since breakfast, and my stomach is growling.

"I can hear the beast needs feeding," he teases with a wink. Then he turns his attention back to the road.

I'm surprised he's so lighthearted, not his usual demeanor, especially after the day we've had. I like it, though. He was always so serious, so…I don't know, responsible. I'd love to think I have something to do with this different side of him, although I'm sure the fact his buddy, Evans, should make a complete recovery, and both he and Kai should be released tomorrow, is part of it.

For now, Lena is going to stay with Jake and Rosie. Yanis had offered one of his spare bedrooms, but she didn't want to be a *fifth wheel in a budding romance*. Her words, not mine. She felt her presence wouldn't stand out as much at Jake and Rosie's, given their one-year-old daughter, Tessa, holds all their attention.

She's lying. She just wants the baby snuggles.

I don't blame her. I remember the first time I shot someone and I was trained for it. It shakes you to the core. Not that Lena is oblivious to what we're sometimes faced with in our line of work. Aside from Yanis, she's probably the most informed PASS employee. But it's one thing to hear it told, read reports, or see images—it's a different ballgame when you're living it.

"By the way, what was the story with Bill?"

Yanis had gone to talk to Evans while I stayed with Kai. Poor guy had been full of apologies. As if he could've anticipated getting hit with a Taser from behind. I wanted to hear what the detective had to say, but I didn't want to walk out on Kai. Besides, it had been interesting to watch our determinedly single office manager trying hard not to ogle Kai's substantial shape under that sheet. I can see the appeal, until Yanis enters the room, of course.

"He's had an eye on Sarrazin for a few days. This morning he tailed him out of Denver, and just past Glenwood Springs, a dark SUV pulled alongside and bullets started flying from the rear driver's side. He cut off on the byway, but they caught up with him at the gas station."

"Did he get a good look at them?"

"Yeah. He passed all that on to Aiken." He glances over and grabs for my hand. "Also...he thinks he found the house where they took you. A large mountain lodge four miles from where you were found."

Four miles? It had felt like forty at the time.

"Really?"

I shiver at the memory of that night and unconsciously rub the back of my thumb on my leg. I don't want to think about what might've happened if I hadn't gotten myself out of that place when I did.

There's still something nagging at me and I can't quite put my finger on it.

"Yeah, Bill didn't have a chance to dig into ownership but Aiken's team is looking into it."

"Good. Did he get a chance to talk to Sarrazin?"

"Aiken?" Yanis darts a look my way and I nod in confirmation. "No. They're keeping him sedated and he already has a lawyer posted by his bedside."

Figures. They don't waste any time putting the muzzle on.

While Yanis pulls into the restaurant parking lot and runs in to grab us some food, I replay the day's events in my head. This morning's meeting almost feels like it was a week ago, so much happened in the interim. I shiver remembering the soft voice seconds before the blinding pain of the Taser hit me.

Suddenly uneasy, I scan the parking lot around me. A couple walks out of Aztecas and gets into a truck three spots down. I turn back to the restaurant and find Yanis watching me through the window. I keep my eyes on him, forcing a smile he returns, but with my right hand hit the central lock.

When a few minutes later he walks out, a paper bag in hand, I quickly disengage the locks. I don't know why I'm so jumpy.

"Everything all right?" Yanis asks when he gets behind the wheel, handing me the bag of food.

"Yeah, I'm fine."

I keep my voice light and breezy, but it doesn't seem to fool Yanis. The man is too perceptive when it comes to me.

"You locked the doors," he says, hitting the ignition. "Bree?" he adds when I don't immediately respond.

"I feel…unsettled," I admit.

"That's understandable." He reaches over and gives my knee a light squeeze. "A lot has happened. We may occasionally deal with violence in our line of work, but that's usually targeted on others. In this case you were the focus. I'd be worried if you weren't affected."

He makes a valid point, an insightful one. Maybe

it's as simple as that; some lingering trauma.

When we get to his house, I fall on the food as soon as my ass hits the couch. Yanis chuckles as I devour the first of the two burritos he was smart enough to get me. He always takes good care of me.

God, I love this man.

The last bite I'm about to pop in my mouth freezes midair. *I love him*. There's no qualifications to that thought this time. No buts, no reservations, no fear, and no walls.

"What's wrong?"

A look of concern washes his features as he sets his burrito down on his plate.

My throat is suddenly thick with emotion and I can't seem to manage more than a light shake of my head. I have a degree in psychology, I know the sudden wave of emotions is in part because today left me feeling defenseless. But that doesn't make it any less real.

"Come here…" He plucks the food from my hold and drops it on my plate before hauling me onto his lap, his arms banding around me. "Talk to me," he urges in a demanding tone.

Too overwhelmed to speak, I take his face in my hands instead, feeling the soft bristle of his short-trimmed facial hair against my palms. Warm blue eyes search my face as I press my lips against his, tasting the salt of my own tears.

"You're scaring me, *Tygrys*," he mumbles against my mouth, right before he takes over the kiss.

Dinner forgotten, he slowly strips me—showing his feelings with gentle eyes, dominant mouth, and worshiping hands—until I'm straddling his lap, my body as naked as my love for him.

With hurried hands I pull his shirt over his head, our mouths fusing back together after the brief separation. As his strong hands dig into the cheeks of my ass, I work on the buttons of his fly. A delicious shiver ripples over my skin as his long fingers track down my crease and find my slick center. The moment his cock springs free, I wrap my fist around the silky, hot steel, and I moan down his throat.

Our moves are instinctive, yet precisely choreographed, as his large hands lift me up while I line up his length at my core. Then he breaks the kiss, lays his head back against the couch, and watches as he lowers me carefully, filling me inch by luscious inch.

Time stands still.

With our bodies anchored together and our eyes locked, no words are necessary to let our hearts speak. Still, I want him to hear.

"I love you."

One of his hands lift up to my face, brushing a strand of hair behind my ear. Then he traces the contour of my mouth with his fingertips before leaving them pressed against my lips.

"Say it again."

My mouth curves under his touch.

"I love you."

His eyes close on the last syllable.

Then he lowers his hand, tracing my neck and chest with his fingers, down my belly to where we are connected. I watch his nostrils flare as he rolls the pad of his thumb over my clit, sending a charge through my body. His eyes snap open when my pussy contracts around him, heat blazing from their depths.

His hands find my hips, his grip almost painful as he lifts me slightly.

"Hold on to the back of the couch," he growls, his mouth barely moving.

I curl my fingers around the rigid frame behind the pillows and grab on tight as he powers up inside me.

My feet are planted in the seat, my legs are burning, and my fingers are cramped in a desperate attempt to hold on as Yanis fucks me hard from below. He appears to command every movement, yet in leaving me on top, control is in my hands.

Our lovemaking a perfect display of the balance we are finding.

CHAPTER 26

YANIS

"Mom."

My eyes meet Bree's over a quick breakfast at the diner before we head to the office. Hers widen.

"Did your brother tell you?"

"Tell me what?"

"I can't believe he didn't mention it." She sounds put out. "We told him last week."

"Told him what, Ma?"

"I should've called you myself, but he said you were busy and he'd pass it on."

"Things have been crazy for all of us," I offer in defense of my brother.

In all fairness to Dimi, he has an infant at home and still managed to keep up with his share of the load these past weeks.

"I understand that, but now you're not prepared," she persists.

"For crying out loud, Mom," I growl, fast losing my patience. "Would you please tell me what you're calling about?"

Bree is pressing her lips together in an attempt to keep from laughing, and I shoot her a glare.

"We're moving!" Ma cheers enthusiastically. "To Grand Junction," she adds when I don't instantly respond.

It's on my lips to say "Finally," but instead go with, "That's good news."

Hopefully by the time they get here we'll have things back in our control. Bree gives me the thumbs-up.

"I know, right?"

"When are you listing your place?"

"Oh, we already sold it. Crops and all. This really nice guy from Cheyenne wants it as his hobby farm, handed over a check right away."

I drop my head back and look up at the ceiling. Hobby farm, my foot. They'll be lucky if the check clears.

Jesus, my parents. Lovable but utterly clueless.

I hope to God they didn't get ripped off. They have a decent acreage and even if their house is not much to speak of, the land is prime. I have a suspicion that was the attraction.

"I can hear you thinking, Yanis," she scolds me. "But don't worry, it was a fair market price and the check cleared before we signed the papers."

I can't hide the sigh of relief, although I still wonder what constitutes a fair market price in my parents' minds. They still exist in the seventies.

"When do you have to be out of there?"

"We already are," she says cheerfully. "Rolled out this morning. Packed everything in the old travel trailer."

The shock must've shown on my face because Bree leans over the table and puts a concerned hand on my arm.

"This morning," I repeat.

"Crack of dawn. We just stopped in Craig…"

Fuck me. Craig is a couple of hours northeast of here. Two and a half at most.

"…because the trailer is swaying a little. Your dad is going to reload it for better balance."

I shake my head. That damn trailer was ancient when they got it twenty years ago. It's a miracle it hasn't spontaneously collapsed yet. My instinct is to drive out there, but with our situation here so fluid, I don't want to go too far. Maybe I can get a flatbed over there to load the thing up.

"I'll send…"

"Stop right there," she cuts in firmly. "Your father and I are fine. We picked up a value-pack of bungee cords and have three rolls of duct tape in case of an emergency, and your dad is good with his hands."

He has a green thumb, yes, but I wouldn't trust the rest of his fingers.

"Call me when you get closer to town." I lock my eyes with the amused ones across the table. "Bree now lives with me, but we'll figure out a place for you to stay."

It's fascinating how the light gray color instantly darkens as her amused look turns into a full-out glare.

"Sure," Ma says easily. "Wouldn't be for long. We already have a real estate agent looking at properties for us."

"Here? Who is it?"

Part of me already suspects.

"Nicest girl, Dimi recommended her. Name of Megan Denny?"

So much for our nice relaxed morning after yesterday's madness.

Neither of us finish our breakfast and I slam a few bills on the table. I'm going to have to kill my brother, but that'll have to wait until I clear the air with Bree, who is pissed. I can venture a guess why, but I wait until we're in the Yukon before I broach it.

"It makes sense. My parents can bunk at the apartment until they find a place."

She turns on me with her mouth open disbelievingly.

"That's your reasoning? It makes sense? Well, if that doesn't make me feel all warm and cuddly inside," she snaps, and swivels back around, looking straight out the window, her face tight.

"It does. You're already here," I defend myself. "It's not like you weren't going to end up there permanently anyway. You're just wasting rent money."

"Rent money," she echoes in a dull voice.

I watch her throat move as she swallows and realize I've really upset her.

"*Tygrys*, part of me has always known I had that

house built with you in mind. Even when I was determined to ignore my feelings for you."

Some of the tension leaves her profile and I catch her biting her lip. Taking a calculated risk, I reach out and with a hand to her cheek turn her head my way. A lot of the angry heat is gone from her eyes.

Progress.

"You love me."

She stubbornly presses those lips together but eventually nods.

"Yeah…" I smile and brush a thumb over her soft cheek. "And I've always loved you."

Instantly her expression softens and a faint blush appears on her cheeks.

"You know that, right?"

She shrugs.

"It helps to hear it."

"I told you—"

One of her eyebrows lifts up to her hairline.

"No. All you said was something about it being on your lips to tell me you *fucking* love me, if I recall correctly. You never gave me the words."

In my mind that had been a declaration, but I can see now it wasn't exactly well-executed. So I take her face in my hands and lean in to run my nose along hers.

"I love you, Brianne Graves. More every day, and I don't want to miss a single one of them. Please, move in with me?"

Her lips slowly curve up, revealing her pretty,

white smile.

"I will," she responds but when I go to kiss her, she puts her hand against my lips, adding, "Next time, try leading with that."

BREE

I'M SURPRISED TO see Lena at the office.

She looks up nervously when we walk in the door, her relief evident when she sees it's just us. I walk straight to her and wrap her in a big hug.

"I never got the chance to properly thank you yesterday," I tell her, taking a step back so I can look at her. "Being kidnapped once was enough of a blow to my street cred. Getting nabbed twice would've decimated it. I owe you big time for not letting that happen."

I'm glad to see her grin back at me.

"I'm just glad I didn't accidentally hit you, 'cause I'm pretty sure the boss would've fired my ass."

Yanis grunts affirmatively behind me.

"Heard from Kai?" he asks, decidedly changing the topic.

"He called Jake last night, who said he'd pick him up this morning, Boss." She walks to her desk and grabs a few message slips. "Couple of people left messages."

He takes the messages from her and flips through them as he walks away.

"Bree, get hold of Joe Flynn. He left a message, see what he wants and tell him he can relax," he orders, stopping halfway to his office.

Back in bossy mode, which is a hell of a lot different than the loving, attentive guy from last night and this morning.

I mock-salute him, which earns me a narrowing of his eyes before he turns on his heel and shuts himself inside his office. I head for the kitchen to grab a coffee before I tackle Flynn.

"Gosh, I'm getting all the warm fuzzies," Lena comments sarcastically, having followed me. "How can you stand it?"

I snicker at her eye roll.

"There's more to him than meets the eye," I volunteer, wiggling my eyebrows.

"If you say so. I'd rather not know."

She leans her shoulder against the doorpost as behind her Jake and Kai walk into the office. I lift a hand to try and warn her, but Lena's on a roll.

"If you ask me, men's attributes are highly overrated. You can get battery-operated replacements that don't bark orders and always show results. I can hook you up."

With that she turns, only to run face-first into the chest of a dumbstruck Kai. The man looks like he's been hit with a Taser again. I squeeze behind them, clapping Kai on the shoulder in passing.

"Glad to see you up and about."

I'm still chuckling at Lena's mumbled apology, and hasty retreat to the reception area, when I sit down at my desk and pick up the phone.

"Flynn's Fields."

"Joe Flynn, please? It's Bree Graves at PASS Security, I'm returning his call."

"Just a moment, please. I'll patch you through to him."

I boot up my computer while I wait.

"Flynn."

He sounds like he's outside somewhere.

"Joe, it's Bree at the PASS office. You called?"

"Oh. Yeah, I heard something about a shooting at your office yesterday. Is everyone okay?"

It doesn't surprise me. The sheer number of emergency vehicles in our parking lot yesterday had been quick to draw local media. Dimi had dealt with them.

"We're fine, thanks, and it looks like you can rest easy. Sarrazin was injured and is currently in the hospital under FBI custody."

There's a slight pause before he responds.

"Wow. I didn't expect that. Good news, though. Did he say anything?"

I wave distractedly at Dimi sitting down at his desk, a big bakery box in front of him. I'm instantly hungry, having eaten only half of my breakfast. I forcefully turn away from the temptation and stare out the window, focusing my attention on the call.

"As far as I know he hasn't. Last I heard he was still sedated after surgery, but even if he wasn't, we're not likely to get much out of him, he had a lawyer by his bedside."

"I guess that was to be expected," he comments. "So what happens now?"

"That's up to the FBI. I assume there's going to be an in-depth investigation of his involvement in a series of crimes that will likely include the damage done at your vineyard. I'm sure the feds will be in contact at some point."

"Okay, I'll wait for that. Guess I won't need the extra security anymore."

He makes a good point, but it's not my call. I glance over at the closed door to Yanis's office.

"I'm sure the boss will be in touch with you about that at some point," I suggest. "Right now, he's dealing with the aftermath of yesterday's events, but I'll tell him you brought it up. For today at least Shep should be there."

We exchange some meaningless pleasantries before I end the call and turn to Dimi, who shoves the opened box of donuts in my face. I dive in with both hands. A girl's gotta grab her fuel where she can get it.

"Yeah," Yanis barks when I knock on his door five minutes later after scarfing down the treats.

He looks up and raises his eyebrows as I walk in.

"Save any for me?"

He waves a finger at my face and I quickly wipe the powdered sugar from my mouth.

"I think there's a few left."

Between the four guys in the office and myself, it doesn't take much to kill off a dozen donuts. Lena doesn't eat sugar, something I've never been able to understand.

"Better be," he grumbles. "Did you talk to Flynn?"

"Yeah, he'd heard about yesterday."

"Hard not to with those damn reporters monitoring their police scanners twenty-four seven. I'm sure it was all over the news this morning."

"I guess. Anyway." I take a seat in one of the visitor's chairs across from him. "I mentioned Sarrazin is in FBI custody and that they'd likely be in touch with him at some point. He wanted to know about the extra security and I told him you'd be contacting him about that."

"I'll call this afternoon. I want to talk to Fillmore first, give her a heads-up first. Spoke to Aiken. They ran the plates on that van parked behind the building. Fake and VIN-number filed down. He says their lab can probably recover the number but it's gonna take some time."

"And Sarrazin?"

"Still sedated. He's fighting some infection. His mother has arrived, although no sign of stepfather dearest."

"Probably hiding in one of his mansions," I observe with more than a hint of bitterness.

Guys like this are like eels in a bucket of snot; hard to grab hold of.

"Yeah, that was another reason Aiken called. His tech guy is scrambling to pull together any and all electronic evidence against Sarrazin and Albero——deeds, financials, phone records, the whole nine yards—before they have a chance to bury it. He's requested our help, or more specifically Radar's, to dig into the ownership of that mountain lodge Bill flagged. They need something solid before he can request a warrant."

"I'll go tell him. I can help, it'll give me something to put my teeth into. I don't want sit around twiddling my thumbs and waiting for something to happen."

I get up from my chair and move to the door when Yanis calls me back.

"Bree…"

"Yeah?"

I turn and watch him round his desk, stalking toward me. When he's close enough, his hand slips around my waist, pulling me flush against him. I have to tilt my head back to look at him. He promptly takes it as an invitation, slamming his mouth down on mine in a hard kiss that instantly fuels the fire that always seems to burn hot between us.

"Love you," he growls when he finally lets me come up for air.

"Not that I don't appreciate it…" I grin up at him, "…because I do, but where did that come from?"

He shrugs, kisses the tip of my nose, and lets me go.

"Well," he starts when he's seated behind his desk again. "I was hoping you could handle my parents when they show."

My mouth falls open in disbelief.

"So that was to butter me up?"

I try to hang on to my snit but the deep rumble of his rare laugh melts it away.

"It was you who suggested next time to lead with that."

CHAPTER 27

YANIS

I STACK THE chicken on the platter my dad hands me and turn off the burners on my grill.

"Come and get it!" he hollers as he walks inside.

Bill—who I picked up from the hospital this afternoon—chuckles in the seat I guided him to when he offered to keep me company outside. His arm will be in a sling for a few weeks to keep it immobile while his shoulder heals, and since he has no family waiting for him in Denver, I offered him the spare bedroom.

Of course I checked with Bree first, who was immediately on board, and it was Ma who decided it was occasion for a family dinner. At my house.

We had a chance to catch up while I was manning the grill. Evans explained, despite being sidelined by the brass, he'd been digging around a little. Asking a few too many questions—apparently of the wrong people—and had been put on cold cases. He put in for a leave of absence, which was readily granted. Someone seemed glad to have him out from underfoot.

He used his 'time off' wisely, though. He'd tried to retrace Bree's steps of that night, marked off a perimeter on the map where the log home had to be located, and circled any houses he could see on Google Satellite. Then he started driving around. It took him half a day to find it, proving how little fucking effort the police were putting in.

He was about to turn into a dead-end street he'd marked as one to check out, when he spotted a Range Rover coming down the mountain. He recognized the man behind the wheel as Sarrazin and stayed on his tail. Bill had been living out of his car ever since, afraid to take his eyes off the man.

I glance inside where Willa and Ma are bustling around the kitchen and my brother is lounging in front of the TV. Bree is bouncing baby Max, who apparently is grumpy around dinnertime.

"You're a goner."

Tossing back the dregs of my beer, I turn to find him grinning up at me.

"That's envy talking," I tell him.

"Damn right it is," he confirms, as he twists in his seat to look at Bree. "Hope you know how lucky you are. Before you know it, she'll be lugging around your own spawn."

I'll be damned if that doesn't sting.

Turns out it's true what they say; you don't realize you want something until it's too late to have it.

"Not an option," I state quietly.

I sense more than see his head swivel back and

meet his solemn eyes.

"That's a damn shame," he finally says.

"We should probably head in before they send out a search party."

A fussy baby Max is passed from hand-to-hand during dinner so everyone has a chance to eat. When it's my turn, the little guy falls asleep on my chest and my mother practically melts in her seat.

I've been expecting a comment so it doesn't surprise me when Ma pipes up.

"You're gonna make a great dad one day, my boy," she says, beaming.

My eyes instantly shoot to Bree, who is frozen on the spot with a stack of dirty dishes she just collected in her hands.

"Ma…" I caution, getting to my feet. "I'm forty-six, how about I be a great uncle?"

"Pffft. Plenty of men have babies later in life," she says with a stubborn set to her chin.

I firmly hold the baby against my shoulder with one hand and close in on Bree, slipping the other under her hair and curving my fingers around the back of her neck. Ma watches us and zooms in on Bree.

"You know Rosie was in her forties when she had Tessa," she persists.

My mother can be like a bulldozer once she clamps on to an idea and I can tell she's digging her heels in. Already I feel Bree growing tense under my hand.

"Enough, Ma," I growl.

"But—"

"Anna…" Dad weighs in, his eyes on Bree.

Ironically, for all of his cluelessness most of the time, my father is the more intuitive of the two.

"It's okay," Bree announces, drawing the attention as she locks in on my mother. "I can't have children, Anna. Lost that ability a long time ago."

I watch the color drain from Ma's face.

"Oh dear…" she mutters, wrapping her hand around a shawl knotted at her throat. "I didn't know."

"I realize that, which why I'm explaining it to you. I'm sorry if that's a disappointment."

"Don't apologize for that," I snap, getting annoyed.

I give her neck a squeeze, but she steps out of my hold and turns to face me.

"Your mom has a right to be disappointed, Yanis. I sure was, and so were you not that long ago. I'm not apologizing for something I had no control over, but I can certainly be sorry for bursting her bubble."

It shouldn't surprise me Bree has an understanding perspective on the situation and I find myself nodding in agreement.

Behind me I hear Bill mumble, "Total goner."

Dimi bursts out laughing. Guess it wouldn't be a family dinner without some controversy but as soon as it flared up, it's over.

Not that much later I close the door behind my parents, who were last to leave.

"Ready for a beer?" I ask Evans, who's leaning back on the couch.

"No alcohol with the meds I'm on. I'll take a water,

though."

"Shit, that's right. Mind if I have one?"

He waves me off.

"Nah, not much of a drinker these days anyway. It doesn't bother me."

Bree walks in from the kitchen and I catch her around the waist, pressing a quick kiss to her lips.

"You okay?"

She nods. "Yeah. I'm fine."

"Can I get you anything?"

"Wouldn't mind a beer."

When I return with drinks, Bree has joined Evans on the couch. I take one of the club chairs.

"Have you by chance had an opportunity to call Benedetti?" Bree asks him.

"Actually, I spoke with him briefly last week. He asked me to come down and meet with him. I was supposed to drive out there for a lunch meeting on Friday but I won't be driving anytime soon. He's looking for someone right now and it looks like I might be out of commission for a bit."

"It's your shoulder," I point out. "Not your head. I imagine if he's that hard up for an extra set of hands, he'll happily settle for a sharp mind to help take off the load."

He throws me a dubious glance but then Bree puts in her two cents' worth.

"I totally agree, and there are other ways to get there than driving. You can always fly."

Evans snorts. "If I wanna pay an arm and a leg."

"Maybe worth it if it nets you a fresh start," I suggest.

He doesn't look too convinced but nods anyway.

"I'll think about it. For now, I'm gonna hit the sack, I'm wiped."

I take his spot on the couch and pull Bree against me to watch a bit of the news. There is no longer any mention of a shooting or any ongoing investigation. Looks like the powers that be have managed to suppress any reporting on the subject. Half an hour later, Bree is nodding off on my shoulder.

"Bed."

"Bossy," she retorts in a sleepy voice.

"I'll show you bossy," I threaten, pulling her up off the couch with me.

Her eyes, half-closed earlier, are suddenly blazing with heat.

"Promises, promises…"

BREE

"FOUND SOMETHING."

Radar comes walking out of his office.

"I had to dig deep for this one," he shares with a grin in my direction, as he walks past my desk and sticks his head into Yanis's office. "Ownership of the mountain home is listed to a trust fund."

I hear a chair squeak and a moment later Radar backs up to let Yanis through.

"Name?" he snaps as he leads the way into Radar's office.

I quickly get up and follow the men in.

Radar pulls up a document on his screen.

"Martha 12/24/88."

"Looks like a date," Yanis says.

"Maybe a date of birth?" I suggest. "What is Sarrazin's birthday?"

Radar flips through a notebook on his desk.

"June twenty-seventh. Same year though."

"Who is Martha?" Yanis wants to know. "Any connection Sarrazin?"

"None that I can find, but I can tell you who is listed as managing trustee." Radar turns to us, sporting that smug grin. "None other than Patria Holdings."

"Did they create the trust?"

"I haven't dug quite that deep yet."

"Dig," Yanis instructs him. "Find out who Martha is. I want to know who set it up, when, and who the beneficiary is. Aiken will need every sliver of information you can dig up to get a warrant. If they can get a forensics team in there, they may be able to find traces of blood or other DNA evidence tying Sarrazin to Bree's kidnapping or the murder of Robert Connell, the floater they found in the reservoir."

"Gotcha."

"Call me if you find anything. Bree and I are heading out to Flynn's Fields shortly."

That's right, I almost forgot with this morning's rush to get Bill on his flight to Durango and the pile of messages waiting for us when we got to the office. Turns out even our brief stint in the local media was enough to generate a flood of new inquiries into our services. I guess taking down the son of a crime lord is good advertising.

Anyway, we're supposed to meet up with Shep at the vineyard to take down the surplus PASS cameras we installed. Yanis is dragging me along for the ride, still not willing to let me get too far out of sight. His justification was I could go over the final accounting with Joe, but I see right through the excuse. He wants me close, and frankly, I don't mind.

"Let me grab my stuff," I tell him, heading for my desk.

Five minutes later we're on our way to Palisade.

Shep is waiting when we pull into the parking spot beside his truck.

"He's not here."

"Who? Flynn?"

"Yeah. The girl in the office says he's running a bit late. You wanna wait for him or get going on those cameras?"

Yanis looks at me.

"Don't mind me. You guys go ahead, I'll wait for Flynn inside. I'll call you when he gets here."

"I'll walk you in."

This from the man who used to send me off on assignments by myself to places like Kenya. I roll my eyes at him.

"I've been walking just fine, Yanis. My ankle is all better," I offer sarcastically.

Maybe not *all* better—I still get the odd twinge or

two—but well enough to make my own way to the office.

"Humor me," the stubborn ass says.

Shep chuckles and rather than make a scene to further his entertainment, I start moving to the main building, not surprised when I hear Yanis's footsteps crunch on the gravel behind me.

He opens the door for me and waits just inside as the receptionist points me to the rustic leather chairs in the waiting area. When I take a seat, he shoots me a mock-salute before heading back out.

Men.

I pull out my cell and check emails for something to do. Maybe ten minutes later the phone rings and I look up to see the receptionist answer.

"Flynn's Fields, how may I help you?"

The woman's eyes come up and meet mine as she listens for a moment. "Yes, Mr. Flynn. She's here waiting for you." A brief pause and then, "I will, sir. Yes, I can do that."

She hangs up the phone and gets to her feet.

"Ms. Graves, I have to run a quick errand, but Mr. Flynn has asked me to make sure you're comfortable. Why don't I show you to his office, he said he shouldn't be too long. Follow me."

I get up and follow the woman down the hall, past the tasting room PASS has used for the past couple of weeks to a set of large, ornately carved wooden doors at the end. She shows me into a comfortable office with an oversized rustic desk and a seating area with a fireplace and furniture matching that in the lobby.

"Have a seat," she indicates the couch before leaving the room, closing the door behind her.

Nice space. It's almost as big as my entire apartment. Large windows frame the vineyard beyond. Nice view too. If I had to work here, I'd probably spend more time admiring the view, or sneaking out the back entrance between the windows, than doing anything productive.

My eyes drift to the stone fireplace—oversized, like the rest of the room—with the vineyard's logo branded into the thick slab of raw wood serving as a mantel.

Something stirs in the back of my mind and I get up for a closer look.

The logo looks to be a stylized landscape, bordered by some grapevines and overlaid with two capital letters F in Celtic script.

It's somehow familiar, just like the scent of Pine-Sol that seems to cling to the wood of the mantel. It's the smell that triggers the memory.

I've seen one with a logo just like this before. I didn't examine it too closely at the time—I was in too much of a hurry to get away—but I'm willing to bet when the FBI gets their warrant for the mountain lodge, they'll find the exact same logo branded into the fireplace there.

Then I notice the simple arched steel fireplace stand holding a brush and an ashpan.

But the slot where the fire poker is supposed to be

is empty.

"Ah, I was wondering how long it would take you."

I swing around at the voice to find him standing in the open back door. The easy smile on his face looks the same, but the steel in his eyes matches the weapon in his hand.

CHAPTER 28

BREE

"I SUSPECT ANGELO took it," Joe says, shrugging. "Probably for the same reason he used the lodge."

I brace when he casually walks toward me.

There's nothing casual about the gun he's holding, though. That thing looks dead serious.

"Why would he do that?"

The chuckle seems genuine enough.

"Because he's an idiot and I like playing with him. Letting him think he has all the power. It makes him cocky, and predictable."

With his free hand he points at the mantel.

"Put your hands up there."

I contemplate whether I should risk going for my sidearm, but he seems to pick up on my hesitation.

"Don't even think about it. There's an AR-15 aimed at your lover's head. One sound from you will have it explode into something unrecognizable."

I'm willing to take a risk on my own life, but

there's no way I'll risk his. Obediently, I place my hands on the mantel and feel him press the barrel of his weapon behind my ear.

"That's better," he murmurs, as he uses his other hand to search me for weapons.

I'm divested of my phone, my sidearm, and he finds the blade on my belt, but completely misses the small Sig I have in my ankle holster.

"Were you there?" I ask to keep him talking.

"At the lodge? No, or that bastard wouldn't have gotten us in as much trouble as he did." He chuckles again and I feel his breath brush against my cheek. "And I wouldn't have had to clean up after his ass."

I wonder who he is referring to when he talks about 'us.' Does he mean Albero? Is Joe somehow linked to him? I have so many questions, but right now I'm more worried about his arm reaching around me. With deft movements he one-handedly fastens a zip tie to my wrist.

I focus on the blond hair on the back of the hand and the faint scar that disappears in the webbing between his ring and pinkie finger.

It's the same hand I saw on Bobby Lee's ass in that picture from the Attorney General's campaign party. The one in which Sarrazin's eyes were shooting darts in his direction.

"Remember, just one wrong move or sound from you, or if you force me to shoot you here, Yanis will get a bullet as well."

So that's the plan, he's taking me somewhere else

to end me.

Good. As soon as we're out of range and Yanis is out of danger, I have a fighting chance, but in the meantime, I want to get as much information as possible.

"What was Bobby Lee to you?" I ask, as he moves to my other hand and puts a tie on that wrist as well.

"A fuck. A lousy one at that."

His hand goes to my belt which he loosens and for a moment I worry he has more than killing me in mind, but he pulls the belt free from my jeans without touching the buttons.

"She was a means to an end. Angelo needed a reality check after hounding the bitch for so long."

He takes one of my hands from the mantel and threads the belt though the zip tie on my wrist before slipping it back through the belt loops around my waist.

"Unfortunately, it only made the son of a bitch try harder to get in her pants."

Then he pulls down my other hand and does the same before feeding the belt through the final two loops on that side. Finally he buckles it tightly, effectively trapping my hands to my waist, rendering them more useless than they would be tied together.

Even if I could stomach dislocating my thumb again, it's impossible now.

Clever.

"Why does it matter to you?"

Knowledge is power. That's the only thing I have

going for me now.

He turns me to face him.

"It doesn't, but it matters to the old man. He'd put a bullet in Angelo's head if that wouldn't draw even more attention to the *famiglia.*"

"You work for him? Albero?"

He throws his head back and laughs. If I didn't know better, I'd call it an attractive laugh. A wholesome one. I can see why he fooled us all.

"Not exactly," he finally says, grabbing me by the back of my neck.

He gives me a shove toward the back door, but I dig in my heels and twist out of his hold, glancing back at the fireplace mantel where he left my blade and sidearm. With my hands tied to my sides, I won't be able to get to my ankle holster. I need to buy some time.

"If you're not working for him, then why do this?"

"Money." He shakes his head. "Isn't it always about love or money?"

Grabbing my arm, he propels me toward the door again.

"Did you kill Bobby Lee?"

I'm trying to give Yanis an opportunity to clue in something is wrong. He has a well-developed sixth sense I hope is twitching right now. I just pray he's careful, because somehow, I don't think Joe is bluffing about having a gun aimed at Yanis.

He sees right through my attempts to slow him down.

"Full of questions, aren't you?"

It's not a denial.

When he pulls open the door, I take a step back. A navy van with the same vineyard logo is parked right outside, the sliding door already open.

"Did you?" I turn my head to look at him.

"Does it matter? It was a loose end that needed taken care of. You're another."

"To protect Sarrazin," I offer.

"To protect family," is his response.

His fingers bite into my arm as he shoves me outside.

YANIS

"ONE MORE."

Shep takes the other side of the ladder and helps me carry it around the back to the other end of the large barn where the vats are stored. There we prop it up against the side when my phone vibrates in my pocket. I hold up a finger to Shep, indicating for him to wait while I answer the call.

"Mazur."

From the corner of my eye, I see Shep start climbing the ladder anyway. I'm about to tell him to hang on when Radar starts talking.

"Hold on to your hat. This is gonna blow your mind," he says excitely.

"Talk to me," I snap, my attention fully focused on the call.

"I found the grantor for Martha 12/24/88."

He pauses for effect but I'm quickly impatient.

"And?"

"Delmer Beauregard. Our friend the Attorney General."

My mind goes into overdrive, trying to come up with reasons Colorado's chief law enforcement officer would have created a trust fund with Colorado's largest crime lord at the helm. Not to mention why said crime lord's son would choose a property owned by said trust to abduct Bree to.

Different scenarios present themselves—with blackmail topping the list—but that only raises other questions.

"And get this," Radar continues. "He's been feeding the fund for the past thirty years or so with monthly deposits, but Patria wasn't given control of the fund until twelve years ago."

Seems like every detail we uncover launches even more questions.

"Interesting. Did you figure out the significance of the name? Martha?"

I look over at Shep and notice him three-quarters of the way up the ladder, frozen and intently focused on something.

"Oh yeah. Martha Jean Ancaster, former secretary to then lowly associate for Ginsberg, Wong, and Associates in Denver, Delmer Beauregard."

Shep looks down at me and I can tell from the look on his face something is amiss.

"December twenty-fourth, nineteen eighty-eight,

she gave birth to a child at Swedish Medical Center," Radar continues in my ear as I watch Shep hustle down the ladder.

"Let me guess," I volunteer. "Beauregard's illegitimate offspring? Our trust beneficiary?"

"In one, Boss. But you'll never guess who."

Shep reaches me just as the blue winery van I noticed arriving earlier drives off and a ripple of unease rolls over my skin.

"We've got trouble," Shep rumbles, and I almost miss what Radar says.

"Joseph Flynn Ancaster."

My eyes dart to the main building.

Bree.

"He's got her," Shep confirms.

"My ride," I yell at him, already running for the parking lot when I realize Radar is still on the line.

"Boss? What the hell is going on?"

"I've gotta go."

I jump behind the wheel and toss my phone at Shep.

"Find the number for Aiken, get him on the phone. Now."

Over the tops of the vines, I can just see the blue van turning at the end of the service road. Instead of heading south toward town, I watch it turn left toward the highway.

"Boss, go easy," Shep warns when I floor it after the van. "Flynn isn't alone. A second guy is driving which means—"

"I get it," I snap.

One driving means the other has his hands free. They can't see us coming, or Bree will be dead before we can get to her.

By the time I get to the highway and turn east toward the mountains—following the van four vehicles ahead of me—Shep is relaying information to the FBI.

Half an hour later, I watch them take the cutoff for Old US Highway 6 along the Colorado River.

"What's happening?" I ask Shep, who just reported the new directions to Aiken with whom he still has an open line.

"They've got a chopper. About to take off. He says it'll take him about half an hour to catch up."

"Fucking pray we've got that long."

About five miles down the road the van turns right onto Stone Quarry Road which—according to my GPS—crosses the river before leading into the mountains.

From there we wind through a maze of smaller roads and, with barely any other traffic, I'm forced to fall back farther. At some point I'm afraid I've lost them, when I spot a cloud of dust to my right. I turn onto the logging road, hoping they don't pay attention to their rearview mirrors, because as easy as it is for me to spot him, he'll be able to see me too.

"Where the fuck are they?" I ask Shep, who has been relaying every twist and turn we've made so far.

"Coming in as the crow flies," he reports. "Five

minutes from our location."

On the right side we pass a wide cutout with a skid-mounted fuel storage tank, right before the road makes a turn into the woods.

"Passed an open space with a green storage tank, heading into the trees," I hear Shep update before spitting out a few choice curse words. Then he tosses my phone on the dashboard.

"What?"

"Lost signal."

Ahead of us the van isn't visible anymore, and when I glance up at the thick canopy covering the road, I realize we aren't either.

"They won't have much of a visual. *Fuck!*"

I slam the heel of my hand hard on the steering wheel.

"What's that?" Shep points up ahead where it looks like the trees open up. I immediately slow down. "Let me go check it out," he says, his hand already on the door.

The moment the Yukon rolls to a stop, he's out, slipping into the trees on the side of the road. I'm tempted to go after him, but grab my phone from the dashboard instead. I have no bars, but I try calling Aiken anyway.

It rings twice and then I hear a crackle before the line goes dead. *Sonofabitch.* What a clusterfuck.

Shep pops out of the trees and motions for me to join him. I grab the rifle from behind the passenger seat and slip out of the vehicle, carefully closing the door without latching. With no ambient noise from traffic even the slightest sound will carry far.

"Looks like an old hunting cabin. Van is parked out front."

BREE

"WHAT IS THIS place?"

I couldn't see much from the small window in the back of the van and every time I tried to turn my head, Joe would press the barrel of his gun harder to the base of my skull. Every pothole and rut we hit on the way, I was afraid the thing would go off.

From the pressure building in my ears, I could tell we were heading up in the mountains, but it's still a bit of a shock to the system when I'm hauled out of the van. From the dry dust of the mesa to the lush green and mountain air in less than an hour by my calculations. Yet a lifetime removed.

"Ask Sam, he picked the location."

I never got to see the driver. He got in after me and never spoke. Besides, I was too distracted by Joe, who I managed to keep talking. More so the closer we got to our destination.

I now have a much better understanding of the connection between Albero and the hold he has over the Attorney General and Joe himself. The man is mercurial in his manipulations.

When Joe mentions that name, however, all my attention is on the figure rounding the front of the van.

"You?" is all I manage.

Sam.

The man who bought me a greasy cheeseburger and lent me the shirt off his body in the back of a stretch limo. Who had been part of Bobby Lee's security detail, *that* Sam. No longer that friendly charmer, but a steel-faced, cold-eyed mafia henchman.

"I forgot," Joe chuckles behind me. "You two already met. Sorry we don't have time for a proper reunion, but I have to get back to the vineyard. Where to, Sam?"

"Round back," he says, leading the way around the ramshackle cabin.

The moment I see the massive firepit and the large pile of logs stacked beside it, I know I don't have a lot of time left. A good hot fire this far away from civilization is a good way to get rid of a body. I just don't particularly want it to be mine.

"On your knees."

Joe pushes down on my shoulder until my knees buckle under me. I drop my ass to my heels right away so my hands are lined up with my ankles.

"So that's it? You kill me and think your problems will be solved? Do you really think I haven't shared everything I know already?"

I keep talking to distract from my careful movements.

"What you've shared isn't important. What you can testify to is."

I pretend to scoff at his comment, even as I struggle not to shit my pants.

"That's not even a spit in a bucket compared to the irrefutable evidence the FBI already has compiled," I bluff, slightly shifting my back out of Joe's line of sight.

I've never been so grateful for the magnetic flap on my ankle holster. Had it been a snap or Velcro, I wouldn't have been able to slide the little Sig into the palm of my hand.

"Maybe on Angelo and the Don, but I'm not even on their radar."

"Are you sure?" I ask, while gauging my ability to shoot Joe from my position.

I stand a better chance of shooting Sam and using the few seconds it'll take for Joe to realize what's happening to get to my feet. With Sam disabled, it would make better odds for me.

Before I can rethink what I'm doing, I change the grip on the gun and turn my body toward Sam, hoping I angle my wrist sufficiently to hit his body.

The sound is sharp and echoes as I watch the man grab for his gut. I only hesitate for a moment, but when I try to get my feet under me Joe is already there, his boot kicking the Sig from my hand.

I feel his hand grab hold of my hair, pulling me up, as the cold steel of a barrel presses into the base of my skull.

Then I hear a shot and find myself falling face-first into the firepit.

CHAPTER 29

YANIS

I ABSORB THE rifle's recoil and watch both figures pitch forward.

When I start running, yelling sounds behind me, which I ignore. Nothing's going to stop me.

It was risky with Joe standing so close behind Bree, his gun pressing against her head, but I didn't have the luxury of waiting for a better shot. He would've killed her.

Bree's body is pinned facedown under Joe's much larger form, his head a bloody mess. I grab his arm and with some effort pull him off her. Her hair and the back of her shirt are covered in blood and I can't tell if it's hers or Joe's.

"Bree…Christ, baby," I mumble to myself as I carefully roll her over.

Her front is covered in ash and dirt.

"I'm okay," she says, her gray eyes looking up at me.

I do a quick visual scan, noticing bleeding from a

cut to her forehead. Her hands are strapped to her belt with zip ties and I reach for my knife to cut her loose.

"You're hurt," I disagree, willing my shaking hands steady as I slip the blade between her wrist and the bindings.

She reaches the hand I just freed to the wound on her forehead.

"A scratch. Guess that's what happens when you break your fall with your face."

A joke. She's fucking cracking a joke when my heart is still thundering in my throat. I clench my jaw and concentrate cutting the other tie loose without slicing her wrist.

"You could have a concussion," I grumble.

"I'm fine, Yanis," she says softly, putting a hand on my arm. "You're a great shot."

Good thing I didn't have time to think before I put the crosshairs on the back of that fucker's head and pulled the trigger. Bree is the only woman I know who would go through an ordeal like this, a gun to her head, end up pinned under a dead body, and still calmly compliment me on the accuracy of my aim.

"Is he dead?"

She glances over at Joe's still figure.

"Very."

I grab both her hands and help her to her feet. It's only when I wrap her in my arms, I notice we've been joined by Shep and two FBI agents.

"You good, Bree?"

She turns and smiles at Shep.

"All good. Thanks for tracking me down."

Aiken is standing off to the side, barking into his phone, while his colleague is giving first aid to the man Bree shot.

"I've got Flight for Life coming in for that guy," Aiken announces as he joins us. "I'll need someone to head over to that clearing back there and guide the medics in."

"I'll go," Shep volunteers and jogs off.

"I also got in touch with SAC Sanders, who is notifying the Garfield County Coroner to pick up this one," Aiken continues after thanking Shep.

Then he turns to Bree.

"Do you feel up to talking?"

I feel her affirmative nod.

We're sitting on the ramshackle porch of the cabin, while waiting for the coroner to arrive, listening to Bree relay the information she was able to draw from Flynn. Some of it Radar had already revealed to me, but some of what she got from Joe was news.

For instance, the fact Joe had first been introduced to the Albero family when Sarrazin, his college roommate, brought Joe home for Thanksgiving break twelve years ago. Right around the time Guiseppe Albero was being tried for money laundering. Now Attorney General, Delmer Beauregard, had been the Assistant District Attorney prosecuting him back then.

Joe mentioned he despised his father, who kept him and his mother controlled and quiet with money, but wouldn't acknowledge Joe's existence.

At the time he was introduced to Guiseppe Albero, the man had been actively hunting for leverage on the dogged prosecutor and Joe happily provided him with the ammunition to exert pressure on Beauregard. In turn, Albero had been eager to make Joe his new protégé since his stepson was more interested in frat parties and chasing skirts.

"He said Guiseppe Albero treated him like a son. Something his own father failed to do," Bree shares.

"He never even hit our radar," Aiken confesses. "I mean, we had his name along with all Sarrazin's other college buddies, but he must've been keeping a low profile because no flags went up."

"He gave me the impression he spent his time cleaning up after Sarrazin," Bree suggests. "Wasn't too happy about it either. Which brings me to another thing," she adds. "Bobby Lee. That was Joe in the picture from that campaign party Radar found, with his arm around Bobby Lee. The one that shows Sarrazin looking all kinds of pissed off. Joe made it sound he was just taking one for the team, in hopes that would cure Sarrazin's obsession with the woman."

I snort. "That clearly didn't work."

"No," she confirms. "And he called her a loose end that needed to be taken care of. I was another."

Aiken suddenly grins wide, looking at my girl with open appreciation, and I feel compelled to drop my arm around her shoulders in a not so subtle claim.

"He miscalculated on that one, didn't he? Probably

not used to a woman with your kind of steel. That's not something you see often in those circles."

At that moment a white van, with 'Coroner' in a decal on the side panel, rolls up to the cabin closely followed by a Garfield County Sheriff's cruiser. Their arrival effectively cuts our debrief short. I'm sure it'll be resumed at a later time. First Joe's corpse needs taking care of.

Aiken makes introductions and walks the coroner and sheriff over to where the body is still lying facedown in the firepit. The Flight for Life helicopter has already come and gone to pick up Sam. Since we're out in the boonies with limited numbers, I ended up sending Shep along with him since the other agent who came with Aiken was busy processing the scene.

After the coroner does a brief exam, the body is moved to the van, and Aiken makes arrangements with his team in Denver to pick Flynn up from the Garfield County Morgue tonight.

It's been a couple of hours and—although I cleaned some of the blood from Bree's face and hair with the help of a bottle of water—some traces still remain and her clothes are caked with it.

"If we're done here, I'm gonna get Bree home so she can get cleaned up," I tell Aiken. "We can catch up later."

"You know I have a chartered helicopter waiting," the bastard addresses Bree directly. "I can get you there much faster. Be happy to give you a lift. Besides, it would give us a chance to discuss a spot I have available on my team."

I'm about to tell him what I think of his offer, but Bree beats me to it as she slips an arm around my waist. I'm not sure whether it is to show her support or to restrain me in case I can't hold my temper.

"I'll stick with Yanis, both for the drive and the team. But thank you, I appreciate the offer."

Aiken looks at me and winks.

"Can't blame a guy for trying."

BREE

"HAND ME ANOTHER slice?"

I reluctantly open the pizza box I've been hoarding and Yanis dives in, grabbing one.

For a man who claims fruit on a pizza is sacrilegious, he sure has taken a shine to the Hawaiian pie I purposely ordered. Ignoring my glare, he shoves half the slice in his mouth while David Aiken snickers.

"Balls of steel and has no problem keeping up with you guys, even in appetite. Despite the questionable taste in pizza," Aiken comments around a mouthful.

"Give it a rest," Yanis bites, like he's been doing all afternoon every time the FBI agent needles him. "And don't dis the pie, it's pretty good."

Jeers go up around the large conference table where all our guys, the two FBI agents, and Bill Evans— who made his own way back from the airport—are eating. We're just taking an early dinner break during our debriefing before Aiken heads back to Denver.

Shep is back already, having grabbed an afternoon flight after one of Aiken's agents relieved him from guard duty. Sam—whose last name turned out to be Grossman—was taken to Denver and had surgery to repair the hole I blew in his intestines but is expected to recover. I'm not sure whether to be relieved or upset about that. The bastard played me like a pro, was prepared to kill my boyfriend, and appeared to enjoy building a pyre to crisp me on.

Aiken seems to think he'll be able to turn the man with a little pressure, but I'm not so sure. Time will tell.

The feds will definitely need something more to bring any charges on Albero. So far, they have a case against Sarrazin but unless they can prove widespread conspiracy, those charges are independent from the Albero family. Anything attributable to Joe died right along with him.

The FBI agent is planning to return to Denver to deliver a formal death notification to Martha Ancaster, Joe's mother. She apparently just returned from a European river cruise, which explains why Sarrazin was able to use the mountain lodge for his nefarious plans.

Even though he doesn't have proof of culpability on Guiseppe Albero, Aiken is determined to disrupt the dangerous influence he has with the highest-ranking law enforcement officer in Colorado and the resulting widespread corruption. Delmer Beauregard is the weak link in that chain and nobody's arguing the man needs to be brought down.

At my request, Yanis drove me straight to the office instead of home first. I took a long, hot shower in the locker room and changed into clean clothes. That and a full belly is all I needed to feel half-human again.

"Should I put on more coffee?" Lena asks, sticking her head into the conference room.

"You don't need to stick around for that," Yanis tells her. "Why don't you head home?"

"I, uh…"

Her hesitation is evident and I get it. It may be unlikely someone will come after her at this point, but you never know. Better safe than sorry.

"Wouldn't it be wiser to stay vigilant for now?" I offer. "We should be breaking up this party soon anyway. It's getting late, you may as well hang around and wait for Jake."

"I can do that," she answers, a little too eagerly.

Across the table Jake nods at her and Yanis leans close.

"Smart call," he whispers, giving my shoulder a squeeze.

"Goner," I hear Bill mutter, and a collective snicker goes up from the peanut gallery.

Forty-five minutes later, we drop Aiken off at the airport on our way home. He's leaving two agents behind to accompany Sarrazin back to Denver when he's released tomorrow.

The man will have his hands full when he gets back.

When we leave the airport, I twist in my seat and look back at Bill.

"So how was Durango?"

"Good. Been years since I was there, I'd forgotten what a nice place it is."

"And the meeting with Benedetti?"

"I've got a month to recover and get my shit in order—give my notice, sell my house, pack up my stuff, find a place there—and I start December first."

My grin is wide and heartfelt. I like Evans, he's a good guy and I'm sure he'll mesh well with Benedetti.

"Congrats."

"Yeah, good news," Yanis says, glancing in his rearview mirror.

"Appreciate the tip."

"My pleasure."

I straighten in my seat and Yanis puts a hand on my knee, throwing me a wink.

"All I need now is to find me a woman like you," Bill pipes up behind us. "Unless I can convince you to drop this deadbeat and head for the mountains with me?"

"*Fuck me*. You too?" Yanis reacts and I start laughing.

"Can't blame a guy for trying," Bill comes back with.

Yanis turns to me.

"I'm gonna have to lock you up in the house," he grumbles.

"Don't you dare," I threaten him. "Or I might take

him up on that."

This time when he meets my eyes, his are amused.
"Oh yeah?"

"You bet. I've never had so many attractive offers."

CHAPTER 30

YANIS

"*I* DARE YOU to tell me you've had a better offer than this."

Bree wears a cheeky smile at my words until I bend down, purse my lips, and blow a breath over her distended clit. The resulting full body shiver running through her puts a smug grin on my face.

"Quit teasing," she scolds me when I lift my head again.

"Let me get this right, you're accusing *me* of teasing?"

Her mouth sets in a stubborn line and she tries to roll away from me, but with her legs over my shoulders, and my hands holding her thighs in place, she's not going far.

"Yanis!"

"Haven't moved, *Tygrys*."

This time I take the bundle of nerves between my lips and suck lightly, but the moment I feel her thighs start to press against my ears I lift my mouth.

She lets out a frustrated yelp and flings a pillow at me. Maybe I've teased her enough. The truth is, this dragged-out anticipation is taking its toll on me as well.

I lift myself from between her legs, crawl up her body, and am about to settle my hips in the cradle of hers when I suddenly find myself on my back, Bree straddling me.

"Payback."

The promise is delivered with a sly little grin.

She proceeds to do exactly that, subjecting me to the sweetest torture until she has me pleading for release.

She finally puts us both out of our misery when she takes me deep inside her. Both already well-primed, it's a short, wild ride to an explosive climax.

"That was fun," she mumbles, draped over me as we both catch our breath. She lifts her head and her eyes twinkle. "Can we do that again?"

I bark out a laugh.

"Fuck, Bree, I'm gonna need more recovery time than that."

On the nightstand my phone starts buzzing. An opportune reprieve.

Bree reaches over and grabs it, checking the call display.

"It's Aiken." She winces as she hands it to me. "It's also nine thirty. I'll call Lena, tell her we'll be in shortly."

She rolls off me and out of bed as I sit up and

answer the call.

"Tried calling you at the office. Catch you at a bad time?" the agent asks.

I look over to see Bree walk into the bathroom with her own phone to her ear, naked as the day she was born. My dick instantly stirs again.

Christ. Age hasn't diminished her effect on me.

"Just running a little late."

He chuckles on the other end.

"Been a busy few days," he observes.

"That it has."

It was two days ago I almost lost Bree again, and although she seems to have bounced back just fine, it's left a mark on me. It would be easy to fall into the trap of thinking the threat is now gone with Flynn dead and Sarrazin in federal custody, but I know the true power behind this mess was not with those two men.

Albero is still out there and with Beauregard in his pocket, we can't afford to dismiss him.

"What's up?" I ask, as I listen to the shower turn on in the bathroom.

"Have you seen any news this morning? Read a paper?"

"No, I haven't."

"Okay, well, let me update you. I spoke with Martha Ancaster yesterday morning. She hadn't been informed yet her son died, so the news came as a bit of a shock. According to her their relationship had been strained in recent years."

"She tell you why?"

"Not specifically, but I got the impression she was aware of his relationship to the Albero family and not happy about that. She made it clear she holds his father responsible."

"Understandable."

"Yeah. Anyway, she must've gotten busy right after I left because this morning, I turned on the news and Beauregard's face was all over it. She sent copies of a paternity test Delmer had insisted on thirty-some years ago to local and national networks and planted the seed of his involvement with organized crime. Massive exposé and the reporters are digging. My phone has been ringing off the hook this morning with demands for a full investigation into the Attorney General's alliances."

The grin on my face spreads involuntary when I feel some of the lingering weight leave my shoulders. With his credibility in question, not only his power, but his usefulness would diminish. One down, and only one left to go.

"Glad to know they're finally reporting some positive news."

"You and me both," Aiken says, laughing. "Feeling a lot better about matters this morning."

"For sure."

"One more thing and then I'll let you get back to whatever you were doing when I called." I hear the smile in his voice, which means he has a pretty good idea. "Sam Grossman is talking. Didn't take much after he realized it could easily be made to look like he had a much larger role than he actually did. Decided to turn state's evidence in the case against Sarrazin, and cooperate with any investigation into the old man in return for protection in the WITSEC program."

I swing my legs out of bed when I hear the shower turn off. Too bad I'll be too late to join her.

"And the good news keeps on coming," I observe. "Albero must be feeling the heat."

"I'm sure he is. Especially since Sarrazin's pretrial hearing is scheduled for tomorrow."

"Do you think he'll make bail?"

"Not likely with the charges against him, but I've learned to never say never."

"Keep me up-to-date."

I'm already heading for the bathroom.

"Will do."

Ending the call, I toss the phone back on the bed and push open the bathroom door. Wrapped in only a towel, Bree is in front of the vanity, rubbing lotion on her arms.

"You seem happy," she comments, looking at my distorted reflection in the steamed-up mirror.

I walk up behind her, my front brushing up against her back.

"I am. Very happy."

To illustrate I rock my hips, pressing my revitalized cock to the swell of her ass.

"I can tell." She leans her body into mine. "Good news?"

"Yeah. I'll tell you about it later."

I reach for the shower faucet to turn the water back on and then in one deft move peel the towel from Bree.

"Hey! I already showered."

With one hand spread wide on her lower belly, and the other covering a breast, I turn her toward the stream.

"I think you missed a few spots," I whisper with my lips against her ear, as I dip a finger inside her pussy. "I can take care of those for you."

She rolls her head back against my shoulder, tilting her chin to smile up at me.

"Is that so?"

"Hmmm."

I sandwich her between my body and the tile shower wall, and press my lips to the side of her neck as I work my finger inside her.

"Yanis?"

"Yeah, baby."

"Best offer I ever had."

BREE

"WHAT TIME ARE you leaving?"

Yanis looks up from his desk.

He's supposed to pick up Bill and give him a ride to the airport. Evans is returning to Denver after his follow-up doctor's appointment yesterday, and Yanis is heading to Salt Lake City this afternoon to meet with a new prospective client.

"I need about twenty minutes to get this proposal finished up and then I'll head out. I should be back tonight, though."

"Okay. I guess I'll say goodbye now."

I round his desk and bend down to press a kiss to his mouth. One he immediately claims as he slips his tongue between my lips.

We tend to minimize public displays of affection at work, but in the relative privacy of his office all bets are off.

I smile down at him when he finally lets me up for air and move out of his reach.

"Be safe. I'll wait up for you."

A wolfish grin spreads over his face.

"We'll have the house to ourselves," he points out.

"Yes."

The grin disappears and his eyes heat as he looks in mine.

"Be naked when I get there. We have some christening to do. We'll start with the kitchen."

A warm tingle starts low in my belly at the promise in his words.

"Maybe," I tease.

I slowly back out of his office, only to bump into Dimas who stands right outside, his hands clamped over his ears and an expression of abject horror on his face.

"Just so you know, I'm never eating at your house again," he announces.

I snort in part amusement and part mortification

before darting for my desk. When Yanis leaves a while later, he stops by and leans in.

"*Naked*," he whispers in my ear before walking away.

"I can hear you," Dimi barks from the desk next to mine.

I'm left with a blush on my face and a smile on my lips.

It's been a week since I ended up facedown in a firepit with a dead man on top of me. I can't say the experience hasn't resulted in some vivid nightmares on a few occasions, but each time Yanis was there, his warm body and sleepy voice quick to banish any lingering chills.

Surprisingly, living under one roof hasn't really required much of an adjustment, despite each of us having lived alone for so long. Maybe it's because even when we weren't a couple, we were in tune with the other. You don't work closely with someone for that many years—especially someone you have a history with—and not develop a good sense of who they are.

We already know most of each other's likes and dislikes, habits and quirks, and even with Bill as the proverbial fifth wheel, moving in together has been a notably easy transition.

Mind you, we've had lots to distract us. Among other things there are Yanis's parents, who are still bunking in my apartment. They've seen a few properties and this afternoon they're viewing one place—about ten minutes east of Yanis's…I mean *our* house—for the second time.

Anna asked me to come, mostly because Yanis won't be here and Dimi has his hands full at home, I suspect. Although, she claims she needs a woman's input. I'm not quite sure how helpful I'll be but I'm game. I like hanging out with his parents. They ease the ever-present ache in my heart my own mother's loss left behind.

"I HAVEN'T BEEN out this way," I comment from the back seat when Max drives us out of town.

The few houses I can see from the road are set back a ways and look to be expensive. Understandable with these views.

We've just passed what could be considered a mansion on our left when the road turns to gravel. About two hundred yards farther, Max turns into a long driveway that meanders through a copse of trees before the farmhouse becomes visible.

It's definitely older and more modest, sitting atop a hill with nothing but nature surrounding it.

"It beautiful."

Anna twists in her seat and smiles back at me.

"It is, isn't it?"

When we pull up to a couple of cars already parked in front of the house, I see a familiar figure step out of the front door.

Shit.

The real estate agent, forgot about her.

She's all smiles for the Mazurs until she spots me getting out of the car.

"Megan, right?"

I step forward offering my hand. Killing with kindness is the best way to defuse a tense situation. Or so I hope.

She can barely hide the sour expression on her face yet has no choice but to put her limp hand in mine.

"I'm sorry, I don't know your name."

Like hell she doesn't. She's the kind of woman who probably did some research on her perceived competition.

"Oh, I'm sorry," Anna twitters with a nervous chuckle. "This is our daughter-in-law, Bree. You haven't met?"

"No," Megan says.

"We have," I answer at the same time. "Except no formal introductions were made," I add quickly.

"I see. Glad that's been remedied." Anna smiles at the woman. "Our oldest son, Yanis, has finally come to his senses. He's been in love with Bree for decades," she exaggerates, "but it's taken him this long to make his move. We couldn't be happier."

She's laying it on so thick I'm pretty sure this encounter was the objective to my coming all along. Sneaky.

I'm grateful for the distraction when the owner joins us outside. Clive is an old man, if I were to guess

I'd say north of eighty, with a kind smile but sad eyes.

As it turns out his wife of sixty years passed away this past July and as he explains, he's lost his motivation to keep the farm going. With neither of his children interested in taking over, he's decided to sell.

He takes us on a tour of the house, which is dated, but well-kept and looks to be in sound condition. Then he leads us to the barn where some farm equipment is stored, which he indicates will be part of the sale.

Finally, Clive opens a door into what may have been a tack room and gestures for me to lead the way.

"Oh, my goodness," escapes me when four little furballs stumble over each other to get to me.

I love dogs. Used to love taking care of Radar's pup, Phil, when he was on assignment, but I haven't had much of a chance since he and Hillary got together.

I go down on my knees and am assaulted by four wriggling bodies and wet kisses as the four vie for my attention. Their mother is a pretty English Shepherd who sidles up beside Clive, her head at his knee as she keeps an eye on her brood.

"Each of my kids want one, which means I have two left to get rid of. I can't bring them to my new place in town."

"Max and I have decided to take one," Anna says, stepping into view. "That one is left."

She indicates the smallest of the litter, a tricolor female who has rolled on her back at my knees so I can scratch her round, pink belly. I smile when one of her back legs starts twitching as I rub a certain spot, but my eyes are sharp on Yanis's mom.

"Why do I get the feeling I'm getting railroaded?"

Anna does her best to look innocent, but Max laughs heartily.

"Because my wife is a terrible actress."

"I am not!" she sputters indignantly, oblivious to the fact she all but admitted she planned this whole thing.

IT'S A LITTLE after eight when I hear the front door open.

"Hey."

I get up off the couch and walk up to Yanis, who is shedding his coat. As soon as his hands are free, I slip my arms around his waist and lift my face for a kiss.

"I like coming home like this," he mumbles against my lips.

"Hmm. How was your meeting?"

"Good. Signed a one-year contract for their new facility, which should keep us busy. Construction starts early next year."

"That's great. Have you had dinner?" I ask, slipping out of his hold and moving toward the kitchen where I've shoved the pan of lasagna back in the oven to keep it warm.

"No. I wanted to get home to—What the fuck is this?"

Guess he found my little surprise sleeping on the

couch where I left her.

I smile to myself but straighten my face before I turn around to where Yanis is scowling down at the puppy.

"*That*, is Lucy and she's ours."

His eyes narrow as they come up to meet mine.

"Ours?"

I nod. "Blame your mother."

I have no qualms throwing Anna under the bus after she manipulated me.

He looks back down at the puppy, who is just starting to wake up and wags her tail happily when she sees a new friend. He ignores her advances but is instantly on alert when Lucy suddenly starts barking in the direction of the front door.

Yanis is already moving before the doorbell rings. I quickly move to pick up the pup, who is attempting to get down from the couch on her own, and am alarmed when I catch Yanis pulling his weapon before yanking the door open.

"The fuck are you doing here?"

CHAPTER 31

Yanis

I'D BEEN EAGER to get home to Bree, fully intending to follow through on the promise I made her earlier.

Instead, I come home to her still dressed, a sleeping dog on my couch, and the fucking Don of the Albero family on my doorstep.

This does not make me happy.

It's a similar scene to the one many years ago, the man himself casual, hands in his pockets, and two of his goons a few steps behind him but definitely more alert. Guiseppe is clearly older, but when he lifts his head to look at me, his eyes are as sharp as ever.

I curb the desire to put a plug in him when his glance drifts over my shoulder to Bree, who I can sense behind me. I have no doubt she has her gun drawn.

"I want you to know your woman has nothing more to fear from Angelo," he starts, his voice raspier than I remember. "I've made sure of it."

"Right," I bite off, making it clear I don't trust him. My tone doesn't seem to affect him.

"I've watched you, you know?" His head slowly bobs up and down as he speaks, but his eyes don't waver. "I'm the one who recommended your company to Joe. I've been keeping my eye on you over the years, watched you build a reputation for yourself and thought maybe this was an opportunity to bring you into the fold. Turns out you were even better than I gave you credit for. I should've snapped you up the first time I knocked on your door. You'd have made an excellent lieutenant. But now?" He looks me up and down. "Now, I wonder if you'd have had the stomach for my line of work."

He dissolves into a rattling cough and spits out a wad of phlegm on my front steps.

As disturbing as it is he's clearly kept his eye on me, I don't get the sense he's here with violence in mind.

"What do you want, Albero?"

He shakes his head.

"Just to tell you it's over." He glances over my shoulder again. "No one's gonna touch your woman or anyone working for you." I can almost hear Bree's teeth grind at that comment even as Albero's eyes return to me. "Payback in kind for the peace of mind you gave me twenty years ago."

With that he abruptly turns away and walks toward the black sedan at the end of my driveway, his henchmen right behind him.

I feel Bree's body pressing to my back as she peers around the side.

"Did that just happen?"

I almost jump out of my skin when my phone starts ringing in my pocket. I pull it out as I see the vehicle's taillights disappear down the road. Shutting the door, I check the screen where Aiken's name pops up.

"Aiken, you'll never guess who—"

"Sarrazin was found dead an hour ago," he interrupts, stopping me in my tracks.

"What?" Bree wants to know.

I hit speakerphone and sit down on the couch.

"Say again?"

"A guard found Sarrazin shanked in the showers at Englewood."

Englewood Correctional Institute is a federal prison in the Denver area, where Angelo Sarrazin was remanded earlier this week by the pretrial judge after denying him bail.

"How is that possible?" Bree asks, as she sits down on the couch beside me. "Wasn't he just transported there?"

"Guess the Albero family has enemies inside," Aiken offers.

"I don't think so," I contribute. "Seconds before you called Guiseppe Albero stood on my doorstep and the first thing out of his mouth was Bree was safe and Angelo would no longer pose a threat. I thought he meant he muzzled him."

"You mean the old man had him killed? His own

son?"

I look over at Bree, who has that little mutt in her arms, her eyes wide on me.

"Stepson. And yes, that would be my guess. Sarrazin likely knew too much for the old man's comfort."

It's silent for a beat.

"He was at your door?"

"Yup."

"I have a fucking surveillance team on his house."

Bree snorts and when I glance at her again, she has her face buried in the pup's fur but her shoulders are shaking. My mouth twitches.

"You may wanna let 'em know he's flown the coop."

"Yeah. Guy's got balls," Aiken concludes. "And we've got nothing concrete to haul him in for, dammit."

"Maybe not, but you've got a crooked AG you can go after," I offer. "The man used his position to manipulate law enforcement officers into either looking away or downright breaking the law. I'm guessing you won't be bored."

The agent barks out a laugh.

"Little chance of that. I'd best make some calls. I'll be in touch."

He ends the call and I toss my phone on the coffee table. Then I twist in my seat, facing Bree.

"Now. Where were we?" I point at the creature on her lap. "I believe you were explaining to me what that thing is doing here."

"Her name is Lucy," Bree corrects me and proceeds to dump the animal on my lap.

Apparently scowling doesn't work with animals, because she is totally oblivious and happily tries to climb my body to get to my face. I pick up her wriggling body and lift her to eye level.

"You're gonna take a shit on my rug, aren't you?"

The pup lets out a little yelp as she licks the air in front of my face.

"Your parents adopted one of her brothers," Bree supplies.

She tells me about the farm, the old guy and his dogs, and my parents' decision to put in an offer on the spot after Bree gave the place her thumbs-up.

The whole thing has Ma's fingerprints all over it. She plays up the hippy-dippy senior part, but it's mostly smoke and mirrors for a cunning mind.

I sink back in the couch, dropping the pup to my chest, and am immediately rewarded with a bath and a beard trim.

"No," I say firmly, tapping her on the nose. "No chewing my face."

She sits back on my chest and tilts her head to one side and then the other as if she's listening to me talk. Then she curls in a ball and promptly falls asleep.

I turn my head to glance at Bree and notice her face has gone soft as she looks at the dog.

"Isn't she adorable?"

"She's a shit-disturber, I can tell," I counter.

"She is not. Look at her, she's a little lamb."

"She's a cockblocker," I insist. "We should've been christening the kitchen by now."

Bree grins and moves closer, leaning in to kiss the damn dog on my chest first before shifting her attention to me.

"See? Already I've been downgraded to second rank," I grumble.

This evening definitely did not go as planned, but with my feet on the table and two warm bodies snuggled up against me I can't really complain.

BREE

"LUCY!"

Yanis's booming voice blasts from the house.

I look over to where the pup had been chasing her first snowflakes just seconds ago. She's nowhere to be seen now, but there are tracks in the thin layer of snow leading underneath the deck. Little terror. I wonder what she's been into now.

I got home myself only ten minutes ago and let her outside for a pee. It started snowing as I was picking up a few groceries on my way home from the office. The plan was to have dinner ready by the time Yanis got home, but apparently, he's back early.

He's been in Vegas this past week, tasked with the security for a series of three back-to-back concerts by a famous—albeit aging—R&B star at one of the older casinos on the strip. PASS is starting to make a name in the entertainment business, which is an abrupt departure from the mining industry, where most of our previous contracts came from.

The Vegas deal is the third new contract this past month and the second entertainment one. I have to say I enjoy them more. They're short term, high energy, and no two are alike. The only thing I made Yanis swear is never to ask me to put on a dress and impersonate a star again.

"That fucking dog," he complains, walking out of the house with the remnants of one of his sneakers in his hand.

Oh dear. I may have forgotten to close the walk-in closet in our room. She likes to hide in there and use our footwear as chew toys.

"She missed you and she's teething."

It's a weak defense, but aside from her penchant to decimate the occasional shoe, Lucy is an absolute sweetheart. Smart too, she already knows a handful of commands. And, she does adore him.

Yanis stops a hairbreadth away, his larger form towering over me.

"She's a menace."

"You needed new ones anyway." He glares at me with narrowed eyes so I decide to change tactics. "You're home early."

I put a hand to his shoulder and lift up on tiptoes to press a kiss to his stubborn mouth.

"Snow's supposed to get worse and I didn't want to get stranded in Vegas," he grumbles.

"That's probably smart. I want to hear all about

Vegas, though." I pluck the mangled shoe from his hand before lacing my fingers with his and tugging him toward the door. "Let's grab a beer and you can tell me all about it while I start on dinner."

He doesn't answer but he doesn't resist and I indicate for him go in ahead of me, quickly tossing the shoe over the railing before I follow him inside and close the door behind us. I'm sure Lucy will come out of hiding soon. Hopefully, by then, I'll have him distracted enough he won't notice.

"So? How was Cooper Grey to work with?" I ask, setting a beer on the island in front of him.

"Not bad. At least smart enough to stick to the protocol. I've never seen so many middle-aged women trying to relive their youth." He fakes a shiver. "More fake eyelashes and artificial cleavage than you might see at a drag queen convention. Fucking screaming like teenagers, tossing bras and panties at the stage. Grown women, if you can believe that."

I make a sympathetic sound and don't share that if there was one other man who could get me to strip out of my panties, it would be Cooper Grey. Talk about hotter with age.

Yeah, best not share that.

"How have things been here?" he asks and sips from his beer.

"Quiet." I add the sliced peppers to the bowl of veggies for the stir-fry I have planned. "I spoke with Bill a few days ago. He's moving into his new place in Durango this weekend. He starts on Monday."

"We should take off for a couple of days after Christmas. Go see his new digs."

I look up and smile at him.

"I wouldn't mind that." I pull the wok from the cupboard and set it on a burner, adding some EVOO and a splash of sesame oil for fragrance. "Your parents are settling in at the farm. Your mom wants us to come over for Sunday dinner."

"You know that's going to become a standard request now they live here, right?" he asks with a smirk on his face.

"I figured, but I don't mind. I like family time."

He shakes his head, but does it smiling. "I'll remind you of that when they start driving you nuts as well."

"Not gonna happen," I assure him when I suddenly remember another phone call from earlier in the week. "Oh, you know who else called? David Aiken. He wanted to know if we'd heard anything else from Albero. Turns out we were the last people who reported seeing him. The man looks to have disappeared from the face of the earth."

"What do you wanna bet he's retired to a beach in Central or South America somewhere, living out the rest of his life?" Yanis suggests.

With no one left next in line, I guess it's possible he's hung up his hat.

"Could be."

A scratch at the door draws my attention. Lucy is covered in a dusting of snow, showing her doggy smile, indicating she wants to come in. I slide the door open for her but at the last minute she dives for something that was out of view and proudly carries it inside, dropping it at Yanis's feet.

His mangled sneaker.

I fully expect him to throw another fit but instead he starts laughing. A full-on belly laugh that fills me with a feeling of contentment I've never experienced before.

I'm happy. Truly and completely happy.

EPILOGUE

BREE

"*Z*APPA! DROP IT!"

I turn to see Max senior chasing after Lucy and her brother. The two are running off into the fields, side by side with one of baby Max's diapers they must've stolen from the trash can precariously stretched between them.

Yuck.

Yanis chuckles at the dogs' antics and his little nephew presses his ear against my new husband's broad, rumbling chest. The dogs are not the only ones thick as thieves. Mini Max adores his uncle and vice versa.

There might have been a time when seeing those two together would have been painful, but aside from a mild tinge of melancholy, witnessing the unconditional love between them is a thing of beauty.

We got married this morning in a simple ceremony with family and friends. Friends who make up our extended family. Growing up with only my mother and no other relatives to speak of, I always dreamed of big family get-togethers like this.

It's still a little chilly, being only the first weekend of April, but it's a nice sunny day and it's beautiful out here.

"You look like a happy bride."

Hillary—who is hugely pregnant with her first, only a month away from her due date—sits down beside me on the bench.

I grin at her.

"I'm just happy."

She throws an arm around my shoulders and tugs me close, leaning her head against mine.

"You can tell me to fuck off," she starts. "But I have something I want to ask you. Actually, two somethings."

I lift my head and turn to face her.

"What's that?"

"Well…" She glances over at Radar who is watching her from a distance. He's hanging out at the barrel grill with the other guys, all keeping an eye on the meat I'm sure. "Radar and I were talking and we want to ask you and Yanis to be godparents for the baby."

I've suddenly lost the ability to speak as a giant lump gets stuck in my throat.

"Oh God, I didn't mean to upset you," Hillary starts rambling. "That's why I didn't say anything until I checked in with you. Forget I—"

"Yes," I manage, unable to keep the tears at bay.

"Yes, I…I mean *we* would be honored."

I think by now just about everyone in our extended family is aware Yanis and I won't be producing offspring, which makes this gesture even more meaningful.

"Yeah?" Hillary makes sure, a happy smile spreading on her face.

"I can't wait. Word of warning though; I reserve the right to spoil my goddaughter rotten."

They wanted to keep the little one's gender a surprise so everyone at the office has been placing bets, not only on the sex of the baby but the date of birth. I called for a girl born May second.

Hillary laughs. "I expected nothing less."

I look over at Radar, who isn't hiding he has his full attention on my tête-a-tête with his wife, and nod. He smiles wide.

"As for my second request," Hillary continues. "I was wondering if you'd consider being my birth coach."

"Me?" I'm a little shocked and more than a little excited at the request. "I don't know anything about childbirth."

"I know more about childbirth than I care to some days," she responds dryly. "I need someone who can keep me focused. We're planning a home birth with a midwife."

"What about Radar?"

"He'd rather I deliver in a sterile room surrounded by doctors, nurses, and all necessary emergency equipment, but will go along with any decision that makes me happy. He's just very nervous about the whole thing."

I glance over at him again, noting he's returned his attention to the group he's standing with.

"How does he feel about having me there?"

"Relieved."

Tessa, Jake and Rosie's year-and-a-half old, walks over and drops a handful of dirt on my lap.

"Bah!"

"Yes, bah," I echo back at her. Her face is dirt-streaked and she wears half the sandbox Max built for the kids.

"Up!"

Her grubby little arms reach for me and I give up on the cream-colored dress I wore for the occasion, and lift her up on my lap.

With the little girl tucked in my arms, my chin resting on her strawberry blonde curls, and my eyes shiny, I smile at Hillary.

"I would love to."

YANIS

I WATCH BREE from a distance and smile as Tessa slaps a hand against her cheek, leaving behind a dirty streak.

Bree seems oblivious and snuggles the girl a little tighter.

I've worried from time to time, wondering if maybe it would get difficult for her to be surrounded by babies, but the woman I'm looking at seems happy.

My wife.

Fuck, if anyone had told me this would be where we'd end up, even as recently as spring of last year, I'd have declared them delusional. Turns out I've been the one fooling myself for so damn long.

I lost her once by my own volition and was lucky enough to find her again. There is nothing I won't do to warrant she's never lost again.

The ring on her finger and the family surrounding us are just the first steps. I'm going to spend the rest of my life ensuring she stays as happy as she is today.

"You did good, Brother," Dimi walks up and plucks his son from my arms. "Made everyone suffer through your fucking awful mood for fifteen years, but watching you with her—it was worth it."

"Not sure whether to thank you or lay you out," I grumble, but there's no malice in my voice.

"Thank me. Your ball and chain is watching."

Sure enough, Bree is looking at me, her expression one that expands my heart tenfold.

"Love you," she mouths.

I'm frozen like a lovestruck fool of advancing age, wondering what I did to deserve a rich life like this and a woman like her.

Then my father hollers behind me, snapping me out of my rose-colored trance.

"Yanis! Get the hose out, will ya? Your dog is covered in baby poop."

Damn mutt.

THE END

ACKNOWLEDGMENTS

First and foremost, let me thank YOU, my readers. Some of you have been patiently waiting for Yanis and Bree's story and I genuinely hope you enjoyed it!

I'm always grateful to my list of usual suspects.

My editor, Karen Hrdlicka, and alpha reader and proofreader, Joanne Thompson. They make me look so much better than I am.

My agent, Stephanie Phillips of SBR Media, who finds new folks to love my books all the time.

My publicists, Debra Presley and Drue Hoffman and my PA Krystal Weiss of Buoni Amici Press. These ladies make me look professional and on the ball. Believe me, I'm not.

My beta readers—Deb Blake, Pam Buchanan, and Petra Gleason. I'm so lucky with these three. Theirs are the last eyes on the manuscript, ironing out the final few wrinkles

My Barks&Bites reader group is amazing. A great, welcoming group of people who love discussing books, having fun, sharing stories, and supporting and uplifting each other. I'm fortunate to have them in my corner.

I'm blessed with my ARC readers, the blogs who support me, and some fantastic colleagues all willing to read and/or support each new book I put out there. I so appreciate you!

My hubs deserves a special thank you. He's not

a reader, he also doesn't really understand what it is that keeps me glued to my laptop all the time, but he's always there, looking after me when I have my nose to the grindstone, and cheering me on!

I love you all!
Freya

ABOUT THE AUTHOR

USA Today bestselling author Freya Barker loves writing about ordinary people with extraordinary stories.

Driven to make her books about 'real' people; she creates characters who are perhaps less than perfect, each struggling to find their own slice of happy, but just as deserving of romance, thrills and chills in their lives.

Recipient of the ReadFREE.ly 2019 Best Book We've Read All Year Award for "Covering Ollie, the 2015 RomCon "Reader's Choice" Award for Best First Book, "Slim To None", and Finalist for the 2017 Kindle Book Award with "From Dust", and Finalist for the 2020 Kindle Book Award with "When Hope Ends", Freya continues to add to her rapidly growing collection of published novels as she spins story after story with an endless supply of bruised and dented characters, vying for attention!

https://www.freyabarker.com

If you'd like to stay up to date on the latest news and upcoming new releases, sign up for my newsletter:
https://www.subscribepage.com/Freya_Newsletter

CPSIA information can be obtained
at www.ICGtesting.com
Printed in the USA
LVHW052014230621
690962LV00015B/772

9 781988 733661